DEVIL'S LUCK

A LOU THORNE THILLER

X X
KORY M. SHRUM

TIMBERLANE
PRESS

DEVIL'S LUCK

Thanks, Sarah!

−K

Thanks, Sarah!

AN EXCLUSIVE OFFER FOR YOU

Connecting with my readers is the best part of my job as a writer. One way that I like to connect is by sending 2-3 newsletters a month with a subscribers-only giveaway, free stories from your favorite series, and personal updates (read: pictures of my dog).

When you first sign up for the mailing list, I send you at least three free stories right away. If free stories and exclusive giveaways sound like something you're interested in, please look for the special offer in the back of this book.

Happy reading,

Kory

AUTHOR'S NOTE

TRIGGER WARNING

This book includes descriptions of child pornography and rape. These moments are short and allusive and you can usually see them coming. As an author, I tried to keep the emotion and gravity of the situation realistic to the story without gratuitous embellishment. However, please skim or skip these passages, with my complete support, if they will hurt or bother you.

Kory M. Shrum

For Uncle Craig,
my biggest fan

1

Spencer Halliday hobbled down the checkered hallway. The two-inch difference in length between his left and right legs accounted for his gait, but he was determined not to be slowed down by it.

"Where's Diana?" he called out, without stopping. A sheet of paper trembled in his hand as he swung his arms to steady himself.

The woman in leather pants leaning against the wall looked up from her phone.

"Surveillance room." She blew a bubble until it popped, a large pink film spreading across her lips. She licked it away with a swipe of her tongue. "Why? What do you want now, Quasi?"

Only Blair was brave enough to call him this to his face.

No matter. What was she to him anyway? The scent of grass and sweat wafted off of her. Dirt was smudged across her upper arm. Spencer supposed she'd just returned from a raid.

Dirty, disgusting, he thought, his mouth pulling into a sneer. *My Diana would never be so unkempt.*

And Diana was the only one who mattered.

"Diana," he called out. "Diana, I have something!"

He shuffled past Blair without answering, the bald spot on his head reflecting the flickering fluorescents above.

He burst through the closed door and found her in the dark, staring into the blue light of a computer terminal. Her face was scrunched in concentration. This glow made her look like a fresh corpse still tormented by its gruesome death. Her blonde hair, pulled into a severe ponytail on the top of her head, was toned silver.

"What is it?" she asked blandly, a hint of annoyance in her tone.

"Look at this."

"No," Diana insisted. Her blue eyes were made bluer by the glow. "I can't take my eyes off him."

Spencer sucked at his upper lip with his considerable underbite. "But I finally got a match on the DNA results you wanted."

"What DNA results?" she asked, again not looking away from the screen. "How can he smile so much? He smiles *all* the time. *Why?* What do you have to smile about, you bastard?"

Spencer ignored this. Diana often mumbled to herself when concentrating. He continued undeterred. "There's a match for the coffee cup and a five-dollar bill. In New Orleans."

At this Diana did look up. The lines in her face smoothed out. Her eyebrows lifted in surprise. "Really? New Orleans?"

"There was a blood sample collected from"—he looked at the sheet again—"Julia Street station. It's definitely her."

"How recent?"

"March."

"If the blood was collected in March, why am I only now hearing about it?"

Spencer shifted his weight. *No, no.* This wasn't going how he wanted. He'd imagined Diana's joy at the news. He imagined her slipping her arms around his neck and—what?

Biting him maybe.

Or perhaps shoving him against a wall before pressing her tight body into his. Delicious rewards for his efforts.

He shivered at the thought.

But there was no joy. She was scowling at him.

His anxiety spiked electric along his skin. "I don't know. A lag in processing? The NOPD has been understaffed since Hurricane Katrina. Their police force hasn't recovered."

Her reaction made him doubt himself.

Foolish, he thought. *I shouldn't have told her.*

Maybe letting her know about the match would put her on a collision course with the woman. Diana's obsessive mind would make it impossible for her to let such a trail go. He could only hope that Lou was long gone and the trail in New Orleans cold.

Because the Lou woman frightened him. She wasn't to be trusted, especially not with someone so precious as Diana.

But if Diana had learned that he kept things from her—
She'll kill you.

Desire ripped through him at the idea.

"New Orleans," Diana murmured to herself. "I haven't been there in years."

Spencer shifted uncomfortably against the pressure building between his legs. "Why do you care so much about her?"

"You mean, why do I care about finding someone like me?"

No one like you. Never anyone like you.

Instead he said, "You must've known there'd be at least a few."

"Spencer," Diana began, and the hair on the back of his

neck prickled. It was her voice, pitched low. He knew that voice. It promised violence.

She pushed back her seat and stood. She had a hand on his throat before he'd seen her move.

Her heat radiated like the sun across his face and neck.

His mind babbled. *I want I want I want—*

Her eyes were black now, the inner blue cannibalized by the room's shadows. "I want to know who she is and what she has, Spencer. It's obvious she has connections and assets that I don't."

"No," he said, too quickly. His tongue darted out from between his lips. If only he could taste the air like a snake, taste *her*. "No, I just—I just wondered if this is about Winter."

Spencer already knew the answer. For Diana, *everything* was about Winter.

Diana affected a shrug. "So what if it is? Would that matter?"

"No." Spencer didn't like how high and tight his voice sounded. "You're free to—"

Diana tightened her hold on his throat and drove him back. His head hit the cinder block wall, ears ringing.

"I *am* free to do whatever I want. And what I want is for you to find me the best PI in New Orleans."

Her mouth was over his now. *Hot. So hot.* He wondered if those lips could scald him.

"A PI?" he repeated, his dick hardening.

She must've seen the ache in his eyes. With a wicked smile, she slid the fingers from her free hand into his hair and gripped it. Then she pulled so hard tears sprang to his eyes. A small whimper escaped him.

She put her lips close enough to his ear that her words tickled when she spoke. "The best PI in town. Someone who can find her."

"Okay," he mewled, squirming beneath her. His fists opened and closed at his sides. He wanted to touch her, wanted more than anything to put his hands on her body.

But that was not allowed. He was *never* allowed to touch her unless she said *the word*.

"Spencer," she whispered into his mouth.

Please, please, please, he thought. *Please say it. Please say*—

She released him, stepping back out of his reach and taking all the heat with her. "Don't disappoint me."

2

Piper Lynn Genereux rested her weight against the door jamb, watching the six-foot-tall drag queen lean over the sink to peer into the mirror. With steady hands, fake eyelashes were glued and pressed to each eye. The lightbulb overhead hissed, but neither noticed. Piper was mesmerized.

Their eyes met in the mirror.

"You're pretty," Piper said reflexively.

Henry laughed. "Don't sound so surprised."

"I'm not surprised," she said defensively, uncrossing and recrossing her arms. She'd seen Henry in drag countless times. "I'm just saying you've gotten really good at this."

"I've come a long way from plastic pants and Aqua Net, yes," he said. "Thanks again for letting me use your bathroom. My apartment is too small for three queens."

Piper could only imagine how difficult it was for Henry to share a bathroom with his boyfriends, especially now that she was reminded how much work getting ready was for him.

"What time do you go on?" she asked, offering a tissue so he could dab the fallout from his mascara.

"Eleven. I go on right after Mustang Mary," he said. Their eyes met in the mirror again. "Are you coming?"

In truth, Piper had hoped to go to bed early. She hadn't slept well the night before. Too many strange dreams only half remembered. But with Henry's hopeful face pouting at her, *no* wasn't an option.

She rubbed her nose. "Sure. I'll come."

"Will you bring a girl?"

"*A* girl?" Piper snorted. "You make it sound like I have more than one. Dani and I aren't even official. Besides, she's working late. She has a deadline."

"What about the dangerous one? You could bring her instead."

Piper frowned. "I don't have a dangerous girlfriend." *Or any girlfriend.*

Henry removed a glob of mascara from the wand. "Leather jacket. Mirrored shades. Looks like she eats flesh for breakfast and drinks blood for dinner."

Piper laughed. "Lou? She's not a cannibal."

"I'm just saying she's got a man-eater vibe. I haven't seen her in a while. I thought you were into her."

"I was," she admitted. "But now I'm not."

"Because..."

This was dangerous territory. It wasn't that Henry was forbidden to know about Lou. It was that *no one* was supposed to know about Lou.

"It's not like that," she said. "We're friends."

"Just work friends?" he asked, adding stick-on jewels beneath his eyes.

"More than that," she said. He'd seen Lou pick her up from the bars. Work friends don't do that. Nor did the word acquaintance work after all that had happened between them.

Lou had saved her life. And she loved her. At first she'd

been certain it was an intense romantic love. Now she knew it was deeper than that.

Best friends? she wondered. *Is she my best friend?*

"How much *more?*" he asked, rummaging in his makeup bag.

"You're such a perv. I said nothing was going on. We're just close."

"I mean, without a doubt, Dani is gorgeous, but I'm trying to understand why you passed on Lou."

Lou passed on me. "She's way out of my league. So is Dani, but at least that seems like a mountain I can climb."

Henry snorted at the innuendo. "I know what you mean. There was this hot barista at the Starbucks."

"Poydras or Canal?"

"Poydras. He was thick as hell and had this amazing butt."

"You're quoting Todrick Hall again," Piper said.

He didn't seem to register this comment. "But then I started talking to him and found out he's a double finance and plant biology major at Tulane. He wants to revolutionize the coffee industry and create a coffee with negative emissions that will save the planet while we *drink* it." Henry scoffed. "Definitely not the barista I thought he was."

Piper saw the popped button on his sequined bodice. She tried to refasten it. "What kind of barista were you hoping for?"

"The kind who only works for beer money, I guess."

Piper had no idea what any of this had in common with her and Lou. "Well, good thing you already have two boyfriends."

"I'm always shopping for my third."

The button finally snapped into place. "I'm aware."

"And now you have a hot girlfriend and you and Lou are disaster friends," Henry said, dabbing on foundation where he'd over wiped.

"What? No."

"You work together at the detective agency, right?"

Piper couldn't even imagine Lou managing the register at Madame Melandra's Fortunes and Fixes. "Yeah, but—"

"Your job is to hunt criminals, catch bad guys, clean up messes. It's all drama, drama, drama. Didn't Dani end up in the hospital?"

"That was more of a journalism accident." A complete lie, given that a Russian mob boss had cut off her finger and had beaten her half to death.

Henry arched a brow. "Sounds disaster-y to me."

"Stop saying that."

"It's not a bad thing! It just means that your relationship is based on drama, rather than, I don't know, a shared love of churro sundaes or boy-hunting."

Piper scoffed. "We're real friends."

Though admittedly, there are a lot of bodies, she thought glumly.

"It's just that people like us, with shit parents, we tend to have certain types of relationships. We attract the drama. It's hard to make real connections with people. Disaster friends come and go. That's okay. It's as it should be. That's all I'm saying."

I don't want Lou to come and go.

"We aren't disaster friends," she said again, lip stiff. "We connect."

Henry arched a brow at her hard refusal. "Okay. Whatever you say, sis."

LOU THREW THE DUSTY TOWEL INTO THE HAMPER AND observed her gleaming apartment. She'd cleaned it top to bottom for the second time that week, and considering her minimalist style and near-nothing possessions, this was...

Ridiculous, she thought. *I'm losing my mind.*

She was no less restless than when she'd begun the project six hours ago. All that scrubbing and organizing hadn't expelled any of the energy itching along her spine. What had she hoped to accomplish?

Perhaps nothing, but she'd run out of options. Her guns certainly hadn't helped.

She'd begun with those, of course. She'd drawn the curtains and pulled her entire arsenal from the myriad of hiding places tucked around the apartment. She'd disassembled, cleaned, and reassembled each gun carefully. She'd counted ammunition. She'd sharpened her blades and rewrapped fraying handles. She'd repacked her medical kit and made fresh rags.

Still, she couldn't settle. She needed to *do* something.

I need to hunt.

Her shoulder twinged. The stab of pain slid up the side of her neck like a knife.

It was a reminder that even cleaning was a gamble.

Her shoulder refused to heal, at least not as quickly as Lou wanted it to. When the bullet had grazed her collarbone, the doctor had warned her it would be at least six months before she could use it.

Be grateful the bone didn't shattered.

"Grateful," she murmured, and sank onto the edge of the mattress pressed beneath the windows.

Behind her, the St. Louis night was vibrant. The illuminated arch stood like a starlet on the riverway carpet. Headlights from boats swept the moonlit waters. A half-moon hung tilted in the sky like a spotlight.

Her hands smelled like bleach. *For all the wrong reasons*, she lamented.

What had she done before, when the restlessness was this

bad? When she was a moment away from pulling the skin off her body with her bare hands?

She grabbed her leather jacket off the kitchen stool and stepped into the converted linen closet.

Once upon a time it had shelves for towels. The shelves had been removed to make room for her body.

Now it smelled like sawdust from her recent sanding, another desperate, itinerant task. When her fingers brushed the wall, they came away powder-soft, a thin film coating them.

She pulled the door closed and darkness swelled. It slid over her face and hands, along the side of her throat, and pooled at the back of her neck. It was like a cat rubbing against her.

She surrendered to it.

The world thinned, a gossamer curtain falling away into nothing but pitch. A compass, unseen but felt, whirled inside her. It searched for a location to latch onto, two points to align in the dark.

Something snagged, and the sense of weightlessness evaporated and gravity returned.

Lou stepped from the shadows toward the sound of voices.

"I'm thinking of Todrick's *I Like Boys*," a gruff voice said.

"I love that song," Piper said, shifting her weight against the door where she leaned. "Such a bop. It'll be fun to dance to."

The kitchen was dark and quiet, as well as the open living room adjacent. At the start of a hallway was the lit bathroom where Piper stood, ankles and arms crossed.

She turned away from the light of the bathroom toward Lou, as if sensing her arrival. Then she did a double take, eyes widening.

She stepped away from the frame and slammed her index finger against her lips.

"What?" the gruff voice asked.

"I thought I heard something," Piper said. She made a frantic knocking sound with her hand.

Lou understood, lifted her hand, and rapped against the closed door beside her.

"Coming," Piper called. She opened and closed her front door, her eyes never leaving Lou's face. "Hey, Lou-blue. So nice of you to *drop in*."

A bedazzled head popped out of the bathroom, looking like an exotic bird checking to see if the coast was clear of predators. His face sparkled.

Lou remembered this one. *Henry*, she thought. Or was it Harry?

"Oh hey," he said. "We were just talking about you. Are you coming to the show tonight?"

Piper looked as interested in this answer as Henry.

"I have work," Lou said. To Piper, "I came to see if you wanted to join me."

"Ohh," Henry said with a dramatic gasp. "Fun crime-fighting stuff? Are you going to *cuff* someone?"

He waggled his eyebrows.

Piper let out a nervous laugh. "We aren't cops, H."

"Well, either way, duty calls. Do you care if I finish up here and lock up after I leave?" he asked.

"You're assuming I'm going to go. What about your show?"

"Pfft. Girl, you've seen me shake my ass a million times. You're not missing anything. Go save the world."

"Grab a coat," Lou said quietly.

"What's that?" Henry poked his head out of the bathroom.

"Good luck with your show," Lou said, pitching her voice louder.

He smiled and tilted his head. "Thanks, girl. Have fun with the handcuffs."

Piper grabbed a coat off the back of the kitchen door and forced her arms through the sleeves. As they stepped into Piper's stairwell and shut the apartment door behind them, Piper made a show of stomping on a few of the stairs, but they never reached the floor below, which opened onto King's detective agency.

Instead, Piper felt an arm hook around her waist the moment before she was jerked through the dark.

Piper might have been disturbed by this, the sense of compression and falling, if she hadn't traveled in Lou's special way many times before.

When the world reformed around them, it revealed a pine forest. The smell of sticky sap, pungent and thick, saturated the air. The air was also noticeably cooler, which explained Lou's insistence on a jacket despite the ninety-degree weather holding New Orleans hostage.

"Oh, wow." Piper sucked in a deep breath. "It smells like Christmas up in here."

Lou was looking at the GPS watch on her wrist. The screen illuminated her face green and created deep shadows beneath her lips and nose.

Moonlight shifted through the clouds, giving Piper the impression of spirits wandering between the creaking trees.

"Not that I don't love coming to the forest in the middle of the night, but, uh, what are we doing here? The creep factor is *quite* high right now."

"We're looking for a body."

"Oh, that's nice. I feel better already," Piper deadpanned. "What body?"

"One of Fish's."

The mere mention of the serial killer they'd captured five months ago brought the situation into clearer view. This wasn't the first time she'd been invited to a find-a-murdered-body dig-along. In fact, they'd uncovered fourteen bodies more than the thirty Jeffrey Fish had confessed to since his arrest in March.

Piper's suspicions were confirmed when she saw the two shovels propped against the tree, their blades glinting. And the sight of the shovels told Piper two very important things.

First, Lou was going crazy and running out of ways to self-soothe. That explained why she smelled like bleach.

Second, Piper needed to do the digging.

Lou stepped carefully through the low-lying ferns until she seemed to settle on a spot. She checked her GPS watch again.

Something cried shrilly overhead, thrashing the branches as it passed.

Just a bird, Piper told herself. *Maybe a bat.*

"Where are we?" she asked.

"Ohio. The Zaleski State Forest." Lou grabbed a shovel. "It's here. Beneath me."

"*No.*" Piper knew better than to question Lou's amazing abilities, one of which meant she could find anything she was looking for. What she objected to was the shovel in Lou's hand.

"No," she said again, pulling at the shovel. It didn't budge.

"Okay, so you're still stronger than me, but I don't need to tell you that shoveling will destroy your shoulder, do I? Do you remember what happened last time?"

Because of course there had been a last time. Lou insisted on trying to dig up every body they found and it never ended well. Lou's stubbornness seemed as infinite as her high tolerance for pain.

"Maybe I can do it this time," Lou said.

"And maybe you'll keep on being wounded for the rest of your life. I know this is hard for you, but please just wait until the full recovery time is up and you get the doctor's approval, okay?"

Lou relinquished the shovel and Piper stumbled back.

Damn, she's strong.

Lou looked away. "I should get Dani to help you."

"Don't bother. She's got an editorial deadline." Piper put the tip of the spade into the earth and pressed hard with the heel of her sneaker. The earth broke open easily. Maybe it'd been raining.

Lou dropped into a crouch a few feet away.

Piper didn't mind shoveling with an audience, but twenty licks in she asked, "I'm in the right spot, correct?"

Lou gave a nod barely registerable in the dark. If the moonlight hadn't been abundant, Piper would be digging blind.

She was sure the canopy cover helped keep the forest cool, and there was a light breeze. She could hear water somewhere in the distance, and smelled it too. A nearby river or stream likely cut through the woods.

And yet despite the coolness, a thin line of sweat formed on her brow and the back of her neck as she labored.

The wooden handle turned in her grip, growing slicker. The muscles in her back were already talking to her. Her hands began to ache.

Lou seemed to pick up the thread where she'd dropped it. "We need Dani to report the body. She's the one with the media contacts."

"If we find a body you can just send Dani the coordinates. These journalists need almost nothing to follow a lead, man. They're like bloodhounds."

Piper was about two feet down when she asked, "Where'd you get the shovels?"

"I borrow them from a ditch digger in Alabama."

Were ditch diggers still a thing? "He knows you're borrowing his stuff?"

"No. And I put them back in a slightly different place each time."

"Don't do that!" Piper said, pausing to wipe her face. "Poor guy will think he's losing his mind."

Then she thought glumly, *Maybe we're all losing our minds.*

She was three feet down when she asked, "We do stuff, right?"

Lou's face was unreadable in the dark. Part of her cheek and jaw had collected moonlight, but her eyes and mouth were invisible.

"I don't understand the question," Lou said.

"Do we do stuff?"

"Can I have an example?" Lou inched forward into the moonlight, revealing her face.

"Do we hang out, go to the movies—you know, *stuff?*"

"We've had pizza in New York."

"Yes!" Piper said. "Though that was a lunch break in the middle of the Bennigan case."

"We went to that party in Italy," Lou added. "You got drunk."

Piper frowned. "It was a mob boss party. We went so Konstantine could get the name of that stalker for you."

She stopped shoveling and tried to catch her breath.

"Have we really not done anything that's not related to bad guys?" She frowned. "You picked me up from my mom's house when—no, wait. You came because King sent you."

Piper didn't want to think about that night anyway. Her mom with a needle hanging out of her arm and her abusive boyfriend wielding a shotgun as if that is an appropriate reaction to someone wanting to move out.

"We watched all seven seasons of that show," Lou said. "The one with the dragons."

Piper pumped a fist. "Yes. Yes, we did."

"It wasn't very good. Though I liked the fight scenes."

"You would. But worst ending ever."

"We're still watching the one about the killer who hunts killers."

"*Dexter.* Oh, and there's *Killing Eve*! I want to see that one. Wait." Piper's excitement vanished. "Is that all we do? Eat and watch television?"

"We are supposed to leave for the road trip Friday."

"Right!" Piper's enthusiasm returned like a loyal dog. "Road trips are excellent for bonding. There's music and snacks and talking. Wait, what do you mean, supposed to? Aren't you still coming?"

"Yes," Lou said. "But things come up."

"Nothing will come up," Piper said. "We're going and we'll have the time of our lives."

She shoved the end of the spade down into the hole again —and cracked something. "I think—"

"Let me," Lou called, and hopped down into the hole.

Using her fingerless-gloved hand, Lou brushed away the disturbed earth until two black sockets gazed up at them.

3

L ou and Piper stood on the street outside Madame Melandra's Fortune and Fixes with two duffels sitting between their feet. One was stuffed with Piper's clothes, her wallet, and a neon blue phone charger.

Piper was hot. The day had barely started and she could already feel the heat thrown over her like a thick blanket. She just hoped that whatever car Dani chose from the rental place had a working air conditioner.

Staring at her feet, the black bag finally came into focus. Piper frowned. "What's in your bag?"

Lou grinned, her eyes safely guarded behind her mirrored shades. Her hands rested in the pockets of her leather jacket.

How she could wear it in this heat, Piper didn't know.

"Probably guns," Piper guessed. "But hopefully also underwear."

Lou snorted. "What makes you think I wear underwear?"

It was Piper's turn to giggle.

A Lexus rolled up to the curb. From the driver's seat, Dani gave a friendly honk and waved.

Piper pointed at the trunk and it popped open. She threw

the bags in and went to the passenger-side window, motioning for Dani to roll it down.

"You didn't have to rent such a posh car. We would've been fine with a compact."

"It's mine," Dani said, and gave a sheepish grin. "My mom wanted a new car, so she gave me her old one. And it's only got ten thousand miles on it, so I thought we could just break it in."

This is the old *car?* Heat crawled up the back of Piper's neck. *Must be nice.*

"What's wrong?" Dani asked when Piper opened the door.

"Nothing," she lied, sliding into the passenger seat. "This is great."

Dani adjusted the seatbelt across her chest. "I'll drive first. I'll be good until at least Houston."

Piper gestured to the I-10 sign. "We need to stop at a gas station for snacks."

"Got it," Dani said, the good humor still seizing her expression.

At least someone is having a good time, Piper thought. They hadn't even started and Lou looked bored as hell, stoic as a statue in the backseat.

When Piper had first thought of the road trip idea months ago, she'd been excited.

Lou had gotten shot and almost died, and as she lay in a hospital for days, all Piper could think about was how Lou needed more good things in her life. It was true they watched TV and went out to eat. They'd been in a bar together a few times. But that wasn't enough.

The road trip was the shift they needed. With music and hours on the highway with only the summer wind in their hair, they could make real memories. Good, drama-*free* memories.

Take that, Henry, she thought. *And this way, if the crime-fighting ever ends, Lou will still have a reason to be my friend.*

Because Piper knew nothing lasted forever. King could close the detective agency or decide to retire for real given his age—and then what? What reason would Lou have to stay in touch with her?

This will be fun, Piper insisted. She wasn't sure who she was trying to convince. *Everyone is going to have a great time, and Lou—*

"Do I just sit back here?" Lou asked, poking her head up between the seats.

Piper pinched the bridge of her nose.

"There's the playlist," Dani offered.

"Good idea." Piper connected her phone to the car's Bluetooth system and turned on the playlist she'd made.

"I added a few NIN songs since you said you liked them. And I've got a lot of Alanis Morissette, some classic rock, Beyoncé, Ludacris, Paramore, and—"

The speakers began to thump.

"What is this?" Lou asked.

"'Imma Be,'" Piper said, adjusting the bass on the stereo. "The Black Eyed Peas."

Lou's facial expression was unreadable.

This will work, Piper told herself. *We'll have fun. We'll make memories. And no one is going to get shot.*

LOU SAT IN THE BACK OF THE CAR, TRYING TO IGNORE THE throbbing ache in her shoulder. She wasn't sure why her body would ache after just sitting. It wasn't getting the workout it would in a firefight or even the taxing movement of pulling a gun.

Dani and Piper sang off-key to "Toxic" by Britney Spears.

Piper looked back at her hopefully, then pretended to

extend the invisible microphone she held in her fist out to Lou.

"I'm hungry," Lou said into Piper's fist.

Piper undid her seatbelt and leaned into the backseat. "We've got Doritos, Pringles, gummy bears—"

"Doritos."

"That's my girl." Piper popped open the bag and took a chip for herself. "Mmm, ranch."

But eating the chips only temporarily distracted Lou from the pain in her shoulder and the boring backseat.

As she counted the highway markers and noted the *San Antonio 134 miles* sign, she wondered how she was going to get through this.

"For dinner, I'm thinking about Taco Bell," Piper said.

"Oh god, no," Dani said. "Taco Bell goes right through me. Can we do Burger King? They've got a veggie burger."

"Fine. I like their milkshakes."

"Let's do dinner at seven," Dani said, glancing at the clock on the dashboard. "We can switch then."

"Burger King at seven," Piper confirmed, tearing open the bag of gummy bears. "I'm going to get the Whopper with cheese. And a Dr Pepper."

"Thought you wanted a milkshake?" Dani asked, cracking her window a little more.

"*And* a milkshake. What about you?"

"Probably a Sprite."

Piper nodded as if she'd barely heard this. "How do you guys feel about 'Where Them Girls At'?"

Lou counted the minutes to seven with growing restlessness. When seven passed with no Burger King in sight, she was agitated. 7:20. 7:42. 7:53. 8:23. Her foot bounced in the well behind Dani's seat.

The world darkened and shadows filled the car like rising

water. They slithered across her muscles, making her flesh crawl. The gentle pull inside her grew stronger.

She strained against it, willing herself to stay in her seat, the thin beams of moonlight like ropes to salvations.

"We could pick something else?" Dani offered, glancing at the clock. "I don't need a veggie burger. I could go for a—"

Lou felt the shadows around her soften, deepening. *I can't—*

"I'll get it." She exhaled and gave herself over to the darkness. The car, the music, Dani and Piper's soft conversation all bled away.

They were replaced with fresh night air and starlight.

Lou looked up and saw the Burger King sign. It felt good to be on her own two feet. She sucked in a lungful of fresh air. It smelled like garbage, a huge dumpster standing below the lit sign. She didn't care. It was still heavenly.

Inside, she ordered the food, getting three sodas and the milkshake into a carry carton. She gripped the sack of food in her other fist.

She stepped out into the night and wondered if she really needed to go back right away. Maybe she could wander for a bit.

But then they might stop somewhere else for food.

A guy on the sidewalk wearing a Burger King shirt lit a cigarette. "Have a good night."

"You too," Lou said, sidestepping into a shadow between the building and dumpster.

Then she was back in the car.

"Lou!" Piper cried. "Where did you go?"

"I told you." Lou held up the food. "I got dinner."

"No," Piper whined. "We gotta hit the drive-through. We gotta—"

"Thanks, Louie," Dani said. "Can I get that Sprite?"

Lou handed her the soda. "Here's your veggie burger."

"Amazing! And ketchup for the fries! Babe, help me out." Dani was giving Piper a look Lou didn't understand.

Piper rubbed the back of her neck again, accepting the milkshake Lou offered. "Yeah, thanks."

They ate in silence, Piper tearing open little packets with her teeth and squeezing sauce out onto the wax paper.

When the gas light came on, they pulled off the interstate.

"Let's just stop here," Dani said, pointing at the hotel across from the gas station. "We've already done twelve hours today. That's enough. Maybe we'd all do well to get out of the car for the night."

"I didn't even drive," Piper said.

Dani handed her the keys. "You can start tomorrow."

PIPER OPENED THE HOTEL ROOM TO FIND THEIR BAGS PILED against one wall. On the desk was a note scribbled on the hotel's stationery:

I'll be back in a couple of hours. ;) – L

Dani came up behind her and put her chin on her shoulder. "What do you think the wink face means?"

Piper huffed. "She thinks she's giving us some privacy."

"That's nice of her."

"Is it?" Piper asked, throwing the keys down on the desk beside the note.

"Come on," Dani said with a grin. "This'll be our bed. Lou can have that one."

The look in Dani's eye drew a nervous laugh from her. "Are you implying—?"

"Oh yeah, I'm *implying*." Dani came up onto her toes so that she could kiss Piper's lips.

But Piper broke the kiss first. "I can't. I'm sorry. She could just pop in at any time."

"She's got her compass thingy," Dani said, undoing the button on the top of her shirt. "I think she'll know when it's safe to come back."

Piper liked the look in her eyes. They were dark and hungry. Her hair was cascading over one shoulder as she looked up at her through thick lashes. That look alone was almost enough to undo Piper.

"I can't," Piper said, and this time it was harder to say. "I don't want to be thinking about Lou while I'm..."

She let the insinuation slide.

Dani sat down on the edge of the bed, kicking off one of her boots. She was noticeably colder.

Well, now I've screwed up, Piper thought. *Left and right today.*

"You seemed a little *irritable* today."

Piper looked at the luggage on the floor and then at the note. "Do you think the road trip idea was stupid?"

Dani frowned, shrugging out of her shirt. The sexy look was gone with the clothes as she rummaged in her bag for a night shirt. "No. Why would it be stupid?"

Piper sank into the desk chair and covered her face. "I don't know. I guess I had this big plan in my head that we'd go on this epic adventure and eat snacks, and listen to music and talk, but this whole trip she's just been sitting in the back of the car, *grimacing*."

"Honey, Lou's never been a big talker."

"I know. But I wanted us to bond, you know? I wanted us to have moments like real friends."

Dani unhooked her bra. "What do you mean, *real* friends?"

"Right now we're disaster friends. We hang out when there's a bad guy to hunt or kill or someone to save or if everyone is being held captive by some psycho. What if that's the only reason she talks to me? Out of necessity?"

Dani pulled a Tulane t-shirt over her head and swept her

thick hair up into a messy bun. "Listen. You know that Lou is different. A road trip with Lou isn't going to be like a road trip with me. You've got to accept that. Just try to have fun with her the way things are."

As things are.

But *as things are* meant accepting that Lou was distant and unpredictable. Unreadable at the best of times. She could disappear at a moment's notice, and what then? Where would that leave Piper?

Disaster friends come and go, Henry had warned.

No. That can't happen, she thought. *I can't let that happen.*

4

T he hotel room fell away. Lou relaxed against the shift of the world, feeling points in space realign. She felt it first low in her chest. In the solar plexus, it came as a tug forward, the compass inside her reaching out for its destination. Then her mind dilated, opening like night-blooming jasmine to the darkness consuming her.

But there was only silence, soft shadows, and the smell of water.

When the world reformed around her, she was in a dim bedroom. A man slept beneath a plush green comforter covered in gold fleur-de-lis splattering the fabric. His chest rose and fell softly with his breath as moonlight made the pillows glow. Behind her, the high arched window overlooking the Arno River was open, filling the room with a gentle August breeze. Even though it must be three or four in the morning, Lou could still feel the heat of the day in the air.

She stepped up to the end of the bed and Konstantine stirred.

He rolled onto his back, revealing the pistol gripped loosely in his right hand.

He must've had it hidden under his pillow, she thought. *He pretended to be asleep until he could grab it.*

She pushed her mirrored sunglasses up on her head and smiled. "Bad dreams?"

He left the gun on the bed and sat up on his elbows. His eyes raked her body. "You look good to me."

She arched a brow. "Smooth."

"I thought you were with Piper," he said, careful to inflate the *i* in her name.

"We drove all day." She sounded exhausted even to herself.

Konstantine gave her a knowing smile. "Was it difficult for you? Traveling the way we mere mortals do? I bet when the sun went down it was harder."

"It's a waste of time," she said. "I don't know why she insists on doing it this way."

"It's an American pastime," Konstantine said, lying back against the pillows and putting his hands under his head. Lou noted his bare chest, letting her eyes scrape down his torso, with no attempt to hide her thoughts.

"How's your shoulder?" he asked.

"The same." She wasn't sure why she'd admitted that. It was the truth, but it sounded dangerously close to whining.

Louie Thorne did not whine.

"Do you want to lie down with me?" he asked. "Or do you need to get back?"

She shrugged out of her leather jacket and reached down to unbuckle her boots. She kicked them off onto the floor as she climbed into the bed.

Konstantine moved over, lifting the comforter so she could slip inside.

"I told them I'd be back," she said.

"I'll be sure to keep you awake then," he replied with a devilish grin.

When he moved in, placing the length of his body against

hers, warmth radiated through her. Without realizing it, she moved in closer. He placed a kiss on her throat. Then another. On the third, she stiffened, her body going rigid with the pain.

He pulled back, his shadowed face pinched. "Sorry."

Her irritation spiked. "My shoulder should be better by now."

Konstantine arched an eyebrow. "First of all, shoulders are notoriously difficult to heal. Secondly, you were *shot*. The doctor said you would need at least six months. By my count you are six weeks short of that."

"Five," she corrected.

The truth was, it had never taken Lou this long to heal. She'd been shot before, many times. She'd been stabbed, and suffered every other type of injury one could when throwing themselves headlong into battle.

"I've never been so—"

"Bored?" Konstantine offered with a smile. "It's good that things are quiet. You're not as capable as you usually are."

Lou dematerialized, allowing the shadows in the darkened room and those layered by his body over hers to provide the gap she needed to bleed through the world.

She reappeared behind him on her side, her good shoulder bracing her, and put her finger to the back of his head. "Bang."

He rolled over and enveloped her outstretched hand with his. "Yes, you're still fast. And you're still strong. But there is nothing wrong with rest, *amore mio*."

The truth was, Lou had never been one for rest. When Aunt Lucy was alive, she made frequent comments about Lou's restlessness, the way she would pace like a lioness in her cage at even the slightest agitation. At times it felt like a current ran through her, a live wire. And if she didn't do something with all of that energy, that desire, it would tear her apart.

"You could rupture your shoulder," Konstantine said. "Then you wouldn't lose months, you'd lose *years*."

All this talk about her shoulder wasn't sexy. It rubbed against her mind like steel wool.

He must've seen the look on her face.

"I don't mean to lecture you. You know your limits."

Her aunt had often accused her of going too far, pushing too hard and not knowing when to quit. That was great when it came to hunting murderers and mafia kingpins. Less so when it came to the care and maintenance of her own body.

She met his eyes. "I haven't gone *looking* for trouble."

"No," he said, and placed a kiss on the tip of her nose. "But trouble will find you sooner or later."

She grinned. "You're one to talk. I seem to remember pulling you out of a burning villa after Nico carved up half your face."

"*You* set the villa on fire."

Lou didn't remember that part.

"Besides," he said. His voice dropped an octave and a hungry look overcame his features. It was the wolfish way he was watching her lips, relinquishing them only to trace the line of her throat and collarbone. "The sooner you're healed, the sooner we can..."

He bit his lower lip.

"We tried that," she reminded him.

Two months after her brush with death, after the bullet tore a hole in the side of her neck, she'd tried to fuck him. When he'd put his hands on her hips and pulled her forward, the sharp pain shattering that side of her body had rocked her. It was a pain unlike any she'd known before, and few on this planet were more acquainted with pain than she was.

Yet she'd been unable to move for several minutes, while

he'd poured apologies into her ears. Of course, that hadn't stopped her from trying twice more.

Now Lou moved to adjust herself on the bed and find a position that didn't allow her shoulder to roll forward, pulling at the weakened tendons there. She settled for lying on her back, her gaze skyward. This left Konstantine on his side, gazing down into her face.

"I must admit…" he began. The hunger was still there in his eyes, but Lou saw the attempt to rein it in. "I'm more than a little jealous that they get to travel with you."

"I took you to New Orleans," she said.

He tilted his head, the ghost of a smile on his lips. "That wasn't a vacation. We went to kill Dmitri."

"There was New York."

He tilted his head. "On our way to kill Nico."

She supposed none of their *travels* could be classified as vacations when one accounted for all the shootouts, hunting, and murder.

"After we get back from San Diego, I'm going to La Loon," she said. "I've been away for too long. I want to check on Jabbers."

"Take me with you," he said, and seeming to hear his earnestness, he looked away.

"Jabbers might eat you," Lou said. "I've never brought…"

She searched for the word. What was Konstantine to her? *Boyfriend? Lover?*

"Anyone," she decided on. "The men I bring are for her to eat. It stands to reason she'd see you and think you're food."

"I'll take my chances," he said with a grin.

Lou arched both brows. "That's because you haven't seen her."

She stopped short of adding, *She's going to scare the shit out of you.*

He considered this for a moment. Then his smile softened. "I trust you."

Her heart clenched as if kicked.

"A trip will take your mind off your shoulder. We can do a proper exploration. I can collect soil and plant samples. We can discover the mystery of La Loon together."

He was searching her face, looking for her answer.

She could admit, if only to herself, that La Loon was a mystery that taunted her. She wanted to know why—of everywhere in the world she could go—she went to La Loon.

It wasn't like she hadn't tried to use her power in other ways. But when she submerged herself in water, it was always La Loon that served as the first stop.

La Loon, with its nightmare landscape of blood-red waters, two moons, and dense black forests. Why should she always slip to that unfathomable place? That said nothing of the monster that guarded the domain.

A beast who Lou was half convinced would tear Konstantine open on the spot.

"I'll take you," she said with a wicked smile. "Don't say I didn't warn you."

5

Screaming ripped through the dark room. Lou came up out of a dead sleep, her gun in her hand.

"No, no," Piper said, holding out a hand toward Lou. "It's okay. She's dreaming."

Piper reached across Dani's writhing form and clicked on the hotel lamp.

"Dani, hey, Dani, wake up. Baby. *Wake up.*"

Dani stopped struggling against her imaginary attacker and grew still in the tangle of sheets. Her heavy breathing continued until slowly, her eyes opened, squinting against the light.

Lou's shoulder burned. She lowered the gun, aware now that she'd pulled it with her left hand, her bad side. Now nerve pain shot up the side of her neck every time a vertebra shifted.

"Was I screaming?" Dani asked, touching her face. When her hands came away wet, she looked at her fingers as if she'd never seen them before.

"No big deal. You okay?" Piper asked, running a hand through her hair.

"I'm so sorry," Dani said, pulling herself up. She pressed her back against the headboard and clutched the covers to her chest. "I'm so sorry I woke you up."

"We don't care about that," Piper said, pushing the hair back from Dani's forehead. Several strands were stuck to the side of her face, plastered there by sweat despite the humming air conditioner.

Dani glanced at the gun in Lou's hand. "I scared you."

Piper made a face over her shoulder. Lou chose to interpret the wide eyes and nod to mean, *Say something nice.*

"I always sleep with a gun," Lou said.

Piper motioned for more.

"In my hand. Like this," Lou added.

Piper rolled her eyes.

"Excuse me." Dani climbed out of the bed. She slipped into her flip flops and crossed to the bathroom. She flicked on the light before closing the door and shutting herself inside.

For a moment the two of them remained where they were, unmoving. Piper stared down at Dani's pillow as if just discovering it empty.

"Does that happen a lot?" Lou asked, putting the gun on the nightstand and trying to roll her shoulder back.

Piper ran a hand down her face. "Yeah. Petrov really messed her up."

Lou imagined that was true. She'd seen the condition Petrov had left the girl's body in after he was done torturing her for information about Lou—information Dani didn't have.

In the hospital, small and broken, Dani hadn't seemed like a formidable investigative reporter capable of destroying Lou's anonymity. She'd seemed like a young woman who'd walked through hell and back, but there had still been steel in her eyes. That more than anything had convinced Lou not to silence her.

"It's worse when she stays over at my place," Piper said, scratching the back of her head. Lou could see the pillow lines cutting across her exposed cheek. "I think she wakes up and doesn't know where she is. But when we sleep at her place, it happens too. She says it happens less when we're together though."

Explains why you sleep together most nights, she thought. She wasn't about to mention how many times she'd appeared in Piper's room in the dead of night just to check on her and in doing so had found Dani asleep in her bed.

Piper continued, the circles dark under her eyes. "I guess I should've realized staying in a hotel might trigger it. New place. New smells, or whatever."

Lou rotated her aching shoulder again. "Some wounds take longer than others to heal."

Unfortunately.

They heard the shower crank on in the bathroom, but it didn't mask the soft crying.

"She'd probably prefer it if we just turned off the lights. I think she's embarrassed," Piper said, and leaned across the bed to flick the switch.

Lou sat in the darkness for two heartbeats. Then she rose from the bed and crossed to the bathroom door and pushed it open.

"Lou—" Piper began.

But Lou had already shut the door behind her. Her compass wasn't always for travel after all. Sometimes it told her where she needed to be, even when she had no need to slip at all.

The bathroom was already half full of steam. The mirror was fogged over and a thin mist was forming on the sink and toilet.

The curtain waved slightly from the force of the stream.

"It's me," Lou said, one hand on the curtain.

"I'm okay," Dani said, her voice thick.

Lou pulled back the curtain anyway.

Dani was sitting in the tub, fully clothed, her back taking the full force of the stream. The water was scalding her skin, turning it red.

Lou crouched down on the floor beside her, the edge of the tub between them.

Spray ricocheted off of Dani's body, splattering Lou's arm and face. She didn't care.

"I saw him ripped apart," Lou said softly. "Petrov is dead."

Dani lifted her face from her knees, her face red with tears. "I know."

"Very dead. Entrails on the ground, head torn off. He isn't coming back for you."

Dani nodded, pushing the wet hair back from her face. "I know. But in my head, I feel like I'm going to wake up and it'll be someone else hurting me. Like there's someone waiting in the wings. Him or someone like him, they're going to come back."

Dani glanced at Lou's arm and frowned.

"You must think I'm pathetic. You've got a million scars. And look at you. You don't fall apart every time you have a bad dream."

Not anymore.

That hadn't always been true. What could Lou tell her about her own nightmares? Of Angelo's face emerging from darkness as he pulled his gun and blew out her father's brains?

Of her father screaming out her name?

How many times had she had that dream, or a variation of it? A hundred? A million?

Yes, Lou knew plenty about bad dreams and the way they hung in the atmosphere long after the dreamer managed to wake. How they burrowed under the skin and crawled along the bones, making it impossible to rest.

Lou followed the girl's gaze down her own scarred arms. Every nick, every cut, every raised scar or puckered bullet hole. She'd been hurt, sure. But she'd never been held down and tortured. She'd never had a finger severed from her hand.

"You're not weak," Lou said, running a hand down her arm, clearing it of droplets.

"Then maybe I'm stupid. Anyone smart would walk away from a job that'll get them killed. Investigative journalists are murdered all the time. Or they're imprisoned, and here I am acting like I can take it, but maybe I can't." Dani sighed. "This is all I've ever wanted to do with my life. Tell the stories that everyone else is afraid to tell."

"Then do it."

"Even if it's stupid? Even if it's reckless and I'm not proving anything to anyone—not even myself?"

"Yes," Lou said, unflinching.

Dani wiped the water from her face again.

"I don't think I could walk away even if I wanted to. Even if it *is* the smart thing to do." Her lips trembled. "God, if it happens again—"

"If it happens," Lou interrupted, "I'll be there."

6

Robert King stepped out from beneath the green café umbrella. Without hesitation, the unforgiving sun beat down on his head and neck. He groaned. The black coffee in his grip immediately felt too hot for consumption.

Iced coffee, the girl behind the counter had recommended, but to King, iced coffee was an abomination. Why would he want to water down his drink when he liked it strong enough to burn an ulcer through the side of his gut?

But standing in the sun with the heat pressing against his mind like a wad of cotton, he was beginning to see the appeal.

King began the slow march back to his office, cutting across Jackson Square, clotted with its pop-up artists and living statues. A girl with a violin played a sad melody beneath the awning of a yarn shop. It hadn't always been a yarn shop, but King was struggling to remember what it was in its previous life.

A souvenir shop? Did they sell t-shirts? It didn't matter to him or the hundreds of bodies cluttered in the square. A young man sat on the curb with a trumpet thrown over his lap. He dabbed at his black brow with a navy handkerchief.

It seemed everyone sought shade where they could find it.

The smell of coffee wafting from his cup was met with something fried and spicy.

He hadn't even fully crossed the square before he felt the sweat pool at his hairline and trickle down the back of his neck. He loved winter in New Orleans, which was much milder than the fierce midwestern climate of St. Louis. But New Orleans in summer was almost too much to bear.

King marched on, noting all of this distantly, counting the steps until he'd be back in his air-conditioned office.

Stepping from the square onto Royal Street, his heart lurched. Even at this distance, he saw the woman waiting on the stoop of The Crescent City Detective Agency. Sweat rolled from his temples. He could feel the dampness under his arms and soaking through the collar of his shirt.

He didn't want to talk to a client right now. He wanted a cold shower.

He wanted to sit in his chair and cool off, sip his coffee, and review the day's objectives. Or maybe he wanted to go by his apartment and change his shirt.

But she'd already spotted him, standing and brushing the dirt from her bottom.

"Mr. King?" the woman called, stepping forward. "Robert King?"

She was blond, blue-eyed, and very pretty. She would've been a welcome sight if not for one problem. King knew immediately who she was.

He forced a smile and extended his hand, inwardly disgusted by its dampness.

"That's me," he said. *Best to play it dumb until I know what she wants.* "Do I know you, ma'am?"

"No, no." A sweet, nervous laugh escaped her. "I'm Abby Smith. I was hoping you could help me find my sister."

Interesting angle, he thought, keeping his smile carefully in place. "Come on in and let's have a chat."

King slid his key into the agency's lock and used his hip to pop open the sticky door. It swelled on warm days like this one and a little extra leverage was necessary to separate it from its jamb.

He entered the office first, looking it over the way one does when an unexpected guest arrives.

Was everything put away? Anything incriminating or too revealing sitting out where it shouldn't be?

The red waiting chairs were empty and dusted. The magazines sat in a careful stack. Piper's desk was clear on its surface, chair unoccupied. He was suddenly very glad that the girls were away for a couple of days. It was good timing. It would give him a chance to figure out what the hell was going on here.

"Can I offer you something to drink?" he asked mildly. "I've got water, tea, coffee, juice..."

"No, no, thank you."

Her eyes were roaming the space as fiercely as his were.

His own desk was not so tidy. Stacks of file folders, a half-eaten sandwich, and his laptop crowded its top. King wasn't worried about the mess, but he was trying to remember which case he'd left open before stepping out.

Sikes, he thought. The burglary case that the local PD had off-loaded to him because they had no leads and no money for another full-time detective.

Was King worried about himself? Maybe he should be, with this viper in his den. But King had a few secrets, too.

He glanced to the back of the office. There were three closed doors. One was a bathroom, one led to Piper's apartment upstairs, and the third—*Shit*.

His first real problem.

King read the name plate mounted there. *Ms. Thorne.*

The labeled storage closet was empty. Nothing in there but toilet paper, paper towels, boxes of unused manila folders, and cleaning supplies. King had also put a few cardboard boxes with tax records in there, on the metal shelves that covered both walls.

He seriously doubted the woman behind him gave a damn about any of that.

But the name plate. Oh, the *name plate* might be worth her time.

Piper had put the damn thing up as a joke because Lou was always using the dark closet as her personal entrance. Lou didn't need a real office. She was an unofficial partner in this agency, sure. Her extraordinary skills helped King more often than not. But Lou came and went as she pleased.

Now would be a terrible time to pop in, he thought. *Don't.*

Lou's possible appearance was only one problem. There was a second, more immediate one.

Was it possible that Diana Dennard, the woman who'd introduced herself as Abby Smith, already knew Lou's name?

If so, that name plate was a dead giveaway.

And her name *was* Diana. Not Abby. King knew that much.

"Thank you so much for seeing me," the woman said, taking the chair opposite King's desk. She'd chosen the cluttered one even before King rounded the corner and sat down in his chair. He was careful to keep his eyes on her face.

Don't look at the door, he thought. *Don't look at the name plate and she won't.*

Because he couldn't exactly go over and take it down now. That would be too obvious.

"You're welcome," King said, fishing a paper napkin out of the drawer and using it to pat the back of his neck and his temples. Once soaked, he threw it into the trash bin under his desk. "So tell me about your sister."

"She went missing back in January. We're from the East Coast."

"Oh yeah? Whereabouts?" he asked, knowing full well they were playing a game. Even in games, sometimes people gave surprisingly accurate information. King had learned this after thousands of interrogations as a DEA agent.

"Philadelphia. She was only a semester from graduating from Temple and then she takes off with this guy, can you believe it?"

"It happens," King said companionably.

"We looked everywhere for her."

"Did you file a missing persons report?"

"Well, no," Diana said, and here her smile faltered.

Oh, she's good, King thought. Her acting skills were superb. She'd been able to, on command, affect the blush of embarrassment.

"We don't want her to get into trouble with the police or anything. We just want to find her and bring her home. She's always been a little rough, if you know what I mean."

"I see," King said. "If you're from Philadelphia, how did you end up all the way down here?"

How did you find her? King wondered. *What scrap of information led you to us?*

Because there were a lot of cities in the world and Lou could travel to most of them before lunch. What had set Diana on a trail to New Orleans? To King specifically? They'd been more than careful. And not just King and Lou. Konstantine kept a close eye, scanning all channels for so much as a mention of Lou.

"My sister loves this city, so I thought I'd check it out," Diana said. "I've been here for about a month, asking around. A guy I spoke to yesterday tells me that he saw a robbery at the Julia Street station in March. I didn't think anything about it because you know how New Orleans can be. But then the guy described my sister *perfectly*. And he said she was *shot*. Shot! If that's true, I have to find her. I *have* to. Even if it means she's dead."

Her voice broke on *dead*, the lip quaking. And here were the tears. Right on time.

King lifted his mug and took a drink. He slid the tissues across his desk automatically.

Diana took one and dabbed at those big blue eyes. "I've been told you're the best private investigator in the city. You *have* to help me find her. Money is no problem. My parents are well off and they want to find her as badly as I do. We'll pay anything."

King knew she was lying. Maybe she had money, sure. But there were no parents back east. And there was the fact that she'd yet to say her sister's name.

He also knew the secret informant was a lie, because King had been there the night Lou was shot at Julia Street station. He was the one who'd compressed the fabric to Lou's bleeding throat and begged her to go to the hospital. He was the one who'd hidden her guns and vest, and washed the blood off his sleeves in the park's fountain before the paramedics rolled up to the scene.

There had been no one there, not a soul except himself, Melandra, Lou, and Mel's ex-husband, Terry, the deadbeat now in jail.

It's gotta be the blood, he thought. *Someone must've collected it from the scene, run DNA analysis. But what had Diana had to compare it to?* DNA had to be compared to something.

He knew Konstantine ran ruthless checks on the internet for photos, data, and anything pertaining to Lou. He guarded her anonymity more fiercely than Lou herself did.

But it was painfully clear to King that they'd missed something.

Or Diana's smarter than the average bear.

"Do you have a photograph of your sister?" King asked.

"No," Diana said, sniffing. "Unfortunately, my parents suffered a bad house fire last year. A total loss."

"Sorry to hear it. That's terrible. Facebook? Instagram?" he pressed.

"No, we don't have anything like that."

Convenient. Secretly, King was relieved. Diana might've tracked her to New Orleans, but she hadn't done it through video footage or wayward photos. In that way, Lou was still a ghost.

"But I had a sketch artist draw this." Diana reached into her leather satchel and offered a piece of paper across the mess of his desk. "I described her to him and he rendered her perfectly."

King took the drawing and surveyed it.

Yes, he did, King saw. It was a good match. The artist had captured Lou's features well enough that King saw Jack in them. Jack, Lou's father, and King's former mentee—until his sudden and tragic death.

What interested King about the drawing wasn't only the shoulder-length dark hair or the leather jacket. It was the fact that Lou wasn't wearing her sunglasses. Day or night, Lou often wore her mirrored shades.

Diana must've looked her in the eyes, King thought. *When?*

"What's her name?" King asked.

He saw the woman stiffen in his periphery.

"Louise. She goes by Lou. But she might be using an alias."

So she did have a name. Sort of. Louie must've introduced herself as Lou, if she'd introduced herself at all. And she must not have mentioned Thorne. Otherwise, it would have been Abby Thorne, not Smith, wouldn't it?

Again he had to physically stop himself from glancing at the name plate on the closet door.

"Will you help me?" Diana sniffed again. "You have to help me."

"I'm very sorry, Ms. Smith. I'm packed to the brim with cases at the moment." He made a vague gesture to the stacks piled between them.

Anger flashed across the woman's face. It was such a contrast to the blubbering, concerned woman she'd been the moment before, King thought, *Your mask is slipping, Diana.*

Then Diana's face crumpled so quickly King couldn't be sure he'd seen the anger at all. "But you *have* to help me. Please. I need to know where she is."

A personality disorder, he thought. The emotional shifts were too severe and swift. Of course, he was no psychologist.

"Ms. Smith, the first thing I would do is file a missing persons report with the NOPD. I have a buddy there, Dick White. I can put you in contact with him. They can put out a bulletin, look around, and do a far better job than I can do with my present workload. Would you like that?"

"No," Diana said, standing up suddenly, forcing the chair back. "No, I wanted *your* help. The police are useless."

Or is it really you don't want any police involved at all?

"I'm very sorry. I simply can't take on another case right now. I'd be more than happy to put you in touch with the right people who can help you."

"No," Diana said, stiffening. She reached across the desk and snatched the drawing from King. "No, I don't need your help. Thanks for nothing."

And with this, she made a big show of stomping from the agency into the ruthless August sun.

As soon as the door slammed behind her, King's first

impulse was to call Lou. To tell her that she needed to be careful, that for whatever reason, Diana Dennard was looking for her. But as soon as this thought came, he shoved it aside, afraid that its very existence might call Lou to him.

He didn't want Lou to come. He wanted her to stay with Piper, heading west, far away from here. Putting her on a collision course with this psychopath—and there was no doubt in his mind that Diana Dennard was a psychopath—couldn't possibly end well.

No, King thought. *It won't end well at all.*

7

D iana pulled a chair up to her desk and opened her laptop. *Lou Thorne, Lou Thorne, Lou Thorne.*

The name had repeated like a mantra in her mind ever since she saw the name plate on the door.

Lou what? she'd asked that night in the diner.

And Lou, with all her damned smugness, had grinned. *Just Lou.*

It seemed a long shot that the PI and Lou had a connection. Yet, she'd seen the detective's face when she'd said, "Her name is Lou."

Then came the refusal to help her. Maybe Lou was Lou Thorne, or maybe not. But the guy knew something about Julia Street station and the woman.

My story was good, she thought. *How did he see through it?*

She bounced her foot impatiently as the computer booted up. She typed the name into the search engine.

She didn't expect to find anything. If Lou was deep undercover, as Diana thought she was, then it seemed unlikely a simple internet search would return much. But she had to start somewhere.

And at first she seemed right. There were no social media accounts. No online photos or work history. No "graduated from such-and-such school."

"Damn," she grumbled at the screen. The room had grown dark around her as search after search turned up nothing.

"Try agencies," the woman leaning against the wall said. She was cleaning her fingernails with a six-inch blade. "These ghosts almost always have law enforcement work histories before they go deep. Otherwise, where do they get the skills from?"

Diana didn't question her sister's logic. Instead, she searched for *Thorne* and every agency pairing she could think of. Thorne because she couldn't be sure what form of Lou was the correct one. Louisa? Louise? Louann? Lora? There were a hundred variations and King's smug reaction to *Louise* made her think she'd been on the wrong track.

Smug bastard, she thought, her fingers striking the keys.

Thorne and *CIA*

Thorne and *FBI*

Thorne and *police department*

Thorne and *Department of Defense*

NASA. Marines. Air Force. Army. Navy. Coast Guard.

Thorne and *DEA*

An article popped up. *One-year anniversary since decorated DEA agent and wife slaughtered in home.*

Something in her gut kicked. She selected the link and began to read all about Jack Thorne and his wife, Courtney. About what transpired one night over fifteen years ago, in an affluent suburb outside St. Louis. How Thorne and his wife were shot to death by the mafia after Jack arrested and charged the son of a Capo Crimini.

At the bottom of the article, after all the details of the

brutal murder had been laid out for public consumption, was a photo of the surviving daughter.

A little girl with brown eyes and brown hair. Sullen. Quiet. Familiar.

Louie Thorne, it read.

Diana wondered if the picture had been taken after her parents' murders. She thought so. There was already something dark and haunted in those eyes.

Diana sat back in her chair, staring at the screen.

"Did you find something?" her sister asked.

"Maybe." Diana pulled up the search box one more time and typed in *Louie Thorne*.

Nothing.

She tried again. *Robert King. Jack Thorne. DEA.*

And there was King's face smiling back at her, his arm over Jack's shoulder.

"An old family friend then," she said. "Looking out for your buddy's kid after he's killed. Guess I walked right into that."

Blair came around the chair and leaned over Diana's shoulder. "Is that what she looks like?" She pointed at the dark, sullen child.

"This picture is at least fifteen years old."

Blair frowned. "Why do you have that look on your face?"

Diana chewed her lip, unsure why the anxiety in her limbs had spiked suddenly. "She's like me. I mean, I already knew she was like me, but I didn't realize how much like me."

Blair gave a crooked grin. "So she's a heartless, obsessive bitch too?"

"Her childhood was destroyed. She coped by fighting back, and she's been fighting ever since."

Blair settled into another chair. "Can I ask you something?"

Diana met her gaze. "What?"

"What do you hope to gain by tracking down this woman?"

"I want what she has."

"And what do you think that is, *exactly?*"

"Money, resources. The things I need to take down Winter."

"And let me ask you this. If you were her and someone showed up and was like, 'Give me your stuff,' what would you say?"

"I'd tell them to go fuck themselves."

"Exactly. Because you work for yourself. You do what you want. Why in the world are we wasting time tracking her down? She's not going to help you. If she's as much like you as you think she is, this will never work. In fact, I'll bet a hundred bucks she won't help you."

"She had no reason to help Jennifer McGrath, but she did," Diana mused. She thought of the night the pervert Jeffrey Fish came to kill the girl. While Diana watched through the window, Fish broke into the girl's house and chased her up to the bedroom with the intention of murdering her.

Once Fish began to rough the girl up, Diana had wondered if she should intervene. It didn't matter to her whether or not the girl ended up dead. Diana had been content to let him wear himself out, and once spent, she'd step in and have her fun. She'd only wanted to make sure Fish didn't see another sunrise.

But before she could decide, Lou had simply appeared.

One minute all Diana could see was Jennifer's wide, kitten eyes and heaving chest. The next, Lou had Fish by the hair, pulling him out of the spotlight of an overturned lamp on the bed.

Lou was good at hiding, at moving unseen.

Diana could use that against Winter.

"If she isn't in it for herself, then she does it for other people," Diana said. "And she isn't hunting mafia bosses, she's hunting serial killers. This isn't about her."

"You don't know she hasn't killed mafia bosses. She could've murdered a hundred of them and then got bored. The point is, you don't know enough about her. Period. You have no reason to believe she'll help you. Why are we doing this, Di?"

Diana had seen Lou in action. She'd seen how coldly the woman had torn Fish from the room. She'd seen the woman's hunger—and her restraint. If anyone could give her what she needed to trap Winter, it was Lou.

"She'll help," Diana insisted, looking at the photo of the kid on the computer screen, the one who'd lost everything but had rebuilt herself into something better, stronger. "We just have to make an offer she can't resist."

8

King spotted Mel at a table before the hostess could pull a menu for him.

"There she is." He pointed at the woman with an Octavia Butler book open in front of her. "Thanks."

He angled his wide body through the gumbo shop's tight configuration of tables, making his apologies as he passed, trying not to bump corners or shake overfilled water glasses. Soft jazz seeped through unseen speakers and the whole place reeked of andouille sausage. Spicy and delicious.

His mouth watered.

Mel looked up from her book and smiled. Her hair was natural, teased out to its full height and pushed back from her face by a soft silk scarf.

"Good evening, Mr. King," she said. The gold bangles on her wrist jingled as she pushed a menu across the table toward him. "You're late."

"My apologies." He stooped and planted a kiss on her cheek, French style. "How are you?"

"Fine," she said, unfolding the napkin across her lap. Then she reached up and fussed with the many overlapping necklaces at her throat, gently untangling the strands with her dark fingers.

"And Lady?" he asked, fondly warming at the thought of the Belgian Malinois.

"At home, napping. Do you want to take her with you tonight?"

"No, she's fine with you." This was a lie. King missed the dog when she was across the hall from his apartment, sleeping with Mel. But he knew that the dog brought Mel great comfort and security. And with Dennard lurking around, it made him feel better to know the Belgian Malinois was close by. It was good protection and that dog would die for her.

"Why are you late?" Mel lifted her water glass and took a sip. "I was about to order without you."

"I had to take the long way around." He lowered himself into the chair. He didn't pick up the menu. He knew what he wanted. "I was being followed."

He'd spotted the tail halfway down Royal Street. It moved like a shadow in his periphery. When he'd bent to tie his shoe, he used the dark, reflective surface of his cell phone to search the street behind him. A man with a hobbled gait sharply turned, pretending to look in a storefront window as he rose.

King had cut across Jackson Square, walked through a souvenir shop and out the back, across the alley and into the adjacent street, squeezing past a young man taking out two large bags of trash. It helped that King's own hip wasn't talking to him tonight as it sometimes did. Watching his tail hobble as he did reminded him to be grateful for these rare pain-free days.

Mel straightened in her seat. "Who was following you?"

"A short man, uneven gait, and glasses. And something is wrong with his hair."

Mel snorted, a laugh half escaping her. "What do you mean, something is wrong with his hair?"

King touched his right temple. "I can't tell if he's got a bald spot here or if it's burned short. But something was wrong with it."

"What can I get y'all tonight?" the server asked. It was a woman in a white apron and black tie.

"Chicken andouille for me," King said. The smell of the sausage in the air was making him ravenous. "With a side of cornbread."

"Cup or bowl?"

"Bowl."

"Butter and honey?"

"Yes, please." King would love some sweet, buttery cornbread this very minute.

"And you, ma'am?" she asked.

"Seafood gumbo for me. I'd like the cornbread too, please. And hot sauce."

"Yes, ma'am. Waters, all right?"

"Yes, thanks," King began, then added, "Actually, can I have a Coke?"

When the waitress left, Mel leaned toward him across the table. "Back on subject, please. You've got a guy following you. Do you know why?"

"Either he's with Diana Dennard or he's a different problem."

"Diana Dennard," she said, frowning and placing one hand on the cover of her book. "Where've I heard that name before?"

"Lou crossed paths with her back in March, when they were both hunting Fish."

Last King heard, the serial killer was still behind bars, having admitted to over forty kills to date. King didn't think that would be the end of it. He was sure Fish would confess to more soon enough.

Every time Lou's restlessness got the best of her and she went out into the night to dig up a new grave, it prompted new confessions from Fish.

"Right," Mel said, shaking her head knowingly. "The other vigilante."

King didn't like that word, *vigilante*. It conjured images of masked avengers blowing up government buildings. Lou—whatever she was—didn't fit that description.

To him, she was an arbiter of retribution. A queen of death. Karma.

Payback.

"Dennard came into my office today pretending to be Lou's sister. She was asking about what happened at Julia Street station."

At this Mel visibly stiffened. King understood why. Mel had been the one to pull the trigger that night, and the bullet that was intended to scare her bully of an ex-husband had torn through Lou's neck.

Mel fingered the necklaces at her throat. "You don't think—"

"There's nothing to find," King assured her. "Konstantine and I thoroughly cleaned that scene. But maybe some blood was collected for processing. It could've been collected and processed as part of Terry's case."

Mel grimaced at the sound of her ex's name.

"Maybe they're reviewing all evidence for his trial," King added.

This wasn't anything Melandra didn't know herself. "I'm sure the prosecution is gearing up."

King noted the candle flame flickering on the table, seeing the light dance in her kohl-rimmed eyes.

"You seem okay with that," King said, accepting the Coke put on the table by the passing waitress.

"Terry rotting in prison?" Mel harrumphed. "Hell yeah, I'm okay with that."

Her smile came easy then. Wide and bright. King thought that her smile came a lot easier these days, now that Terry was out of her life.

"And cornbread," the waitress said, placing a large plate on the table beside a small dish of butter and a honey pot. King eyed the mound of soft white cream.

"Thanks," he managed, but the waitress was already gone.

"They're busy tonight," he remarked. "Will you go to the trial?"

"No," she said. "I've seen enough of his face to last me a lifetime."

She looked out over the restaurant, eyes falling on a young couple with a baby standing up in its highchair. The mother was scolding it softly.

"It's amazing," Melandra said.

King didn't think she was talking about people having babies, so he kept his mouth shut.

"Absolutely *amazing* how we torture ourselves. All those years of guilt and shame, me believing something that never even happened. And for what? I've lost so much time, Robert."

King reached across the table and covered her hand with his. He gave it a firm squeeze. "You've still got a lot of time left."

And she did. Twenty or thirty years at least. She was healthy and not even old enough to retire, though he couldn't imagine her ever doing so.

"I do," she said with a bright smile, turning back to him at last. "And I'm not going to let anyone else take that away from me. Never again."

"That's the spirit," he said, unable to resist the cornbread any longer. He used his fork to smear butter along the top, which melted instantly. Then he drizzled honey before shoving it into his mouth.

His stomach turned appreciatively.

"Do you think this Dennard woman is dangerous?" Mel asked, moving a piece of cut cornbread to her plate, balancing it on her knife. "To us?"

"I don't know. Her operation is underground. I don't think she would benefit from outing Lou, not with the risk that she herself would be outed. Konstantine said that she was running credit card scams to fund her operation. She stands to face real jail time if she moves out into the open. Whereas Lou would only lose movability. There are no bodies or proof of her crimes, so if she were brought into the public eye, it would just mean that she'd have to work harder to disguise herself going forward."

"No more snatching people from the streets."

"Not without proper precautions," King agreed. "But the question is, what does Dennard *really* want with her?"

Melandra's frown deepened. "You don't think she wants to eliminate the competition, do you?"

King tried to imagine Diana hunting and killing Louie. Louie was the most dangerous and capable person he'd ever met. But she wasn't without her limitations.

"I hope not," he said. "I *really* hope not."

"They're still in the shop," Spencer said into the small communications device clutched in his grip. "I can't believe he slipped me like that."

"You weren't careful," Diana said, whispering into the earpiece tucked into the conch of her ear.

She stood on the stoop outside The Crescent City Detective Agency and pretended to smoke. She hated the taste of tobacco on her tongue and fought down the urge to spit. The passersby talked and laughed with one another, stumbling down the shadowed streets on their way to another bar. Diana hated them too. And this city. It was dirty. Noisy. Crowded. Too many piss-scented drunks wandering around.

And any place with too many people was the worst.

Spencer continued whining in her ear. "Excuse *me*. I warned you that my walk is too pronounced. You should've sent Blair. Oh, their food has finally arrived."

She threw down the cigarette. "I'm going in. Message me when they ask for the check."

Diana inserted two steel pins in the lock on the front of the building. It took a minute to find the correct placement, but once she did, she heard the tumbler move and the door popped free of its hinge.

The office was empty. Moonlight poured through the high window and painted the floor and furniture. Shadows pooled at the back of the shop.

Both desks were clear of all debris. She wondered if King took all his materials home with him each night. He must.

She closed the door behind her and locked it.

In King's chair, she ran a hand over the tabletop, but there was nothing. She wiggled the drawer, but it was locked. She tried to use her pins to open it, but this lock was much smaller. She switched pins.

Once the drawer was open, Diana realized she'd wasted too much time. There was only a notepad, business cards, and gum in the drawer. A few pens were scattered as well. There were names on the cards, and scraps of paper, but none of them meant anything to Diana.

None of them read *Lou*.

She closed the drawer. Her eyes fell on the name plate. *Ms. Thorne.*

Diana crossed to the door, expecting to find it locked. But it opened easily. Diana's heart rose in her throat as she pushed the door wider. She wasn't sure what she expected to find in this room. Another desk. Lou herself, typing away, burning the midnight oil?

And what would she say if she came face to face with the woman now?

But there was nothing. At least, not an office.

There was a row of metal shelves against one wall. Against the other, shelves full of the most banal items. Toilet paper, a box of legal pads.

Diana ran her hand along the shelves, but found no secrets.

Her fingers traced the walls, the dips in the concrete bricks. But nothing.

Is this some sort of secret panel? she wondered.

She pushed against the wall, wondering if there was a way to get it to open. Or maybe there was a secret lair.

Maybe there was a whole *world* under her feet. Questioningly, she tapped the floor with the toe of her boot.

But no matter how she picked at the corners or shoved against the bricks, nothing gave.

Irritated, she pulled the door closed behind her.

The room to her left was a bathroom. The room straight ahead was locked.

Diana was able to use her steel pins to unlock it and found a flight of steps on the other side. They ascended into the dark.

Diana threw one nervous look over her shoulder at the dim office. People passed the large picture windows, but the office itself remained dark.

"They still eating?" she asked into her comm.

"Yeah, the guy just ordered another helping of cornbread. This guy can eat."

Diana mounted the stairs and pulled the door closed behind her. Inside, she found an apartment. A clean, shadowed kitchenette, a living room with sofa, coffee table, and TV. A window that shone with moonlight. The sheer white curtain seemed to glow in the moonlight.

Down a short hall was a bedroom and bath. The bed was made, though not tidily.

Diana searched the side tables. She went through the closet and searched the pockets of clothes. She pulled the luggage down from the top shelves and opened a box that turned out to hold a lot of photographs.

None were of Lou. Most featured a blond girl that Diana didn't recognize.

Is this your apartment? Diana wondered, eyeing the blonde in the pictures with her arms thrown companionably over her friends' shoulders.

At first she thought Lou might live here. But now it seemed that wasn't the case. Or at least, there was nothing in the apartment that suggested Lou's presence. No leather jackets or mirrored shades. No credit cards or paperwork bearing her name.

"They asked for the check," Spencer said in her ear. "Might want to get moving."

"Are you giving me orders now?" Diana said, low.

"N-no, no," Spencer said, too quickly.

"I didn't think so."

If this wasn't Lou's residence, it didn't mean she didn't have a connection to this girl. She simply didn't have the whole story yet.

Putting the bags back the way she found them, Diana crossed to the living room.

She scrawled *Piper Genereux* on a scrap of paper, copying it from the internet bill on the counter, and slid it into her back pocket.

She decided on the upper-right corner of the room as a place to put the minicamera. The microphone bug was taped under the lip of the window, beside the sofa.

She decided to tape another under the counter in the kitchen. And a third in the bedroom, inside the lamp.

"They're getting up. They're leaving," Spencer said. His voice was rising, strident with his fear.

Diana groaned inwardly. Spencer didn't have the stomach for espionage. If he weren't a master with technology and as obedient as a dog, she'd have done away with him ages ago.

"Don't get your panties in a twist."

She could already see Spencer in her mind, in his full leathers, his mouth zippered shut to smother his soft mewling.

Her body warmed.

What a lovely way to spend an evening, she thought, content to have something to look forward to.

Casting one last look at the apartment and making sure it was as she found it, she descended to the office. She stooped under King's desk and pulled another bug from her pocket, fixing it to the underside, deeper than anyone would think to look or reach.

She took the note from her pocket and affixed the top with a strip of tape from King's dispenser.

On the outside of the door, she reminded herself as she stuck the note to the door. *No need for King to know I've been snooping.*

Then she stepped out into the crowded, hot night and pulled the door shut behind her.

9

Lou sat in the back of the car and stared out at the desert. It was beautiful, she had to admit. She loved the dry heat. The tall red rocks growing straight up into the sky. The vast, empty landscape was punctuated only with a passing cactus from time to time, and comically, a tumbleweed. She'd thought they were fake, a made-up comic effect for cartoons. In the distance, a coyote trotted toward the horizon. Its ears lay flat when it caught the sound of the approaching car.

The only flaw was the light. There was too much of it. Lou was a creature of darkness in most ways, and here in the desert, shadows were few and far between.

Piper's phone rang. She dug between the console and seat to find it.

"It's King." She answered it. "*Yo.* I've only been gone for a day, man."

Piper's humor fell away. "What?"

Lou sat up between the seats, regarding her face.

"Yeah, hold on." Piper handed the phone out to Lou.

"Is everything okay?" Dani asked.

"I don't know," Piper said, watching Lou's face carefully.

But Lou knew her expression was unreadable. Her mirrored sunglasses would only reflect Piper's concerns and fear back at her.

"What happened?" Lou asked by way of greeting.

"Diana Dennard walked into my office this morning, pretending to be looking for a missing sister. Can you guess who the missing sister is?"

"Did she see the name plate?" Lou asked.

King hesitated.

"King?"

"I'll tell you, but don't come here now. Don't pop up. She might be watching."

The back of Lou's neck itched. "Okay."

"I think she saw it, yeah, and put it together that we know each other. She must have."

"Why?"

"She left a note for you." He sucked in a breath as if bracing for a blow.

A chord vibrated through Lou's body like a tuning fork.

"How did she know your name was Lou?"

"Because I told her."

"Last name?"

"No last name," Lou confirmed.

"I was worried about that. There was a moment when she turned away, right before she stormed out—I think the name plate might've caught her eye then."

Lou said nothing, sensing that King was warming up to tell her the worst of it.

"She's got something else on you."

Of course she does, thought Lou. *She hunts like I do.* Dennard wouldn't have picked New Orleans out of a hat.

"What led her to New Orleans was the blood collected

from Julia Street station, but I don't know how she made a DNA match."

Lou threw her mind back. She thought of the last time she'd seen Diana. They were in an all-night diner in Ohio, not far from the scene of Fish's arrest. Lou had drunk a cup of coffee, refusing to give more than her first name. She thought she'd left a tip, though she had a vague memory of pulling the bills from her jacket and throwing them on the table before leaving.

"Can DNA be pulled from money?" Lou asked. Her back was growing hot against the dark seats. Lou realized Piper had cut the A/C so she could hear the conversation better. "Or a coffee cup?"

"Both," King said. "If the prints were clean, which only happens about thirty percent of the time. I tried to pull prints from the tape she used, but both the note and tape were clean. She must've worn gloves or wiped them."

Lou's irritation spiked. She hadn't expected the woman to pocket her coffee mug after she left. She hadn't even considered the idea that the woman might have access to that sort of technology. And not only the ability to collect and profile DNA but the ability to sweep a police department's private data centers to confirm a match.

Dennard was no amateur.

Don't make the same mistake twice, her father's voice sounded in her head. *You underestimated her once and look how close she's gotten.*

"What can she do with my name and DNA?" Lou asked.

"*What?*" Piper said from the passenger seat. "Who has your name and DNA?"

Lou shook her head, asking Piper to wait.

"I don't know. It depends on what she wants. At first, I thought she'd found out I was at Julia Street station with you. I gave a statement that night, so it was possible she came to me thinking I'd seen something. But she never mentioned that. It's possible she might've come to me by coincidence, hoping to get a decent PI to track you down."

King was being humble. He was more than decent as a PI, but Lou wasn't the type to fluff someone's ego.

He sighed into the phone. "The question is, why does she want you? Did she give any clues when you talked?"

Lou tried to remember the night she sat down with Diana Dennard. The conversation had been interesting. Lou remembered feeling mostly intrigued, that after all her years of hunting and killing, she'd finally encountered someone like herself. Another woman who added counterbalance to the injustices of the world.

"She asked a lot of questions about who I worked for, and what my resources were. What did the note say?"

King hesitated. With a smile, Lou knew he was considering lying. She heard paper rustle and wondered if he was digging the note out of the trash.

"King?"

"She wants to meet. In two days at the po'boy shop on Basin. Across from the cemetery."

Lou said nothing.

"Are you going to go?"

She smiled. "Should I?"

She'd already made up her mind.

King seemed to consider this. "I can't tell you what to do. But keep your eyes open, all right? Be careful about popping in and out of New Orleans."

"All right," Louie said, and terminated the call. She handed the phone back to Piper.

"What's happened?" Dani asked from the driver's seat. She was applying her lip balm a bit too frantically.

And seeing the way she clutched the wheel with her free hand, Lou began to understand why Dani kept insisting on driving even though she could've easily passed the task over to Piper.

She feels more in control behind the wheel. Safer.

"You better start talking," Piper said, wagging her phone at Lou. "What the hell is going on?"

"Diana Dennard is in New Orleans. She came to the agency looking for me and she knows I work with King."

"Dennard," Piper repeated disbelievingly. "The crazy lady we caught stalking Fish? The killer who hunts killers but doesn't give a shit about the women he kills? *That* Dennard?"

"Yes," Lou said plainly.

"And this psychopath knows that you work with King? She figured it out from DNA because you had coffee with her?"

"And because I was shot."

Piper tapped her phone against her chin. "Oh, this is *bad*."

"She wants to meet." Lou tried to consider the situation clearly.

Piper looked at her as if she'd just sprouted a second head. "What? *No*."

To be fair, this wasn't a one-way street.

When Lou learned there was another woman tracking Fish, she'd investigated her, too. She'd learned Diana's name and history. And then what? Nothing. She'd simply wanted to know who Diana was and what she was after. That was where her curiosity had ended.

Was it possible that Diana was only curious about Lou, too?

Piper's mouth hung open. "You can't be serious about meeting her. She's crazy!"

Lou said nothing.

"Unbelievable." Piper pressed her fingertips into her forehead. "I should've never put up that name plate. It was stupid. Totally stupid."

"You're not stupid," Dani countered, her brow scrunched. But she was grabbing her lip balm from the cupholder again and uncapping it. "Stop saying that."

"I don't like it," Piper said. "I don't like her sniffing around. What the hell does she want?"

"I'm sure we'll find out," Dani said, wringing the wheel again. "I don't think she came all the way to New Orleans for nothing."

iper glanced into the back seat and found Lou...*dead*. Not really. She was sure the woman still had a pulse, but Piper had never seen anyone so miserable-looking in her life.

God, this road trip really was a bad idea, she thought, not for the first time since they'd left New Orleans and traveled west along I-10.

"We're almost there," Piper said from the front seat. "You want some chips?"

Lou, who remained reclined on her back, one arm over her eyes, shook her head. "I'm fine."

"Are you?" Piper asked. "Because you look like you've been murdered."

Lou lifted her arm and met Piper's gaze. "Have you ever seen someone being murdered?"

God, leave it to murder to perk this girl up, she thought. Aloud, "No. And I hope I never have to."

She didn't need to ask Lou the same question.

"Look! There it is!" cried Dani. She was pointing over the dashboard at the blue horizon peeking between buildings.

Five minutes later, they parked the Lexus in an empty space opposite the beach.

Dani popped the trunk and pulled out the three chairs and a stack of large towels, and nodded toward the umbrella. "P, will you get that?"

Lou grabbed the cooler, which they'd stopped at a gas station to fill that morning with ice, water, soda, and beer.

Salt hung thick in the air, seeming to settle on the skin like silt. Waves crashed, adding a blanket of white noise to the scene. Gulls cried out as they swooped low overhead.

Then they were set up and watching the water, as if they'd been there all along.

Piper took a deep breath of ocean air. "Oh yeah, baby. Smell that."

Lou didn't appear to be inhaling. She caught Piper staring at her. "What?"

"*Breathe.*"

"I'm *breathing.*"

Dani squeezed her left hand gently. Piper could either interpret this as *Chill, babe* or *It's okay.*

Piper rubbed her forehead. "Hand me a beer, please."

Lou obliged, opening the cooler and shifting the ice around.

"I don't think you're supposed to drink alcohol on the beach," Dani said.

Piper half-buried the can in the sand. "What beer?"

They spent the morning like that. And when Lou stood up around noon and wandered away, to Piper's credit, she didn't call after her and insist that she sit down and enjoy this beautiful day. She didn't even complain to Dani about it.

She simply sat with the itchy feeling in her heart that this had all gone wrong. It wasn't how she'd wanted it to be. And she felt *not okay* about it.

She doesn't like hanging out with me. This isn't fun for her. I'm stupid and boring and...

Lou returned, with three hot dogs and a pocketful of condiment packets. She tossed them onto a clean towel spread on the warm sand.

"Oh, thanks," Piper said, her narrative cut short.

"They also have soft serve," Lou said, pointing at the food stand halfway down the beach. "Twist."

"I love twist cones."

"I know you do," Lou said with a quizzical brow. "That's why I'm telling you."

This cracked what was left of Piper's reserve. "Lou, I'm sorry."

Lou was stuffing half a hot dog in her mouth. "For what?"

"For this whole stupid road trip idea. I thought you'd have fun, but I can tell you're bored out of your mind. You're in the sun all day, which I don't think you love."

"I don't."

"Right? You're a vampire. And it took forever, when you can just pop to a beach with half a thought."

"I can."

"I *know*." Piper tore open a mustard packet with her teeth and squeezed it onto the dog. "But I wanted you to have the experience. And I wanted us to spend time together. But it was stupid. I'm sorry I insisted we do this."

Lou looked out over the water, placing her elbow on her raised knee. "When I go places, I'm just there. I don't see the in-between. In a car, you see everything. All the parts that connect one place to another. That was nice."

"You liked that?"

"Yeah. I did."

The tight coil in Piper's chest relaxed. They stayed on the beach until the sun reached the horizon. The sky melted red, orange, pink. Piper ate a twist ice cream cone and finished her beer.

"We can drive back without you," Piper said, packing up the beach towels and putting the empty cans in a bag to be recycled. "You don't have to do another two days of this."

"No," Lou said flatly. "I'll ride with you."

"Why? It's a monumental waste of time."

"It's a good habit," Lou countered. "To finish what you start."

LOU OFFERED TO CARRY THE CHAIRS AND BAGS UP FROM THE car to the apartment. Without waiting for their permission, she put her hands on what she could and shifted from the dark of the car parked in the alley to the apartment above.

Pain sparked in Lou's shoulder as she made a second trip. It wasn't the blinding pain that she felt two months ago whenever she would raise her arm or take too deep of a breath.

Piper's apartment formed around her and she deposited the first round of stuff onto the floor at her feet.

It took Lou four trips to bring all the stuff from the white-gold Lexus into Piper's apartment. Once she was done, her shoulder throbbed so badly she felt unsteady on her feet.

On the last trip, the door opened at the same time and Dani and Piper stepped inside.

"Whoa," Piper said, wrenching her key from the lock. "Sit down. You okay?"

"My shoulder."

"We shouldn't have let you carry all that stuff," Dani said, reaching into the cabinet for a glass. She filled it with water and put it in front of Lou. "Where's your aspirin?"

"Bedside table," Piper said, putting the water in Lou's hand. The good hand, not connected to her overworked shoulder. "But she's right. I wasn't even thinking about your shoulder. I'm sorry, man. I was just thinking I didn't want to carry the chairs up those steps."

"I'm fine," Lou said. She hated being fussed over. It was like a spider crawling up the back of her neck.

Dani appeared, shaking three ibuprofen into her hand. Lou rolled her eyes up and met Dani's. "I'm going to need at least 800 mg."

Dani shook out another pill before handing it over.

Lou took it with the water, finishing the glass in a single go.

Her eyes kept sweeping the apartment. What was this feeling? Like a gnawing in her gut.

"Did you do something different to your apartment?" she asked, assessing the sofa, the kitchen counters, and the gently humming fridge.

Piper followed her gaze. "No. Why?"

The pain in her shoulder made it difficult to think. It pressed against the inside of Lou's skull, obliterating thought. Every breath made the left side of her body throb.

I couldn't fight someone now even if I wanted to, she thought miserably. *Not without trashing half my body*.

She practically heard Konstantine tsking her in her mind. *You should be resting*, amore mio.

Still she searched the dark, expecting to see someone. "No reason."

11

Diana stepped into the hot stream of the hotel shower. It had been a long day. Both of the scouts she'd sent out to canvass for Winter had come back with nothing. She was too worried to send any more. If he suspected that she was close, he might move his entire operation, and it would take her months, maybe years, to track him down again.

She couldn't bear the thought of losing the bastard a third time.

At her desk, comb in her hair, she turned on her computer. A furious swipe of the keys brought her to a black login screen. A back-door login to the dark net.

Diana put in her password for a fake profile she'd created. *Dwayne6669.*

She repeated this until she'd joined all the available feeds.

Box after box appeared, each containing a live video stream. Three, four, five...

Winter had eight feeds running tonight. Each with a different child featured.

It was the one in the bottom right that caught Diana's

eye. The girl was seven, maybe eight, with bright eyes. The leather dog collar around her throat was connected to a chain on the floor.

A man, black t-shirt, no pants, stood over her. His erection in full view.

A rough knock came at the door. "It's Blair."

Diana opened the door and found her on the other side.

"Did you see the feed?" Blair asked.

"I'm watching it now."

Blair came into the room, crossing to the desk. "No, not this one. The one from the apartment."

"What—" Diana began, but then remembered the bugs she'd planted.

I need some sleep, she thought. *I'm borderline useless.*

Blair's fingers hovered over the keys. Her face was scrunched up in disgust. "Can I close this? Pedophiles sick me out."

"Yeah."

A few furious punches and a new screen showed the angled interior of the apartment. Diana had researched the place after she'd left it. There was no listed tenant for that address. The detective agency, apartment included, was listed in King's name. But mail she'd seen for Piper Genereux had told her a bit. Piper was a student at Delgado Community College and her official place of employment was Madame Melandra's Fortunes and Fixes, an occult shop around the corner.

Diana had yet to figure out if King had the girl holed up above his office like a live-in girlfriend—a girl fifty years younger than him, a nice lunchtime fuck before getting back to the task of investigation—or if he'd rented her the apartment because she worked for his landlady.

She wasn't yet sure how all these people connected to one another. It seemed clear that Louie Thorne was the daughter of King's long-dead comrade, but what about the others? How did they fit together? What did they do?

And were these lives just covers for a larger operation?

Or was Louie's life, her secret life, a mystery even to these so-called friends?

Diana wanted answers.

"Why are you splitting the screen?" she asked, watching Blair's fingers fly over the keyboard.

"It's the live feed on the right, and the recorded feed on the left."

On the right all Diana could see was two girls sitting on a sofa. One had a mug of something in her hand. She looked Latina, maybe, with thick brown hair and coppery skin. The other was blond, a blanket draped around her shoulders. At their feet was a pile of luggage and...beach chairs? Had they had a beach day today?

Diana wasn't even aware there was a beach in New Orleans. Then again, she hadn't been in the city long.

"Look at the left. I want to show you something. Here." The laptop's fan clicked on. Its soft whirring filled Diana's room.

The feed on the left had been rewinding, and now it showed an empty apartment with bare floors and no girls on the sofa.

"What am I—" Diana began.

"Shh, just wait."

This amused Diana, who enjoyed when Blair's intensity showed. It was good to know she wasn't the only one invested in this operation. To Diana, it often felt that way.

"There!" Blair froze the frame, then let it roll forward at half-speed.

Diana saw it. One minute the apartment was empty, the floor bare. The next, Lou stepped into the frame, arms full, and deposited armfuls of crap onto the floor.

"Is there a door there?" Blair didn't take her eyes off the screen. She pointed at the dark corner of the room where Louie had entered.

Diana stared into the deep pocket of shadow. It took her a moment to review the layout of the apartment, but no... *no*, she hadn't seen a door there.

"Keep watching," Blair said.

Diana did. After dumping three bags on the floor and rotating her left shoulder, Lou disappeared through the pocket of shadow again.

Only to reappear, this time with the beach chairs.

"You're *sure* there wasn't a door there?" Blair asked, her voice high with excitement.

Diana hadn't inspected that corner of the apartment thoroughly. Could there have been a false wall? It had seemed like an *outer* wall, and a story off the ground. Could something have possibly been behind it?

"I didn't look close enough," she admitted. She sat forward. "I want to hear the audio."

Blair furiously punched a few buttons.

"I wasn't even thinking about your shoulder. I'm sorry, man. I was just thinking I didn't want to carry the chairs up those steps." It was the blonde talking.

"I'm fine," Lou said.

The blonde looked up from the pile on the floor and frowned harder. The other was tapping pills into Lou's hands.

Lou threw them back with the ease of a junkie. Hell, maybe she was. Diana didn't know nearly enough about her to rule out a history of addiction.

Lou bent and picked up one of the bags from the mix, a small duffel, as the other two prattled on about nothing.

Diana took everything in about Lou. She looked the same as she had months ago in the all-night diner in the middle of nowhere, Ohio. But she was holding her shoulder differently.

It was Lou's voice that broke the spell. "I'll be gone for a while."

Diana leaned even closer to the screen, until she began to see the pixels of the image in front of her.

"No," she murmured. "Don't go."

The blonde seemed equally unhappy to hear the news. "What do you mean?"

"I'm going to La Loon."

"Alone?"

"With Konstantine."

The blonde pouted. "For how long?"

"I don't know. A few days. But if you try to reach me—"

The dark-haired one laughed. "I highly doubt a page or text would go *that* far."

The blonde sighed, visibly unhappy. "Be safe, I guess. I'll tell King."

Then Lou was gone, again through that strange patch of darkness in the far corner, half cut off by the edge of the screen.

I've got to go back, Diana thought. *I have to look at that wall again—if it is a wall.*

"Show me the feed from now," she said.

A few more furious punches and real-time video feed came into full screen, along with the accompanying audio.

"Babe, you've been going on about this for hours."

"I know." The blonde dragged a hand down her face. "I just worry about her. She's supposed to be resting her shoulder and taking it easy, and she's doing a *great* job."

Sarcasm dripped from the girl's words.

The other one laughed. "You're one to talk. When's the last time you had a day off?"

"Touché."

"And besides, at least she's trying. She did sit in the back of a car *both ways*."

"True," the blonde said.

"And now she's going to La Loon, which is sort of like a holiday for her."

The blonde asked, "Do you need to get home?"

"I thought I'd sleep over."

"Oh." The blonde sat up straighter. "What about Tavi?"

Is Tavi her kid? Diana wondered, always looking for connections and pressure points.

"She's with my parents."

"Do you think we've found Lou's home base or what?" Blair asked.

"There might be a problem with the tech, maybe the camera has a blind spot or something. Otherwise, there's a false wall there that I missed."

"Or maybe she can walk through walls. A literal ghost."

Lou had seemed real enough when she sat across from Diana, drinking coffee.

Her eyes flicked back to the screen.

"Is it okay?" the dark-haired girl asked tentatively, visibly fidgeting with the mug in her hand. "If you're tired, I can just—"

"No," the other girl said eagerly. "No, I want you to stay."

Then she was shrugging out of the blanket and coming across the sofa to kiss her.

"Ooh la la," Blair said. "What do we have here?"

Diana barely noticed the make-out session developing on the screen. Her mind kept wandering back to Lou, stepping from the shadows in the apartment.

There has to be a door, she concluded. *That building must have a secret passage or something.*

Did Lou have a secret apartment there? Beneath the agency? Or behind a wall? Or perhaps she made her home somewhere else in the city?

Despite the shadows, it had been Lou, unmistakably. Lou

in the leather jacket and her mirrored shades. Lou with a duffel in her right grip.

But who the hell was Konstantine? He must be somewhat important if Lou would take off with him for a few days.

"Did you put a camera in the bedroom?" Blair asked hopefully as the girls rose from the sofa.

"Not a video feed, just audio."

Blair pouted. "Shame."

And La Loon...She'd never heard of it. Was it code for a hideout? An island in the Pacific or something? Diana had the impression that wherever it was, it was remote. Isolated.

Blair turned away from the video and regarded Diana's profile. "About tomorrow..."

Here we go, Diana thought, groaning inwardly.

"Are you still going?"

"Yes," Diana said, keeping her eyes on the feed without seeing it.

"Do you think she'll come?"

Did she? She had until Lou'd mentioned this so-called *La Loon*. Maybe Lou couldn't spare the time now. "Maybe. Unless she has to go to La Loon right away."

"And then?"

"Then I'll talk to her."

"And then?"

"Then hopefully she'll give me what I need to take down Winter."

"And *then*?" her sister pressed.

"And then *what*?" Diana snapped back. "Spit it out."

"When will it be enough? If you find Winter, kill him, then *what*? Is it going to be enough for you? Can we quit then?"

"Not this again, Blair. It's late."

"So what if it's late?" Blair sat back in her groaning chair. "You never sleep. You hardly eat. And I'm worried this won't be enough for you. *Ever.* You'll get Winter and then *what*? I want you to tell me what your life—*our* life—will look like after you kill him."

Diana looked at the screen without really seeing it.

"What's going to fix this for you? Can you really let all this go after Winter is dead? Or will it be like this forever? You running yourself into the ground and me watching you do it?"

"I don't know," Diana said, and knew with certainty this was a lie.

12

L ou stood at the window of her St. Louis apartment and tried to understand the queasiness in her gut. It wasn't unlike the feeling she had when someone stood behind her. It was accompanied by an itch in the spine and the impulse to turn.

And Lou kept turning, but there was nothing there. The apartment was bright with morning light. It was quiet, undisturbed. A crow passing her window called out then was silent.

There was no one lurking behind her, ready to swing.

Why do I feel like I'm being watched?

She shrugged in her shoulder holster, noting the two guns press into her ribs. The coffee maker beeped, signaling that her brew was ready. She drank it black, enjoying the sweet smell and bitter taste on her tongue.

She was unhappy. She recognized this distantly, with some cold, detached part of her mind that regarded feelings as strange, inconsistent phenomena.

This comprehending part of her mind also understood it was because she was not hunting. She was not doing what it was in her nature to do, and that made her unwell. Melancholic.

Why aren't you hunting? she asked herself. *Why aren't you out there killing some kingpin or wife beater or—*

She knew the answer. It wasn't the flaring pain in her shoulder which came and went like a tide. It was the terrifying suspicion that everyone was right.

King. Piper. Konstantine.

Everyone who kept trying to remind her about her shoulder, her so-called limitations—that chorus of nagging voices plagued her. But she'd yet to think of a better way to scratch that itch under her collar.

She could still ambush, sure. She could appear behind anyone and simply grab them and put a bullet in the back of their head. She could do it with ease.

But that wasn't *hunting*. It would hold no release for her. No challenge.

Lou took another drink of her coffee before setting the mug on the island counter. Then she pulled a stopwatch from a drawer and laid it beside the mug. She turned the stopwatch over and activated the voice command setting.

She took a deep breath. "Go!"

The stopwatch started its timer at the sound of her voice, and as quickly as she could, she pulled the left gun, the one governed by her good, right shoulder.

0.05 seconds.

She tried again, but this time pulled from her weaker side.

0.2 seconds.

She grimaced. Too slow. And worse, just that one pull had her shoulder throbbing.

She pulled again.

0.4 seconds.

Because pain slows you down, she thought.

Realistically, she suspected she could get only one or two

pulls on that side before her arm was useless. Leaving the gun in her hand also posed a challenge. The weight pulled on her shoulder, irritating it.

She wanted to try again from the hip. She took a break, giving her throbbing shoulder a chance to relax.

She refilled her coffee and thumbed through a paperback she'd found at a thrift store that day. In it, the hero hunts the man who betrayed him. When she finished the coffee, she began again. She put on a hip holster, fitting guns into their designated slots.

She pulled from her good side first. *0.03 seconds.*

She restarted the stopwatch and pulled from the left. *0.13 seconds.*

That was better. Maybe because the shoulder wasn't quite as hitched from its starting position.

But what are you trying to prove? To whom?

Lou stepped from her linen closet into the stone casing of a crypt. Startled birds shot from their nests at her sudden appearance. The stone floor scraped against her boots, the walls thick with cobwebs and dust.

A little warm for a nest, she thought, stepping over the broken stone slab that might have once been the door and into the open air. A breeze caught in her hair as her boots adjusted to the uneven ground.

The cemetery spread out in all directions. Coping graves and ledger stones lay interspersed with the vaults and a few crypts. Through the wrought-iron gate, Lou saw the po'boy shop King had spoken of.

She crossed the street carefully, waiting for a white sedan with a donut tire to pass before she approached.

The bell dinged.

Four of the five patrons looked up.

One was Dennard. Her blond hair was pulled back in a severe ponytail, her blue eyes bright with unhinged excitement. Her leg began to bounce under the table as she clutched a basket of fries between her hands.

Behind her a mother pushed battered shrimp into a toddler's mouth as he stood precariously on the seat beside her.

Across the aisle, Lou made eye contact with a man in his forties. What was left of his wispy hair had been smoothed back from his face. His mouth was ajar, as if he'd just heard terrible news. Lou thought he should be wearing a lab coat—something about him seemed...scientific.

The fifth patron had already turned her back to Lou as if uninterested in the new arrival.

A man in a stained apron appeared behind the counter.

"Mornin'," he said with a jovial smile. "What can I do you for?"

Lou walked down the center aisle to the counter. She passed Diana without acknowledging her.

"The fish and shrimp," Lou said after a cursory glance at the menu.

He pulled a pen from behind his ear. "Fully dressed?"

She wasn't sure what that meant, but she was far from a picky eater. "Sure."

"Fries? Pickles?"

"Yes, thank you."

"Anything to drink?"

"No."

He tore the sheet of paper off the notepad and pounded the register keys. "It's cash only here. That okay?"

Lou didn't bother to explain that cash was the only thing she carried. She'd never had so much as a credit card in her name. She simply handed over the bills and thanked the man.

"I'll bring it out to ya," he said, and flashed her a smile. "Sit where you like."

Lou barely noticed the smile. She was watching the parody play out behind her, courtesy of the large mirror stretched behind the register.

The woman in the leather pants sitting alone at a table was making frantic eyes at Diana. Diana waved her off. The man too was watching the exchange, glancing from Lou to Diana and back.

They're all together then.

She suspected the woman with the child and the cook behind the register weren't part of the stakeout, but she wasn't prepared to write either of them off. Should this come to a shootout, or some other altercation, it was better to assume everyone was an enemy.

Dennard had chosen this place. For all Lou knew, she owned it.

Lou pulled out the chair opposite Diana. The screech was terrible and made the woman flinch in revulsion.

She seemed even more shocked that Lou had chosen to sit so close. The small table between them was an insufficient barrier. It was so small, their knees touched beneath its top.

Dennard pushed her chair back as if this would spare her.

Lou said nothing. She left her shades on. It was easier to keep her eyes on the room when she wasn't expected to look directly into someone's eyes.

The silence stretched between them, Diana's partners growing uneasy. When the child suddenly broke into a wail, pushing back at an offered piece of shrimp, both of Dennard's companions jumped in their seats.

Diana and Lou remained unmoved.

Diana ended the silence first. "I didn't realize how alike we were. *Louie Thorne.*"

Lou waited for her to elaborate. After all, who knew what

conclusions she'd drawn about Lou in the five months since they'd last seen each other.

"Did you kill them all?" Diana asked. When Lou didn't answer, Diana pressed on. "The Martinelli family was blamed for your parents' execution. I've got few connections in the criminal world, but the ones I have all say the Martinellis are dead. Even the one your dad put in prison disappeared." Here Diana smiled. "Or did he?"

Lou said nothing.

Diana was undeterred by this. Somewhere in the back a pan flared to life with the hiss of oil against heat. "Then there was your dad's partner. Gus Johnson."

Lou's right hand twitched imperceptibly beneath the table.

"Marked missing, but suspected foul play. There was blood on his recliner and carpet. But no body. His front door was locked from the inside. But you would've been only seventeen or eighteen when this happened."

Lou had still been seventeen when she'd gone to Johnson's house with her father's blade in her pocket. Johnson had been her first kill, payback for giving the Martinellis her father's address in order to save his own skin.

"Did you know King has a missing partner too? Ex-partner? He wouldn't have had anything to do with all of this, would he?"

Chaz Brasso? Sure. Lou had finished him too.

The cook with the greasy apron appeared. His hands were wrapped in surgeon's gloves as he put the basket on the table in front of Lou. He smelled like grease and fried meat.

"There's hot sauce and ketchup on the table. Napkins there. You need somethin' else?"

"No, thank you."

He frowned at Diana's untouched fries. "You don't like yours?"

"I'm letting them cool," she said with a forced smile.

The guy nodded, but he didn't look convinced. "You girls let me know if you need anything else."

Lou started in on the food, intending to leave nothing behind. Lucky for her, the sandwich was delicious, a perfect marriage of sweet smoked meat and vinegar.

Diana continued talking. "If Gus was your first kill, and he's the earliest one I could find, then I'm way ahead of you."

Lou let her talk.

"You've been doing this for eight or nine years, I figure. I've been at it for over twenty-five."

As if this is a competition, Lou thought, taking another big bite.

"I must have a hundred and fifty to my credit," Diana went on, finally putting a fry in her mouth. She left out the word *bodies*, but Lou understood. "Not that I count."

Of course you don't.

"What about you?" Diana asked.

Lou had stopped counting in the high two hundreds, and that was years ago. She was sure she was well over three hundred now, possibly four. Mostly because she'd specialized —no, *thrived*—in large firefight shootouts for a while. Ten minutes of action could put as many as thirty bodies on the ground.

"Well, you got the ones that hurt you," Diana said, as if to cheer her up. Here her eyes took on a wolfish glean. "That's what matters, right? Those are always the ones that matter most."

Here it comes. The pitch.

Diana laughed to herself as if she'd made a joke only she could understand. She put her hands on the table, on either side of her oily food basket.

"It's just *crazy* to me how alike we are. We both saw some horrible shit, lived through some horrible shit, but decided to fight back—good for us. We were both a bit famous for a minute, both disappeared..."

So Diana knew about the first slip. The one that carried Lou from the family bathtub to a pool hundreds of miles away, not without a tangential stop in La Loon.

The manhunt for the missing daughter of a DEA agent hadn't lasted long, but it had hit the local news nonetheless.

"And here we are!" Diana held up her hands as if she marveled at her own assessment.

"Here we are," Lou said flatly.

It was the mania in Diana's eyes she didn't like. She'd seen that look before. In Angelo's eyes before Lou had made him drive his car into the Baltimore bay. In the Russian mob boss Dmitri's eyes when they were finally face to face and he wanted her to atone for the sin of murdering his son.

"The only problem is I *haven't* killed everyone who's hurt me." Diana leaned forward. "I have tried myself, *many* times, to corner this bastard, but he's a snake. But with someone like you, with your resources, I think it'll be possible. *Together*, I think we can take this bastard down."

Lou understood now.

The compulsion to avenge. It was why she hadn't been able to stop after Gus Johnson, or Angelo Martinelli. It was why Lou had torn her way through every man who'd been a part of the wreckage of her childhood, including Chaz Brasso and Senator Ryanson. Even Konstantine had found himself at the end of her gun.

Lucky for him, things turned out differently.

And yet, she also understood something that Diana did not. That once this man was gone—whoever this final target was—she wouldn't be free of the hunger consuming her now.

Worse, something darker, more desperate, would replace it.

Lou had learned this lesson all too well.

"He's the last one," Diana insisted, clutching the basket in front of her. The plastic warped in her hands.

That's what you think, Lou thought. "You weren't hunting him when I met you in Ohio."

Because she'd been hunting Lou's target—Jeffrey Fish. A serial killer with a penchant for pretty blondes like Diana. Though he seemed to prefer them about ten or fifteen years younger.

"Correction," Diana said. "I'd just finished hunting him. But he got away. He has a habit of packing up and running whenever he smells trouble."

"No," Lou said.

Diana started as if slapped. "No?"

Lou had no problem saying it again for the sake of clarity. "I can't help you."

Diana's cheeks darkened, the red spreading out toward her ears and neck. "Do you think I can't pull my own weight? You don't know the bastard. He's slippery."

What could Lou say? That it wasn't Lou she needed? That Diana could manage the job just fine without her and that wasn't the problem? The problem, Diana would discover, was what happened *after*. When there were no more targets. When there was no way to scratch the itch in a way that truly satisfied. When every makeshift target that followed would seem like the ghost of a meal for a long time to come.

That's when the madness came. A death unlike any she'd known before.

Lou had no interest in shepherding her toward it.

Instead, she stood, pushing back the chair. She took her empty basket to the counter and put it by the register. She slipped a twenty into the tip jar, not foolish enough to leave it on the table for a second time. The cook gave her a solemn nod, which she returned.

"Maybe now is a bad time," Diana said. Her voice was

pitched for amiability, but the derision was clear. "When you get back from La Loon. We'll talk then. But think about what I said. Think about it."

There was the hint of a threat to those words.

Lou hesitated at the door, but she didn't look back. She simply pressed forward, stepping out into the bright day.

13

K onstantine stood in his living room, watching the shadows grow long on the cobbled floor. He considered the two bags at his feet. One had a couple outfits, a washcloth, soap, a pop-up tent, and a tightly rolled sleeping bag. The other held slim packets of freeze-dried and dehydrated food, enough to feed them both for four days. There was also his gun, ammo, two lighters, and a firestarter brick as well as the compact sample kit with its little tubes and tools for collection: latex gloves and tweezers.

He wondered if he should bring more than a gallon of water.

Did he want to carry it?

He wouldn't let Lou shoulder any of the burden. He was determined that she rest her injury for the full six months at least, though the doctor who'd put her back together mentioned it wouldn't be unheard of for her to need a year or longer to heal.

And even then, on bad days, the muscles and nerves might bother her all her life.

He wasn't foolish enough to remind her of this possibility,

given how much resistance she'd posed to the minimum six months.

He lifted the bags and found they were manageable, one for each shoulder. He hoped the one gallon of water would suffice.

The pressure between his ears popped.

Lou stepped into the room. Her glasses were pushed up onto her head. She frowned at the luggage.

"What's all this?"

"Specimen collection kit and our supplies."

"For what?"

"For La Loon." And now fearing she'd forgotten, he added, "For our trip."

"We enter through a lake," she said.

He smiled. "These bags are waterproof."

"Yes, but you will have to swim to the surface once we get there."

"That's what this is for," he said, and turned one of the packs on its side so she could see the flotation device fixed underneath. "When I activate it, it will rise to the surface."

She arched a brow. "If you get eaten, I'm not bringing any of this back."

He smiled, stepping toward her. She smelled like food, something salty. He kissed the side of her throat.

He moved to her lips.

"I thought you wanted to go," she said, her breath warm against his mouth.

"I do. But I also missed you."

Lou wrapped an arm around his waist. "You have to stop kissing me if you want to go."

"Do I?" he asked. "Have you tried kissing and..." He didn't know the word for what she did.

"Slipping," she offered.

"Kissing and slipping before?" His stomach knotted as he

realized he might not like the answer. He didn't want to think about her kissing someone else.

Lou pressed her body against his until he could feel the notch of her hip bone against the top of his thigh. He adjusted the weight of the packs until they felt steady.

She took his mouth with hers.

Then darkness, a shift where all the air left him.

It was as if a belt had tightened across his chest. Or perhaps she was sucking all the air, all the life from him.

When she pulled back they stood at the edge of a lake.

She was grinning. "*Breathe.*"

This startled a laugh out of him. He hadn't realized he'd been holding it. "So this is it?"

"La Loon? No. This is the first stop."

She stooped at the edge of the water and scooped up a small leather backpack that he hadn't seen before.

She saw him looking at it. "I brought it earlier."

Konstantine wasn't sure what he'd expected her dumping ground to look like, but this was quite mild compared to his imagination. For him, it had been built to mythical portions. He'd imagined something like Lake Avernus, an entry into the underworld. The gates of hell.

But this lake was much smaller, placid with a thin mist hanging above the water. Frogs croaked out a hoarse melody. Something with wings buzzed past his right ear.

From where he stood he could see a herd of deer drinking on the other side of the water. Small rings formed where their snouts touched the surface.

A doe lifted her head and regarded him with cautious eyes. The others twitched their ears too, but they didn't seem all that surprised to see Lou.

The water was dark, but held the purple sheen of an approaching dawn. And it was much cooler here than in Italy.

"We're in Nova Scotia," she told him, as if reading his mind. "I have another lake in Alaska."

"Is it this beautiful?"

A rustling in the trees above drew his gaze skyward in time to see an osprey open his wings and glide. Its cry echoed as it soared over the lake, heading in the direction of the brightening forest.

Something moved through the trees off to the right, making a small chirping sound unlike any that Konstantine had ever heard.

"Racoons," she said, smiling.

"Racoons," he repeated, committing the word to memory. He had no image to accompany the word.

"Have you ever been out of the city?" she asked, obviously amused.

"Once," he said. The night he and his mother were dragged from their beds by his father's rivals. The night his mother was executed.

The sky began to shift from purple to pink. She lifted the backpack and strapped it to her shoulder. He caught her wince.

"Let me," he said, extending his hand.

"I can do it."

"It doesn't look heavy. Let me take it."

"I don't need you to carry things for me," she said, her irritation spiking.

Konstantine laughed. "I am well aware. But there is nothing wrong with letting someone help you. You've helped me plenty of times."

When Nico had nearly killed him, putting enough metal into his body to end his life, it had been Lou who had picked his ravaged and bullet-ridden body off the stone floor.

Again in New Orleans, when Konstantine had used his considerable wealth and power to outmaneuver Dmitri

Petrov, it had not been for the purpose of saving Lou. In his mind, Dmitri stood no chance against her. He understood that Lou was more than capable of protecting her own life and overcoming such a man.

That aid had been in service of her friends, the ones Dmitri could very well have killed.

"If Piper had a hurt shoulder, would you carry her bag?" Konstantine asked, hoping to shift her view on this.

"I carry her bag anyway."

Konstantine nodded as if his point was made. Then he saw the blank expression on her face and realized it hadn't been made at all.

We take care of the ones we love, he thought. *Because we care, not because they are helpless.*

He couldn't bring himself to say it aloud.

Not when she was regarding him as she was now.

He let it go, giving her a slight nod. He didn't want to begin their adventure with quarreling.

She stepped into the water. The deer on the other side of the lake lifted their heads, watching. But they did not run.

This was the part Konstantine wasn't entirely excited about, but he followed her in.

The water was cold. The chill pressed against his legs and groin. He hissed.

Lou looked over her shoulder at him, smiling. She continued walking backward. "Too cold?"

"No."

"You sure?" she teased, seeming to relish his discomfort.

"I'm *fine*," he said. *I have warm, dry clothes in the bag.*

She stopped when the water was chest high, waiting. She removed her sunglasses and slipped them into the pocket of her leather coat, buttoning the pocket closed.

When he reached her, she slid her arms around his waist.

The intimacy surged through him. He wanted to touch

her back. He wanted to coil his body around hers like a snake, but he had all these bags.

"You'll know we're across because the water will turn red," she said.

His heart began knocking in his chest. He felt his pulse in his throat and temples.

"As soon as you're across you need to swim to the surface and get to shore. There are things in the water that will eat you if you linger too long. Or go too far out."

His fear spiked. "What?"

But she was smiling.

"Are you kidding?"

Her smile widened. "I'm not kidding. Get to the shallows as quickly as you can, but let me get out first in case Jabbers is there. If the water things grab one of your bags, let it go. Don't hold on."

His heart was pounding so hard he found it difficult to breathe.

"Just give me a minute," he began.

"Take a deep breath."

"Okay." He inhaled. "How long does this—"

Lou swept his feet. He sank into the water with his bags. The cold dark overtook him, but her hands were still on his body, holding him close. This was a small comfort.

Then, imperceptibly, he saw the waters lighten, turning from black to red. The cold water warmed.

Lou tugged at his shirt, urging him toward the surface. But this reminder was all that she gave him before separating from his body and propelling herself toward the shore.

She was right about the bags.

Immediately they began to pull him down into the water. He sank, groping for the inflation strings on each side.

Then his boots connected with something and his heart jolted. He shifted, near panic, trying to regain his balance.

A car. He was standing on the roof of a *car*.

He pulled the first inflation string and the pillow expanded. He was pulled toward the surface slowly. Then he pulled the second string and really gained velocity.

Ahead of him, a dark shape shifted in the water, revealing a long serpentine body.

Don't stay in the water, she'd warned him. Her grin had made it seem like a joke, but now he suspected that it hadn't been. Whatever he'd seen—or had almost seen—he didn't want a closer look.

He broke the surface. Lou was already in the shallows, shaking water off her leather coat, flapping the front against her chest. She pushed her hair back from her face and turned to see him swimming toward her.

Her eyebrows raised. "You'll want to swim a bit faster."

He followed her gaze and saw four dorsal fins, pointed and black like those of killer whales, cutting the water ten yards away.

He needed no further incentive.

When he was within reach, she bent and grabbed his bags, tossing them onto land before he could object. But she didn't flinch at the task. In fact, she no longer guarded her shoulder as she had moments before. Her posture had improved and her shoulders squared.

He pulled himself from the shallows and looked at the strange world.

It was unlike anything he could've imagined. The blood-red waters. The distant mountains shimmering with an odd yellow haze. Two moons hung in the sky. Close to the water there was a forest, the foliage so dark it was black. Behind Lou, a wide, open plain traced a cliff. The vertical ridge of the cliffs seemed to shoot straight into the sky. He could not see the top of it, lost in low silvery cloud cover.

On her left the water continued until connecting with the ridge. The only way to go was right, away from the lake.

Unless someone wanted to swim across the water to the opposite shore and the mountains there.

But the pod of dorsal fins made Konstantine think that would be a short trip, and the explorer would never see that shore.

"What do you think?" Lou asked, twisting the water out of her hair. She was checking her gun, wiping it down with a dry handkerchief produced from a sealed pocket.

"It's a nightmare," he said.

"Wait until—"

A screech tore through Konstantine's body. The sound raised every hair on his arms and made his insides quake.

"—you meet her."

Konstantine expected Lou to pull the gun, put it up and ready. But she put it away.

"Lou," he began nervously. Something was crashing through the forest, knocking down the limbs as it passed. The enormous shifts of thrashing branches told him the creature must be massive.

"Stay behind me," she said.

"I—" His words were obliterated by the creature emerging from the forest.

It was bigger than Konstantine had imagined. Its long black body, scaled like a snake's, was one massive muscle, contracting.

Its six limbs carved away parts of the earth as it launched itself toward Konstantine.

He knew then that he was going to die.

"No," Lou said, and stepped in front of the creature, her hand out as if that would stop it.

She looked so small compared to the beast. One swipe and it could knock her away.

Yet it hesitated, but only for a moment. It tried to dart around Lou, its jaws snapping in Konstantine's direction. The muscles in his lower guts loosened. His knees weakened.

He saw that the inside of the creature's mouth was white, and puffy. He imagined how suffocating it would be to go down such a throat.

It screeched again, obviously irritated by this game.

"Konstantine, come here," Lou said, reaching for him. But her eyes remained locked with the creature's.

"No," Konstantine said, finding he couldn't move from the spot. He held one of his bags against the front of his body like a shield.

"I'll remind you that this was your idea," she said calmly. "Come here."

He inched forward until he was just behind her shoulder.

"Give me your hand."

Konstantine wanted to do anything else, but he shifted the bag to his left arm and extended his right hand. Lou took it, moving it toward the beast's face.

"Do you have to—"

His palm touched cool muscle. Large eyes widened, surveying him. Its pupils dilated.

It's very intelligent, Konstantine realized with horror. He could practically see the thinking behind those eyes.

The beast pressed its nose into Lou's abdomen, audibly sniffing her, her neck and chin. Then it sniffed Konstantine's hand again.

"Mine," Lou said, and put her arm around Konstantine. "*Mine.*"

The beast regarded them. The sound it emitted now was more like a cooing.

Lou moved.

Konstantine mirrored her, unwilling to be exposed. "What are you—"

"Let her smell you."

The beast was on him in an instant, easily knocking his bag away.

It bent its head and Konstantine braced himself for the attack, for the searing pain of having his entrails ripped from his body.

But the beast only smelled him. It shoved its snout against his chest and sniffed, then his abdomen, his groin.

"Hey, *hey*," Konstantine said, covering himself with his hands.

Then she was sniffing his neck and ear, his hair.

"I think she can smell you on me. And me on you."

She. Konstantine wasn't sure he could think of this animal as a *she*.

"You've brought other men. Wouldn't their scent be on you?" he asked.

"I don't think it would've been as strong with such short contact. And it's possible I smelled like you then too."

He thought of the nearly two years since the first time he'd touched her. How many kills had Lou brought and dumped in this world in that time? Countless. Had the beast noticed the shift? Was there, in the creature's mind, a *before* and an *after* of Lou's time with him? Had her scent changed for the animal enough that it now recognized the source of that smell?

Lou was placing a hand on the creature's snout. "I didn't bring anything to eat."

It rubbed against her like a cat.

"It—*she* missed you." He found his hands were shaking.

Lou smiled. "Yeah, I think she did."

LOU WONDERED IF HER RELIEF SHOWED ON HER FACE. SHE hadn't expected this to go so well. She knew that Jabbers was very intelligent. She had pushed Lou into the water once, when she was bleeding to death, somehow comprehending that the help she had needed was on the other side.

And now, it seemed she understood Konstantine—despite bearing every resemblance to the men she often brought here to La Loon—was not on the menu.

It was more than that. Jabbers seemed interested in him. Curious. She sniffed him and his bags. She dragged her tongue up the back of his neck.

She watched him carefully. Lou couldn't recall Jabbers ever showing as much interest in *her*.

Despite how it looked, Lou kept a close eye, ready for the situation to sour at a moment's notice. Hadn't she seen YouTube clips where a tiger befriended a goat, only to eat it later?

As Konstantine collected samples of the shore's soil, the lake's water, and plucked one of the black heart-shaped leaves from the forest, she kept her eye on Jabbers.

She noted that he didn't entirely look away from her either. Good. It was smart to stay aware.

There were other reasons to be alert.

She'd never been away from the water's edge before. In all the years her power had delivered her to this strange place, she'd only ever stepped onto the shore, and briefly at that.

It had never occurred to her to move further inland and actually canvass the land.

What if there were more creatures like Jabbers, who did not have their shared history. Would they simply tear her apart—or die trying? And even if Jabbers was one of a kind, that didn't mean there weren't other dangers.

Konstantine must've seen her sizing up the cliffs. "I didn't bring climbing equipment, but we can follow the lake and see if there is a gap at the end, where it seems to connect with the lake."

They walked the plain that stretched between the cliffs and the lake. The grass—if that was what it was—caressed Lou's knees. It was black with a strange metallic sheen to it. When Lou touched it, turning it in the light, it shined like the back of a beetle, iridescent.

Jabbers trailed on her left, seemingly content to follow her guests. Once in a while, she would press her side to Lou's and Lou would pat her hard body reassuringly. To Konstantine, she would sniff his hair, the back of his neck.

It amused Lou. Mostly because Konstantine's terror was thinly veiled.

He bent and opened his case. He snipped some grass and fed the thin strands into a vial. He filled another clear vial with the soil beneath it.

Jabbers stiffened.

Lou pulled her gun.

"What?" Konstantine whispered, staying low in the grass.

"I don't know," Lou said, watching the beast slink forward, toward the lake, her body low. "It looks like she's..."

"Stalking," Konstantine confirmed.

With lightning speed, Jabbers leapt from the shore into the water. Her considerable length disappeared beneath the surface, leaving large rings in her wake.

A moment later she broke the surface with something thrashing in her mouth.

To Lou, it looked like a turtle without a shell for its top half, while the bottom half looked like a dolphin's tail.

Jabbers tore it apart while it screamed.

Konstantine's face blanched.

It occurred to Lou that Konstantine might put two and two together and realize that his brothers died like this, torn apart on the shore by this very animal as Lou fed them to her, one by one.

The look in his eyes said as much.

"She must eat from the lake," Lou said. "When I don't come."

Konstantine put his samples in their carry case and removed a small device. "I wondered. I haven't seen any birds, or small animals. And she's so big. I can only imagine how much she has to eat to survive."

"What is that?" Lou asked, gesturing at the device in his hand.

He followed her gaze. "It's a SUMMA canister. To collect an air sample."

"Is there anything you don't plan to take a sample of?" Lou asked, smiling. So far she'd seen him collect dirt, water, and any plants they'd passed.

"I'd like a sample of her blood," he said with a laugh, nodding toward Jabbers. The turtle-dolphin creature had stopped screaming. Now there were only wet tearing sounds. "And I don't think that will happen."

"No, but you can get some of whatever she is eating before she cleans it all off her face."

Lou smiled, watching Konstantine consider this option as the beast lay on the shore, cleaning turtle-dolphin guts out of the webbing between her paws.

To Lou's surprise, he approached the animal with a cotton pad in his hand.

"If she eats you," Lou began, "it's your own fault."

Konstantine cooed to her softly in Italian and the beast mimicked the sound. Lou snorted.

Show off.

Then, to her surprise, she let him wipe her paw with the cotton pad.

When he returned to his kit, he looked like a kid who just walked out of the candy store with a fistful of free candy. There was a pronounced bounce in his step.

"And there's little bits of flesh in it," he said, stuffing the cotton pad into a jar.

Twenty feet lay between the edge of the cliff and the lake. Beyond was an endless plain. Lou began walking in that direction, interested in seeing the lake from the other side.

"There's a gap. We can pass through here."

Jabbers bounded into her path.

Lou stopped. She tried going around, but again Jabbers sat up on her hind legs.

"She doesn't want us to go this way," Lou said, turning to find Konstantine frowning behind her.

Lou gazed around the animal at the endless stretch of field. More long, metallic grass swung in a low breeze. But the sky was light and unmarred.

What's out there?

"She must think it's too dangerous," Konstantine said.

"For us or for her?" Lou wondered.

"Maybe both."

Lou looked up at the cliffs. "Then let's call it a night."

She craned her neck up to regard the cliff face. It cut from the left into their path. From here, it looked as if the dark mouth of a cave awaited them.

If there was such a cave, she'd much rather sleep off the ground and away from anything that may roam the grasses at night looking for a meal.

It was Jabbers who bounded up the side of the rocks first. Her serpentine body seemed to slide and fold over every obstacle with ease.

Lou relied mostly on her right arm to pull herself up. The incline was very gradual, and a worn path allowed her to ascend without much effort.

Jabbers stopped on a landing a hundred feet off the ground. Lou had been right. It was the mouth of a cave.

"You got a flashlight in there?" Lou asked, staring into the pitch black.

After a short rustle in his bags, Konstantine put a metal flashlight into her hand.

She clicked it on.

The cave wasn't huge, perhaps 220 square feet from its mouth to its curved back wall. Against that wall was a pile of...

She moved closer for inspection, her beam sweeping over the rubble.

"Bones," she said. "There's a pile of bones."

"She piled them so nicely," Konstantine said, his voice still strained from the climb.

Lou snorted.

Jabbers squeezed past Lou to the pile and flopped down onto it. Then she began to roll around like a dog in the grass.

"That's one way to scratch a back," Lou mused.

"Can we eat now?" Konstantine asked, and Lou heard the irritation.

"You're like Piper," she said, tossing her small leather bag against the far wall. "You get cranky when you haven't eaten."

Konstantine was tearing open a food packet with his teeth, rolling his gaze up to hers defensively.

After reconstituting the food with a bit of water and heating it over the small fire he built, they ate their chili mac with beef. Once Konstantine had two packets down, the lines in his face evened out. He was even able to offer her half of his brownie.

Lou took off her boots and shrugged out of her leather jacket. The fire made it too warm to wear it, and she wanted to dry her damp clothes near the flames.

Free of the leather, she stretched her shoulders.

"If this is her cave," Lou wondered aloud, "where are the others? She can't be one of a kind."

The fire threw shadows against the wall, which Jabbers watched curiously until she settled at the mouth of the cave, stretching long and feline against the backdrop of the eternal twilight and placid lake.

"Maybe they are solitary creatures," Konstantine said. "Like jaguars, they spread out and have territories hundreds of miles wide. They only come together to mate."

Lou arched a brow at the word *mate*.

With her eyes on the distant two moons, Lou thought, *There have to be others.* Jabbers couldn't have come from nothing.

"Does it always look like this?" Konstantine gestured at the night. "Are there seasons?"

"I haven't seen anything but this. It's always the same."

"No seasons and the same amount of light? No visible sun in the sky. Well, the tilt of the axis could play a part. And some of the outer planets have incredibly long seasons. Forty years, I believe. But this place has oxygen and life. And it isn't freezing. It can't possibly be too far from a star, can it?"

Lou held her hands toward the fire as he stoked it.

"I honestly don't know enough about planetary systems to guess the conditions where such a place is possible," he continued. "But obviously, this is another world."

Lou had thought of the alien planet idea, though she could not, in her mind, fathom that her ability would take her not only through water but across space.

"I guess I thought it was Earth," she said. "In a really distant future or past."

"Where did the other moon come from?"

She shrugged. "Just the right asteroid came along at the right speed or whatever."

"If this is the *very* distant future, it's possible. But that begs the question, where are the humans? Are there any? Or did they go extinct?"

Konstantine eyed the creature lying at the mouth of the cave. "Did they get *eaten*?"

The fire was cozy and there was something about Jabbers asleep at the mouth of the cave that made Lou feel both safe and uneasy. The creature was guarding them. But from what?

"When we first crossed over, there was a car," Konstantine said. "I stepped on it."

"That came with Angelo," she said, watching his face for any reaction to his brother's name.

"Really?"

She waited, seeing where this might go.

"I didn't realize you could bring an entire car with you," he said.

"I made his chauffeur drive us into the bay. I'd only wanted Angelo, but it brought all three of us and the car across."

She wished she understood the expression he was giving her.

"Has that happened before? Where you've brought entire vehicles or fleets with you?"

"No. I can't do it in the dark."

After a long pause, he flicked his green eyes up to meet hers. "And when he got here?"

Lou said nothing.

Konstantine laughed. "How do you know she is a *she*?"

"I guess I don't. It's just a feeling."

If Konstantine was horrified by the news that his brother—and most of the family—had been eaten alive by this creature, he didn't show it. But they'd made that bed the night they came to her childhood home and shot her parents.

She relived it distantly, the white snap of the gun going off in the bedroom upstairs and the sound of glass breaking. The gate to their backyard flying open and Lou's father lifting her and throwing her into the pool, knowing it would save her life.

It had taken her years to hunt them all down. Years to discern how all the pieces of that one night had played out, and who had been responsible for what.

All of it had delivered her to Konstantine's door.

His mind ran with questions too. That much was clear. But he said nothing, only looking into the flames.

"That scar on your shoulder," he said eventually, pointing across the fire to her.

"She bit me," she said.

He didn't reply, obviously waiting for the story.

"I was taking a bath and I slipped through," she said plainly, conveying none of the terror of what it was like for her then, trapped in a body with a will of its own. This was long before Aunt Lucy showed her what she could do.

It was Lucy who had given her back her life. Aunt Lucy who'd not only taken her in after her parents had died, but who'd taught her that *Lou* controlled her power. It didn't control her.

"When I crawled out of the lake, she attacked me. I fought back. I don't know if I poked her in the eye or hit her nose, but she let me go and I fell back into the water. I reemerged in a swimming pool in a man's backyard. He was cutting his grass when I just walked out of the pool. Bad day for him."

"Must have been terrifying," Konstantine said.

"I imagine he hadn't been expecting me, no."

"I meant for you."

She looked up and found him watching her.

"You were so small."

"So was she," Lou explained. "Well, small*er*. More like a pony."

Konstantine watched the beast on the ledge sleep, her

head tucked toward her tail. As if sensing eyes on her, she peeled open one eye and huffed.

Konstantine looked away first. "She's probably seven meters long now."

"She looks bigger than when I saw her last," Lou said. "It's hard to imagine that she might still be growing."

"How did you become...friends?" he asked.

Lou didn't know how to answer. Were they friends? In a way. But how could she explain the sense of connection she had with Jabbers? How sometimes Lou looked into its eyes and saw herself.

"Slowly," she said to the fire.

Konstantine seemed to sense her reluctance to talk anymore tonight. He removed the two sleeping bags from his pack and laid them beside the fire.

"I don't have pillows," he said, gesturing at the pile of luggage.

She considered making a joke about all the things he'd brought but decided against it. He was the one who was carrying it.

He removed his boots so his woolen black socks poked out the bottom of his jeans. His black t-shirt was tight across his chest. Just in the hours they'd been traveling together, a shadow of a beard had begun to form on his jaw.

She liked the look of it. She wondered what it would feel like to kiss him like that.

He put one hand under his head and regarded her. With the other he patted the sleeping bag beside him. "Aren't you tired?"

Tired was something Lou felt in her mind, rarely in her body. Now, by the fire, her body was relaxed. With a gun and a large knife at the floor by her feet, and Jabbers at the open mouth of the cave, she felt more than safe.

Konstantine was watching her, waiting for her answer.

"No," she said. "You should sleep if you want to."

"You're very beautiful," he said. "I can see the fire dancing in your eyes. Did your mother have brown eyes too?"

"No," she said. "They were blue."

She stopped short of saying, *I have my father's eyes.*

Jabbers lifted her head to regard something in the distance that Lou couldn't see.

Small flaps on the side of her head opened and closed. Lou wondered if those were her ears. Whatever she was hearing was far out of Lou's range.

Truth be told, Jabbers wasn't the most interesting thing in the cave. Konstantine bathed in soft light and looking cozy in his fresh clothes was almost too much to resist.

"Will you lie down beside me?" he asked, his lips looking thick enough to bite.

Lou smiled. She could do one better.

She rose from her place and crossed to him. In a fluid moment, she threw a leg over his lap and settled her weight onto his groin. Her legs squeezed either side of his body, eliciting a groan of pleasure from him.

He searched her face from under dark lashes. "Your shoulder—"

"It doesn't hurt," she said. "Ever since we got here, it stopped hurting."

And strangely this was true.

"But if you—"

"Shut up about my shoulder, or this isn't happening," she said, leaning forward and grazing his chest with hers.

His eyes dilated at the word *this*.

KONSTANTINE NEEDED NO FURTHER ENCOURAGEMENT. He leaned up, seizing her mouth with his. His fingers brushed her skin, finding the hem of her shirt.

Yes, yes, yes, his mind chorused.

"Worry about yourself," she said, lifting off of him long enough to pull her shirt and bra off in one movement.

This only excited him more. A low buzz began to tremor along his skin. With a snap of her fingers, she undid the top of her pants. That small motion felt as if she'd unsnapped something inside of him too.

So long. I've waited for so long.

"You want to—" he began, disbelieving. *So long.*

"Yes." She stepped out of her pants, leaving her underwear on.

"Here?" He craned his neck to look at the beast, who was watching them. Desire pounded through him, but so did a tremor of fear. He found, strangely, that one seemed to intensify the other.

"Here," Lou insisted, a smile playing in the corner of her mouth.

She tugged on the bottom of his pants. He lifted his hips to oblige her. The flames threw shadows across her naked chest and stomach.

He thought of the first night he'd seen her.

Then she was just a girl, no more than fourteen or fifteen. She'd appeared in his bed like a dream. Her thick dark hair had been much longer then. It had cascaded nearly to her waist. Her cheeks rounder, girlish. She hadn't yet acquired any of the hardness she'd accumulate over the years. With her lips parted, split like a cherry, wrapped in the nightmares of her father's death, she was the most beautiful creature he'd ever seen.

And those nighttime visits—as far and few in between as they'd been—had only made him want her more.

Fifteen years, he thought. *I've wanted this for over fifteen years.*

She pushed him down against the sleeping bag, sitting astride him again. She began by grinding her body against his.

Each contraction of her muscle made something in him tighten deliciously.

Their nipples grazed and he shivered.

He felt her moisture through her underwear and longed to touch her. He traced the edge of the underwear with his finger.

"I want more than that," she said, and the air left him.

"Yes," he said, his desperation high in his throat. "Yes."

That's when she pulled her underwear to the side and slid onto him.

A long, agonizing groan escaped him. His hands found her hips, pinning her onto his lap, her soft flesh yielding in his hands. He wanted to sear this image of her into his mind forever. Her naked, covered in shadows and firelight.

The feel of her contracting around him.

It's happening, it's happening, it's happening.

And she felt even better than he'd imagined. Her flesh and muscles were softer than the hard planes of her body had led him to suspect. Her motions gentler than all the aggression she carried like a shield.

His eyes fluttered closed against the barrage of pleasure. It was a wave overtaking him, drowning him.

"Stay with me," she breathed into his ear. She grasped his chin and squeezed.

His eyes fluttered open. "*Sei perfetta.*"

"I don't know what that means," she laughed, low in her throat, before running her tongue along his lower lip. "But I like it too."

14

Diana stood at the window behind the thick curtain and watched King work at his desk. He was leaning back in his chair, speaking on the phone to someone unimportant, about a case she didn't give two shits about.

Yet the voice feed was being delivered to the laptop on the table beside her. "If you want her in, you'll have to talk to the DA. I can't subpoena people. I don't have that authority."

His face broke into a grin, his belly shaking.

The laughter echoed through the line a second later.

A short delay then.

It didn't matter. None of it mattered to her, really, as she replayed Lou's words—or lack of them—over and over in her mind.

Her flat refusal. Her borderline disinterest in Diana as a partner. She'd never felt so *dismissed* in her life.

You'll regret that, Diana thought coldly. *Once you realize what I can do.*

And because Diana was busy orchestrating her plan, she couldn't follow King, Piper, or the landlady Melandra personally now. She sent Blair and Spencer, the two most capable members of her twenty-person team, to do that menial task.

Blair was the only one who knew everything. Spencer, more than most. The rest simply believed they were working on an undercover operation to stop a high-profile pornography ring.

Diana wanted to keep it that way.

When she needed additional tails for Daniella and Piper, she pulled from the workers, saying only that the girls were in danger. They were young enough that it could be true. Not children, but young women were always in danger.

Lookouts were posted in the café across from *The Herald*, the newspaper where Daniella Allendale worked, and they also walked Daniella's neighborhood.

King and Melandra were easier to track. They were creatures of habit, their schedules often overlapping, even sharing a Belgian Malinois between them.

It was a beautiful, obedient dog, Diana thought, and she wouldn't mind having it for herself.

Because Diana couldn't be seen, her access to the group was by proxy. She had the cameras in Piper's apartment, but she also had two lookout positions. Adjacent to Madame Melandra's Fortune and Fixes had been an apartment for rent. Diana paid the exorbitant price—not understanding why everything in the French Quarter was so expensive—and could now look through one of the apartment windows directly into King's with the help of a small telescope. She saw the red leather sofa, a large coffee table, and a sparse kitchen with garish black and white tile that hurt the eyes to look at. Below that, she had a decent view of most of the shop. The register and part of the stairs leading up to the apartment.

A second apartment had been rented on Royal Street, providing a view of King's desk inside the detective agency.

The view didn't stretch all the way to the door marked *Ms. Thorne*, but that was okay. Diana would make do.

Piper had the most sporadic routine of the three. She floated from King to Melandra to Daniella. She also set up a card table in Jackson Square and read fortunes for hours into the balmy night. Sometimes she went to clubs on Bourbon Street and stayed until closing time.

Diana took all this in about them, about their life, and was disappointed that it all seemed rather ordinary.

No one showed up with suspicious packages. No strangers stopped in for cryptic conversations. They were, on the surface, exactly what they looked like—an eccentric group living out their lives in a tourist district—not a front for a high-powered criminal investigation unit.

Maybe things were simply quiet. Lou was "with Konstantine"—a name that had turned up nothing in Diana's search. Moreover, when Diana had tried to search directly for Louie Thorne, nothing had come up either. There were only three articles that she'd been able to find about her father, Jack, the slain hero, and only in the first one was Lou mentioned, and only as a byline.

The girl was not on social media. She didn't appear in any online photos or public records. She didn't have a driver's license or voter's ID. She—

A rough knock on the apartment door.

"Come in."

Spencer shoved the door open with one hand and shuffled into the room. Under his arm was a manila folder, his smile bright.

"What do you have for me?" she asked, already sensing his excitement.

"Something very, *very* interesting."

She looked at the hobbled man with a scarred face and receding hairline.

In truth, Spencer disgusted her. It wasn't his appearance. It was the way he looked at her, spoke to her, *fawned* over her.

But his work and his loyalty were assets she couldn't bring herself to throw away, not when every choice, every resource had to be managed so carefully.

"Show me," she said, sliding the curtain closed. She didn't want King to look up suddenly and see her face.

Spencer pulled two photos from the manila folder. In one, half of Lou's face was cut by the light of a gas station sign. It was a 7-Eleven, and given the sea of Asian faces around her, she would guess the 7-Eleven was in a Chinatown or maybe Asia itself.

The second photograph was a screen capture of Lou in a cobblestoned alley, the collar of her leather jacket pulled up to hide her neck, her eyes hidden behind those damned mirrored shades.

There was nothing in the photos that Diana could see, except Lou.

"What am I looking at?" Diana asked. Irritation nipped at her ears.

"Look at the time stamps."

Tokyo 6:15. Amsterdam 22:23.

"So? She stopped off in Amsterdam before heading to Tokyo." She was traveling *with Konstantine*.

"Look at the time stamps again."

"An eight-hour difference."

"No." He shook his head excitedly. "An eight-*minute* difference. Considering time zones."

She looked at the photos again and did the math in her head.

"You're telling me that in a matter of eight minutes Lou went from Tokyo to Amsterdam?"

Spencer nodded so enthusiastically that his glasses slid down on his nose. He pushed them back up.

"That's impossible. The time stamps must be wrong. Or maybe these were on two different days."

"It's the same day. I'm absolutely sure of it."

"No," Diana said, thrusting the photos back at him. "There's an error. People don't just travel across time zones in minutes."

Spencer's excitement faltered. He was clearly disappointed by the direction this conversation was going. "Maybe they can with the right technology or—"

"Check again," Diana said.

"But if it's *real*," Spencer insisted. "What if it's tech you could use against Winter."

How thoughtful. His enduring loyalty, his permeating desire to help her fulfill her greatest wish. Something warm stirred within her.

"Spencer," she said quietly.

Her tone alone stopped the blabbering. She slid her hand down the front of his chest to his crotch. There she traced the thin outline of the metal cage with her probing fingers.

"Do you like your new gift? You haven't said," she asked softly, her mouth dangerously close to his. This was the sort of thing he enjoyed, she knew.

"Y-yes," he said. "Very much."

"Do you like the idea of wearing a cage for me?" she asked coquettishly. Her nails tapped against the metal wires encasing Spencer's penis.

"Yes, yes I do."

"Would you like it better if I took it off? If I said *the word*."

He moaned, his eyes rolling closed at the thought. "I'd love that. Yes."

She gripped his chin roughly. "Tonight. If you're a good boy and check the time stamp again. Or better yet, tell me where the hell Lou is now."

"Of course. Of course, I will."

At this she let her hand drop and turned away from him, opening the curtain again on the New Orleans street.

Below, King regarded the open file on his desk, tapping a pen lightly against the tabletop.

*Tokyo to Amsterdam in eight minutes. **Ridiculous.***

"And stop reading so much science fiction. It's rotting your head."

15

K onstantine must've replayed the memory three hundred times before breakfast. As he showered, hot water pounding his neck and shoulders. As he brushed his teeth and selected his clothes—a black button-down, tight pants, and leather shoes. As he shaved, styled his hair, pushing it back from his eyes.

As he walked across the piazza, hands in his pockets, and up the steps of the large stone church that served as the Ravengers' stronghold.

Even as Stefano, his right-hand man, gave him the update for the two days he'd been gone, his mind remained in La Loon, fixed on the sight of Louie's naked body awash in firelight.

"Did you hear me?" Stefano asked in Italian. He sighed. The low light sparked in his dark eyes. Today he wore an Armani suit, his nails gleaming from a manicure.

"No," Konstantine admitted. "Just tell me the last part, about Riku Yamamoto."

"They want more money," Stefano said. He waved his hand. "What has you so distracted today? Bad vacation?"

Again, the feeling of Lou sliding onto him, the wet, slick sensation of her contracting. Her hand shoving against his chest and that look in her eyes when—

Stay with me.

His groin tightened.

Stefano arched a brow. "That well, huh?"

"It had its moments," he said, and the moment he was buried to the hilt inside Lou had been the best of it. He was only glad that he had not climaxed instantly, given how badly he'd wanted her and how the years of longing and waiting had made the desire nearly senseless.

La Loon itself was a nightmarish place. It wasn't only the disorienting landscape, or that all its organisms seemed oil-slicked and iridescent.

It was mostly the creature, which despite Konstantine's reasoning terrified him.

It was unlike anything he'd ever seen—or wanted to see again.

The fear his brothers must've felt in the moments before their death—though deserved—must have been immense. Still, as frightening as that place was, and as alarming as Lou's strange connection to it and its ruler, he was glad that he went.

Lou had shown him a part of herself that she'd shown no other man without also killing him. And that meant more to Konstantine than he could articulate.

His phone rang, spinning out a tune on his desk. Stefano fell back, willing to wait for his master's attention. Konstantine appreciated that about his oldest friend.

At first Konstantine wondered if this was about the specimens. He'd delivered his vials to a lab he trusted for its discretion and longed to hear the results, if only because he thought it might please Lou. But this would be an unusually quick response.

It wasn't the lab. Konstantine knew the number on the screen. In English he said, "Hello, Mr. King."

"Hey. Wait, one second. Let this train pass."

The detective's voice was swallowed by the deafening roar of a passing train. The whistle was loud enough that Konstantine pulled the phone back from his ear.

"Where are you?" he asked.

"I had to come down to the train yard to make sure no one could get this conversation with a long-range device. It's too loud for that here."

The hair on Konstantine's neck rose. "What's going on?"

"Diana Dennard is in town, checking up on Lou. I'm pretty sure she's bugged my office and probably Piper's apartment. She might have gotten something into the shop and our apartments too. I can't be sure without being really obvious. She's definitely got tails following us around. A woman in leather pants and a guy that walks with a pretty pronounced limp."

"To what end?"

"She came in pretending to be Lou's sister, asking me to find her. Didn't Lou tell you about any of this?"

"No." Konstantine thought of the notification he'd received upon returning from La Loon. Someone had duplicated photos of Lou in both Tokyo and Amsterdam before his bots could wipe them. He'd been worried the Tokyo photo was Yamamoto's doing. Maybe it wasn't.

"Since I can't search for the bugs or cameras without them knowing we are on to them," King went on. "I was hoping you could take care of that."

"I can try to disrupt the signals remotely," Konstantine offered. "I need the addresses of all properties you think have been infiltrated and also the name of your internet provider."

He didn't *have* to have this information, but it would make the job quicker.

"Why?"

"I can hack routers, networks, anything that they may be using as a signal for their devices."

King rattled off addresses and the name of his provider, while Konstantine scrawled the information on a notebook at hand. Then King asked, "How long do you need?"

"Give me a day," Konstantine said.

"Better than I hoped."

King thanked him and terminated the call.

"About the yakuza," Stefano began, only glancing at the notepad beneath Konstantine's hand. "Chris Litteri and John Christino just returned."

In the face of Stefano's patience, Konstantine refrained from pulling out his computer and setting about the task that interested him far more than politics.

"Yes," he said, putting down the pen. "I'm listening."

PIPER WAS REFILLING THE COFFEE POT WHEN SHE FELT King slip the note into her pocket. Her back stiffened as she repressed the urge to ask, *What's that?*

He'd trained her for this moment. *If I ever slip you a note, it's because something dangerous is happening and I can't speak aloud. Don't do or say anything. Don't react. Just make an excuse to leave and read it somewhere safe. The farther away, the better.*

At the time she'd thought he was being a paranoid bastard. Sure, his ex-partner had snuck into his apartment one night and had almost shot him in the head, and they'd also gotten kidnapped by some Russians, but—okay, so maybe he had reason to be paranoid.

Or this was a test.

She checked the time. It was just past noon. "I was thinking about getting some sandwiches."

"I'd love a BLT," he said, without missing a beat. He took

his coffee and dose of cream back to his desk. "Let me give you some money."

As he handed over the twenty, Piper was careful to look him in the eye.

His gaze betrayed nothing.

Damn, he's good. "Be right back."

The note felt like a stone in her pocket as she jogged down Royal to St. Peter, catching a streetcar at the edge of the Quarter. She rode it for ten minutes until the two women who'd boarded the car with her exited at a stop in the Garden District.

Only then did she pull the note from her pocket, along with her phone, and unfold it carefully in her lap, pretending to look at the screen.

Agency's compromised. Meet me at Blues Bar at 1:15.

That was enough time to get the sandwiches. And a cookie. Right now she could use a cookie.

BLUES BAR WAS A HONKY-TONK PLACE NEAR CRESCENT Park. When Piper walked in with her bag of BLTs and cookies, she expected the doorman to stop her and tell her no outside food.

Instead he nodded toward a closed door across the room. "He's down there."

Confused, she entered the bar cautiously, finding it empty at midday.

"Did a guy—" she began.

He nodded toward the door on the far wall again. Piper had to squint to see it in the dim light. A red bulb overhead made the edges of its frame stand out.

"Thanks." She crossed to the door, opened it, and peered down into the darkness. Four white steps could be seen before the shadows swallowed the rest of the staircase.

Oh man, she thought. *If I get murdered over some bacon...*

She descended cautiously. She kept the sandwich bag close, ready to hurl it at an attacker if one appeared.

But at the bottom of the stairs was nothing more than a concrete bunker and three people standing beneath a single swinging bulb.

"Christ," she muttered. "I thought I was going to get murdered down here. What's going on, man?"

Melandra, Dani, and King all turned at the sound of her voice.

"Did you close the door?" King asked. Piper looked up the stairs to be sure she had.

"Yes, now what's going on?"

He was frowning at the sandwich bag. "You actually got sandwiches."

"Well, *yeah*," she said. "You didn't really want one? Well, I got them cut in half so everyone can have half a BLT and a cookie."

King opened the bag. "There are five cookies in here."

"It was five for two dollars. They're Gino's." When King didn't seem to understand, Piper added, "They're *amazing*."

They passed around the bag until everyone was in possession of half a BLT and a cookie. Piper's had M&M's in it. Mel had taken the chocolate with white chocolate chips and Dani the snickerdoodle. King had passed on the cookie.

Piper thought, *Your loss.*

"How do you know about this place? Are you friends with a guy or something?"

"I know the owner," King said, half of his sandwich in his mouth. For someone who didn't really want a sandwich, Piper thought he was really going at it. "She used to be a cop in Washington. She moved here and opened a bar when she retired in '91."

Piper always thought it was weird how old people knew

everything by year. *I got my teeth out in '83. I bought the house in '01.*

Piper remembered her high school graduation year, class of 2014, and that was it.

"Why the cloak and dagger meeting? What's going on?" Dani asked.

Piper caught her eye and they shared a smile. Dani looked really cute with half of a huge cookie in her mouth. Piper wanted to kiss her but knew this was a weird moment to start sucking face.

"Diana's been watching us, tracking our movements. I found a bug under my desk at work. I have a feeling that she probably put bugs in other places too, but I can't confirm that yet. And I can't get ahold of Lou either."

"She's in La Loon," Piper said.

She took her boyfriend on vacation. Piper didn't like to think about the Italian stallion if she could help it. Something about him got under her skin. But there was no denying that he was super into Lou and would do anything for her, so she let it slide.

"Did Lou meet up with Diana?" Piper asked cautiously.

"Yeah," King said. "She said Diana wanted to hunt a guy together."

"That doesn't sound too bad," Mel said, finishing her cookie and wiping her hands together to rid them of crumbs.

"Except Lou refused her." King sucked mayo off his thumb and wiped the crumbs off his hands with a paper napkin. For someone who didn't want a sandwich, he sure put it away. "I don't think Diana will let it go."

Dani was rubbing the back of her neck. It was a gesture Piper knew well. She did it whenever she didn't like what she was hearing.

"I just wanted you to be aware about the bugs and to tell you to watch what you say in the office until Konstantine is able to destroy the signal. And I want you to check your place."

Piper realized King was looking at her. "What place?"

"*Your* place," he said. "If there's a bug under my desk, there's probably something in your apartment. Maybe even a camera."

Dani choked on her cookie. "Excuse me?"

Her face was reddening. Piper couldn't tell if it was because someone might have taped them messing around or if she was actually choking.

"You can't say that stuff to her." Piper scowled at King.. "You'll freak her out."

"I want you prepared," he said. "That's all. We can't be sure what Diana's next move will be, so we need to be careful."

Dani began wringing her finger. The one Dmitri had cut off.

Mel reached out and placed a hand on her arm. "We're going to be fine, honey. You'll see."

"Exactly. Diana doesn't stand a chance," Piper said, trying to reassure her. "Konstantine's doing his fancy computer stuff, and we're awesome. And we're ready. We're ready for *anything*."

16

———

L ou stood in the closet of her apartment, breathing slowly, her Browning pistol resting across her chest. She rotated her shoulder but found no pain there. It was tight, but that was it.

She felt good. *Really* good.

Better, better, better, her mind was chanting. *I'm getting better*.

King had paged her twice, but it was no emergency. She ignored it. She had plans.

With a smile, she exhaled into the darkness, trying to hold back her elation and excitement. She let the shadows wash over her like moonlit waves.

St. Louis fell away in its place, the honking of a car and screech of a bicycle bell.

Someone was yelling. And then the veil shifted and Lou slipped through.

Prague sprang to life around her, vibrant and hurried.

Lou stepped out onto Charles Bridge. The city was awash in lantern light with a cotton candy–purple sky. A church, or at least Lou thought it might be a church, was framed against that soft sky with its metallic pale green dome of a roof. Somewhere, a large bell began its toll.

A woman with a cart sold circles of cinnamon and sugar dough that looked like bracelets. It made Lou's stomach knot, but she'd eat later.

For now her eyes remained fixed on her target. A short, muscular man. His leather jacket grazed his hips as he marched away from her. She followed him across the bridge, walking past couples hand-in-hand, students with backpacks, and children pinwheeling, arms outstretched.

His boots clicked against stone and Lou fell into step with him, matching his rhythm.

Jiri Svoboda was a middleman. When a riverboat full of heroin docked on the Vltava River, the drug lord made sure it was delivered to the dealers in the surrounding districts.

It was a warm summer night. She was out hunting like she did back in the day. In her life before Konstantine, before King, before Piper and the rest of it.

A surge of nostalgia overtook her, deepening her confidence.

She followed him through the cobblestoned streets, enjoying the sounds of the city waking up at the promise of night. People stumbled out of restaurants laughing. A bus squealed its brakes in front of a Tesco.

Svoboda cut down a side alley.

Lou was on him a heartbeat later. She grabbed the back of his leather jacket and pulled.

He turned, pivoting as if he'd expected her—and if not her, some kind of trouble.

His elbow swung in an arc as the gun slid out of his jacket. Lou grabbed the back of his elbow, redirecting the energy down the same moment she slid him through the dark.

Prague disappeared. Her lakeside sanctuary formed.

Jiri was not perturbed by this shift.

If he noticed that the city around him had disappeared and in its place stood a nighttime forest, his face showed no recognition. Something splashed into the lake, disturbed by the sudden arrival of unwanted guests.

The swing of Jiri's arm turned him away from her. She released her grip and he stumbled into the shallows. He dropped his gun as water sloshed over the tops of his boots. Without stopping, he pulled another from his low back.

Lou had enough time to slip, sidestepping through the darkness, so that when he pulled the trigger, the bullet bit into the pine tree that had stood behind her, spraying bark like wedding confetti.

She reappeared in time to bring her elbow down hard on the gun hand, knocking it free. It hit the water and disappeared. Ripples radiated across the dark surface.

He threw himself against Lou, checking her bad shoulder.

She cried out and went down, hitting the dirt hard. All the air left her on impact.

He was trying to get his hands around her neck. She was bracing him above her with her forearm, but it was her bad side.

That first ignition of pain incinerated her confidence.

Pain rolled through her body, making her spine go rigid. Red bursts danced in front of her eyes.

She managed to get her good arm between their bodies and cross-pulled a blade from her hip.

She drew it across his throat in one fluid moment. Blood sprayed into her face from the split artery, then began to pour. It hit her throat, cascading over the skin into her hair, pooling at the back of her neck.

He coughed, choking. His body grew heavy and slack against her good arm.

When she was certain her shoulder would snap out of

place if she held him a moment longer, she rolled, tossing him to one side.

She sat up, panting.

Her shoulder wouldn't move. The arm was deadweight against her side.

She tried to shrug out of her jacket and get a good look at it, but the movement sent ribbons of fire down her side until her vision darkened.

Svoboda choked out his last on the riverbank then was silent.

The chorus of crickets and frogs that had stopped rehearsing enough for this interlude to play out gradually recommenced their singing.

Lou inched toward the lake. With her good side, she scooped water into her hand and splashed it against her face, wiping away the blood. She didn't want it on her lips. Nothing to do about the vicious globs drying in her hair.

The kill had been sloppy. Pathetic. She hadn't gotten stabbed or shot, which could be seen as an improvement, but now her shoulder was throbbing so badly she thought she might black out.

"I've hurt myself," she murmured, and heard her own disbelief. How was that possible?

Sure, sometimes she was shot or stabbed or thrown into something in the course of a good fight, but she'd never hurt *herself*.

And the emotion she felt now, knowing that if she'd ruptured her shoulder or put herself out of commission for weeks, was that she had only herself to blame.

Anger spiked inside her as she pulled herself to standing. She glanced at Svoboda's body and bent to grab his leg with her good arm.

She'd wanted to take an offering to Jabbers, to thank the beast for not eating Konstantine. But she wouldn't be able to drag this corpse onto the shore. She would do well just to bring it to La Loon and leave it in the shallows for those strange reptilian orcas to eat.

Body convulsing with pain, mind filled with bitter disappointment, Lou slid into the cold water with one thought in her head.

I'm not ready. I'm not ready for anything.

17

Sometimes Diana lamented that her job involved so much time sitting in front of the computer. Tonight she had two monitors in front of her, twice the insult, as sweat trickled down the back of her neck. There was no A/C in this building and the walls themselves seemed to sweat from the heat.

She squinted at the screen, rubbing at her dry eyes. One monitor showcased Winter's feed—nine squares in total, each highlighting a different child.

It was the little boy, maybe six years old, who was getting the worst of it. His abuser kept alternating between raping and beating him, striking the boy over and over across his small back. When the boy bent, vomiting for the third time, she looked away from the grainy image and checked the second screen.

The other monitor was a two-way split feed of Piper's apartment and King's office.

Blair knocked on the door. "Are you going to eat?"

"I already ate."

"What?"

Diana made no answer.

"*What* did you eat?" Blair insisted.

"A sandwich."

"What kind of sandwich?"

Diana scowled at her. "Why does it matter what kind of sandwich I ate?"

"Because you're lying. You've been in this room for seven hours and you haven't left it once."

Diana turned away.

"You're useless to us if you don't eat. And *sleep*."

"You're starting to sound like Mom," Diana said, using a blue bandana to wipe the back of her neck.

"Ouch." Blair threw something and it landed in Diana's lap.

"What's this?"

"A sandwich." She smirked. "Eat it."

She pulled up a chair and sat down as Diana worked to peel back the plastic wrapping.

As Diana ate, her sister watched the screen. When the little boy was thrown onto his stomach again, his mouth visibly mouthing *No, no, wait*, Blair cursed.

"I don't know how you can watch this shit." Blair's throat was tight. "It makes me sick. And furious."

"I don't want to forget what a monster he is," Diana said, forcing another bite of ham, cheese, and lettuce into her mouth.

"Daniel is dead."

Imperceptibly, Diana flinched at the name. *Daniel.* Such a white, suburban name for the bastard who picked her up from school and locked her in a soundproof shed for months. Until she escaped and came back with a gun.

"I'm talking about Winter."

"This isn't Winter," Blair said, motioning vaguely toward the screen. "It's a whole bunch of other sick fucks."

"Winter finds them. He recruits them. Radicalizes them online. He helps them find kids, and worst of all, he circulates this shit across the four corners of the globe. Men all over the world are jerking off to this. These guys are animals, but Winter is the one who feeds them."

"When you disappeared—" Blair began.

"Don't," Diana warned. She didn't want to go down memory lane. Not tonight, while so much weighed on her mind and every time she closed her eyes she saw Lou Thorne stepping from darkness, from nothing.

Impossible. She wouldn't let Spencer's pathetic mewling get to her.

Blair didn't seem to hear her, or she didn't care enough about Diana's wishes to stop. "It was the longest two months of my life. I thought you were dead. I *hoped* you were dead, because being alive meant—well, you know what it meant."

Diana snorted, shoving another bite of ham into her mouth.

Blair prattled on. "All I can think about is that right now, someone is out there lying awake thinking about these kids, wondering where they are, sick to death about them, wondering if they're ever going to come home. They're lying in their beds, staring at the ceiling and asking themselves what they're going to do if they never find out what happened, if they never see them again. How are they going to move on?"

"No one is wondering about him," Diana said, pointing at the little boy.

Blair looked up, obviously irritated by the interruption. "What?"

"He's not a missing child. That's his father."

Blair swore and took a deep breath. "I answered that question for myself. When I was the one lying in bed, worried sick about you, I asked myself how I was going to move on. And this isn't it, Dee. This isn't moving on. I thought if you got the guys that hurt you, you could move on, but you aren't. You just keep finding new targets."

"These kids—"

"You don't care about the kids!" Blair laughed, high and hysterical. "You go hard because you can't stop. You only do it for yourself. When is it going to be enough? *When?* When do we get to live our lives?"

Lou would understand, she thought. *No one is asking her to give up.*

"You don't have to stay," Diana said. "You can leave at any time. Go get yourself pregnant, pop out some kids, live in fucking suburbia for all I care. Go on."

She stopped short of saying, *I never asked you to be here.* Because that was a lie. She had asked Blair, practically begged her. But that was a long time ago, and Diana wasn't so convinced that she needed Blair anymore.

Not when there was someone who might understand her better.

Blair's jaw was set tight, flexing with unspoken words.

The screen flickered. No surprise.

Sometimes Winter's feed cut out suddenly. If he felt the line was compromised in any way, then he always cut and ran.

Then the second screen went dark too, and they could no longer see into King's office, or the apartment.

"What happened?" Diana said, sitting up and tapping the monitor as if slapping it would get it to turn back on.

Blair threw her hands up in surrender. "Yes, what did happen to your precious videos? I'd hate for you to be interrupted in the middle of such an important conversation."

Diana unplugged the computers, rebooted them, checked the server. Nothing.

"Maybe we just lost signal," Blair said.

Diana stood. "It's her."

"You can't—"

"It's *her*. She's done this because she's back."

"You're guessing," Blair said, in a voice one might use to calm wild animals.

But Diana was already lifting the communicator from the desk. She mashed the button with her thumb.

"Operation Retrie—" she said.

Blair shoved her thumb off the switch. "Dee, come on. Take a breath. You don't know—"

Diana wrenched away from her. "Operation Retrieval activates now. I want all teams mobile in five minutes. Go."

Diana slammed the comm down on the desk and gave her sister a pointed look.

"That's *rash*," Blair said, sitting back in her chair and crossing her arms. "What if you're wrong?"

"You'll see." Diana was already to the door, a spring in her step. She craved action after so much inactivity.

"Diana!"

She turned to find her sister staring at her with an unreadable expression. Disgust? Disappointment? Maybe a hint of fear.

She waited for the accusation.

You know our mother lost her mind like this. You're obsessive like she is. You've got to pull yourself back sometimes.

Blair had said this once, after the first time Winter had slipped through her fingers and Diana had blacked out with rage.

That's what you're for, Diana had told her.

But Diana frowned at her now, her disappointment like an itch in her throat. Maybe she had outgrown Blair. Maybe it was time for someone stronger—and more understanding.

Time for someone who was a hunter like her.

Blair thrust the half-eaten sandwich at her accusingly. "At least finish your sandwich."

18

King woke to the sound of Lady barking. It was a high, strident sound of alarm. Then she whined and fell silent. Where was she? Mel's apartment? The stairwell?

Panic rocked through him.

He sat up in bed and opened his bedside table. There in the shadows sat his .357 Magnum. He pulled it out and balanced it on one knee, searching with the other hand for the ammunition amongst the tissues and a bottle of aspirin.

A cold metal cylinder as thin as a finger pressed into the side of his temple.

"Put it back in the drawer," a man said. His voice was muffled, as if his mouth was covered by a cloth.

When King didn't immediately respond, the gun was pressed into the side of his head hard enough to cock his neck to one side.

"*Now.*"

"All right," King said, sliding the gun back into the drawer and closing it. He left his hands palm up on the coverlet in his lap. "Now what?"

"On your knees, hands behind your back."

King slid from the bed to the floor, knowing that if someone had wanted him dead, they would likely have shot him already, unless their plan was to take him somewhere else and do it.

Lovely thought.

His knees creaked, and without meaning to, he threw a glance at the urn on the side table.

A yank fixed thin hard plastic strips across his wrist. They bit into his flesh. Why were they binding his hands behind his back with *zip ties*?

Black cloth slid down over his head and tightened at his throat with a drawstring.

Black sacks and zip ties, he thought. *This can't be good.*

His old claustrophobia rose.

The panic made his heart pound harder as the cloth flapped in and out against his face with each ragged breath.

But it was what he didn't hear that really frightened him. Lady. She should be raising hell right now. Why wasn't she? *Why?*

Before the terror could fully bloom, the butt of a gun struck him hard against the back of the skull.

PIPER WOKE FIRST. SHE'D SAT UP IN DANI'S BED WITH A start. Looking around the dim room, she tried to breathe against the pounding of her heart. But it was only Dani breathing softly beside her.

The room was still. The sliver of the hallway visible from the open bedroom door was also dark.

The apartment was silent. Nothing moved.

She exhaled. *That's what I get for watching* A Quiet Place *before bed.* The movie had been awesome, but not for one's anxiety.

Now every creak meant some monster was going to appear and rip her throat out. Still her breathing felt too loud, her heartbeat more like a battle drum played over a loudspeaker.

Then she saw it. A flashlight swept across the hallway wall, sliding over the bathroom's door frame, momentarily lighting the strike plate.

Without thinking, she sprang to her feet and ran to the other side of the room. She positioned herself behind Dani's bedroom door, pressing her shoulder blades against the cool plaster.

Dani sat up in bed, her mouth opening in question.

Piper shook her head furiously, putting a finger over her lips. She waved for her to lie down.

Dani did, but even from the wall Piper could hear her breathing.

Don't cry, Piper thought. *Please don't cry.*

She saw the end of the gun first, its slender black barrel emerging like a snake from the tall grass. As soon as Piper saw the gloved hand, she struck.

She grabbed the butt of the gun and yanked. Bullets sprayed into the bedroom floor.

Who the hell carries a fully automatic handgun?

Piper's elbow, cocked, slammed into the attacker's face. She felt something give—a nose? Lips splitting over teeth? Something hot smeared across the back of her arm.

She didn't know what she was doing, only that she couldn't let go of the gun. Not until it clicked, signaling that it was empty.

"Duck!"

Piper reacted to the sound of Dani's order, dipping her head low. An aluminum bat swept overhead, connecting hard with a body.

The attacker dropped like a sack of bricks and the emptied gun clattered to the hardwood floor.

In her mind, a mantra: *Lou! Lou, we need you! Lou!*

That's when electricity struck the back of her neck. Her body seized, every nerve in her body on fire.

The blackout was a mercy.

MEL WAS AT THE REGISTER, WRITING DOWN A LIST OF things that needed to be done the following day.

Buy paper towels and receipt paper
Restock the love candles
Search the August catalog for new tarot decks
Call the distributor about the bead shipment
Send newsletter about Back to Ghoul sale

She'd come down into the closed shop with Lady when she realized sleep wouldn't find her tonight. Sometimes making lists helped to quiet her mind enough that she could finally settle down.

And the shop was a comfort to her. It was the smell of incense and wax and the gentle *scratch scratch scratch* of her pen pressing into the yellow notepad.

Lady snarled, jumping up from where she lay at Mel's feet.

Mel lifted her head only to find five guns pointed at her. Large ones, assault rifles by the look of it.

The soldiers holding them stood in full head-to-toe body armor. Her own face, with its ridiculous look of surprise, was mirrored back to her in their dark visors.

"This is a lot of firepower for an old woman," she said calmly, placing her hands on the glass case in front of her nice and slow.

Lady snapped, barking and darting toward the closest soldier—if soldiers were what they were. He—or she—turned their gun and thrust the butt down at the dog.

Lady was too quick, and the hilt slammed into the floor, gouging the wood.

Mel knew how this would end.

She knew that while these people might want her alive—for now—they likely didn't give two shits about her dog.

"*Assez!*" Melandra commanded. "*Restez, ma grande.*"

Lady whined, her ears lying flat against her head.

It was clear that her instincts differed greatly from the words spoken by her mistress, and because of that, a small war waged inside the canine. She snarled, but didn't lunge again.

"*Assez,*" Melandra repeated. She wanted to pet her, give her reassurances. *Je t'aime, ma grande.*

But she would rather save Lady's life than comfort her.

"You leave the dog alone," Melandra said, stepping around the counter, hands up in surrender. No need to give them a reason to shoot her outright. "I'll come just fine."

Tail tucked, Lady returned to her side, sitting down beside her. As she pressed the side of her body into Mel's leg, Mel felt the animal shaking.

"*Restez,*" Mel said again.

Lady's ears twitched, but she was too well trained to disobey.

"*Restez,*" she whispered over and over as they forced her onto her knees, tied her wrists, and slipped the black bag over her head.

LOU HAULED HER BODY OUT OF THE LAKE, HER SHOULDER screaming. The Alaskan night breathed cricket song around her. She needed pills. She needed anything that would quiet the raging burn of her wounded side.

The cooling La Loon waters had helped, but not enough.

I did too much, she thought. *I did too much too soon and I'm going to regret it.*

But she'd killed the Czech drug lord and had carried his body to the shores of La Loon. Jabbers had seemed all too happy to see that things had returned to normal.

Now Lou longed for a hot shower, a good night's sleep, and a fistful of painkillers.

Until the alarm bells rocketed through her. Like a fish-hook in the gut, she was jerked forward.

Dani's terror was the strongest and loudest. It was so strong that Lou found her arms shaking with it.

Lou pulled her gun, able only to fully command her good side, and checked the bullets. They would have to do.

19

Piper came to on the wooden floor of an empty apartment. Or maybe a house. It was the light socket with a white plastic cover that came into focus first.

They were still in the Quarter. She knew the sounds of this neighborhood the way one knows the sound of their parents' voices. She'd been running these streets as soon as she was old enough to hop on the streetcar alone. There was the trumpet music from Jackson Square and Ariana Grande blaring from a nearby bar.

A sudden swell of bluegrass music fought with the Ariana Grande remix, which made her think they were on Bourbon Street, or close to it.

Piper pulled herself to sitting, groaning. The room spun like the time she smashed two hurricanes on a dare.

You never drink liquor sweeter than Kool-Aid, Henry had warned her. And he'd been right.

She groaned. "The hell, man."

"You were tased, by the look of that scorch mark on your neck," King said. He sounded perfectly calm beside her. His legs were stretched out in front of him, his arms behind his back. Beside him was Mel, looking equally serene.

"Really?" Piper murmured. "Some asshole *tased* me?"

And why did they look so calm? Were they really getting so used to these attacks that they could just roll through them now? True, this cozy apartment, though empty, was better than the garage Dmitri Petrov had holed them up in. This place had none of that torture dungeon feel to it.

Only they weren't all perfectly calm.

Someone whimpered beside Piper. She turned and saw Dani on the floor in the fetal position, tears running down her face.

"Oh shit." She scooted across to her. "Baby. Hey, baby. Look at me."

Dani didn't look up. Her whole body was shaking.

"Hey, shhh. Baby. Look at me. Look at me."

"We tried that," Mel said calmly.

Dani rolled her eyes up to meet Piper's.

Piper forced a smile. "See? You're okay. I'm okay. Everything's fine."

Dani's breathing thinned out even more.

"God, why is she breathing like that?" Piper asked.

"She's having a panic attack," Mel said.

"Baby, you've got to slow down. Slow, deep breaths."

Someone snorted, an aborted laugh, and this dismissive sound made Piper look up.

It was Diana. Her sleek blond hair was pulled back in a ponytail at the nape of her neck. Her big blue eyes were round. She looked like a soccer mom with an unhinged gleam in her eye, especially with the gun in her hand.

A woman in tight leather pants leaned against the door to this small room, regarding the scene impassively. Something about their faces looked similar. Maybe the nose or chin. The brow? Piper couldn't be sure.

The room was hot and growing hotter with the six bodies crowded inside it. With the floor and walls bare and Piper's hands tied behind her back, there was nothing that could be used to defend herself.

Piper spotted a gray box on the wall and thought it might be a cabinet, but upon closer inspection, it was only a breaker box.

"Pathetic. I haven't touched her." Diana's voice was surprisingly melodic for a freaking crazy person.

"She has PTSD, you piece of shit! Untie her."

"Please," Dani said, between gasps. "*P-please.*"

Diana rolled her eyes. "She'll live."

"That's more than you're going to do," Piper spat, forcing herself onto her knees. She was trying to position her weight so she could stand. It was harder than she'd thought it'd be. Some distant part of her mind thought, *If we get out of this, I'm going to need to do more squats.*

"When I get out of this I'm going—"

The slap was hard and fast. It rocked Piper off her feet, costing her the ground she'd recovered.

"You'll *what?*" Diana laughed into her face. "You won't do sh—"

Diana disappeared.

One minute she was leaning over Piper, her face glowing with that murderous rage that Piper had seen somewhere before but couldn't place. Then she was gone.

Piper's gaze adjusted to the low light in time to see Diana slammed against the wall, her feet three inches off the floor. She was pinned by the strong hand holding her. She was choking as her boots scuffed black marks against the plaster in their thrashing.

It was Lou who had her pinned against the wall. Lou, dripping wet, her hair, jacket, and shoes all soaked. Small droplets fell from her matted strands onto the floor beneath her.

The gun was in her left hand, but Piper thought it looked like an afterthought. She didn't like the way that arm hung loose at her side.

She couldn't lift that thing if she tried.

The woman in the leather pants pressed a gun to the back of Lou's head. "Put her down."

Lou lowered Diana three inches so her feet touched the wood, but she didn't take her hand off her throat.

"I didn't hurt them," Diana said, clawing at Lou's fist.

"Liar," Piper said.

"I swear," Diana said. "I just wanted you to come. I told you I could—"

Lou shifted her grip on the gun, before opening the power box, revealing a network of circuitry.

"What are you—"

One swipe and the lights went out. Someone pulled a trigger and a bullet bit into a wall, spraying plaster across the room.

"Christ!" Diana screamed. "Don't shoot!"

Then Piper felt hands on her, and the familiar shift of the world rearranging itself to Lou's will.

When it reformed, she was in King's apartment. There was the oversized red sofa. There were the worn records leaning slanted against each other, smelling like the old man's weed. Party lights from the fourth of July still hung on the balcony.

King, Mel, and Dani were all on the floor, trying to right themselves. But they were alone. They were safe.

"I've got scissors in that drawer," King called out, nodding toward the kitchen. "No, not that one. The one on the end."

Lou opened and slammed drawers until she produced a

pair of blue-handled scissors. She snipped their zip ties one at a time.

Mel was up and out of the apartment. "Lady? Lady!"

The door slammed shut behind her.

When Piper's hands broke free, relief hit her like a wave. In the next instant she had Dani in her arms, holding her, rocking her.

"It's okay," Piper said, pushing back her sweat-soaked bangs. "It's over, it's over. Lou is going to kill that stupid—"

King spoke as if Piper hadn't. "She took us but didn't hurt us—why? What point is she trying to make?"

"Because she's crazy," Piper said. "And you're going to kill her, right?"

"I've never killed a woman before."

"Yeah, well, first time for everything." Piper wished she could read that look on Lou's face. She didn't understand it. Lou was a killer. She killed the people who threatened her friends—why wouldn't she just finish Diana already?

"Is she going to be okay?" Lou asked, pushing her wet hair back from her face. Her left arm remained immobile at her side.

"She'll be fine," Piper said, still rocking the woman in her arms. Dani was finally starting to quiet, but her shaking was worse. "When you *kill* Diana."

Then Lady was there. She bounded into the apartment and nosed her way between Dani and Piper.

"Hey!" Piper said.

But Dani took to the dog like a bird to air. She wrapped her arms around Lady's neck and sobbed. Piper decided not to take this personally.

"Go," King said, nodding toward Lou. "Find out what this is about and end it."

Lou stepped back into King's dark bedroom and was gone.

. . .

DIANA FLIPPED ON THE LIGHTS. SHE TURNED A FULL CIRCLE in the empty room, not understanding what she was seeing.

"Are they out there?" she called.

Spencer stood in the doorway, his gun shaking in his hand. "No one came this way."

"Give me that before you hurt yourself." Diana tugged the gun out of his hand.

She pulled open the closet door and ran her hands along the walls. "No. No."

"She disappeared," Blair said plainly. "And she took them with her."

"People don't *disappear*."

"*She* did."

Diana didn't like the fear in Blair's voice. It made her uneasy. The pop of a gunshot made them both turn.

Pop. Pop. Pop.

Something crashed to the floor hard enough to make the house shake. A window blasted open and brassy bluegrass galloped into the room.

In the doorway, Spencer turned.

"No!" Diana stepped around him and into the path of Lou's aim. But this time, Diana had her own gun lifted.

"I'm sorry," she spat, seeing the cold, empty stare that greeted her. "Okay? I'm *sorry*. I took your friends to get your attention. I wanted to show you that I wasn't some incapable loser. I have resources. I can run an operation. And I want your help. That's it. I didn't hurt them. And I think I made my point."

Lou didn't move. Her expression remained unchanged.

Diana's heart knocked in her throat. She swallowed against it. *What can I say? What would I say to myself?*

Blair's breath came in pants beside her.

She thinks I'm about to be shot, Diana noted distantly.

Before she could say anything, Lou whispered, "Why me?"

Diana hadn't been expecting this question. *Why not you?*

She thought Lou understood her own power.

"Who else?" Diana said. "Seriously, who else can do what you do?"

Lou lowered her gun.

Diana tried to seal the deal. "I hate bad guys. You hate bad guys. And my guy is the worst. He's not just a pedophile, he runs a billion-dollar child pornography business underground."

Diana dared to take a step toward her.

"I read about your parents, about your dad," she ventured. Lou's eyes seemed to darken, fill up with black. Diana took a breath and pressed on. "You know how I feel, Louie. I can't eat. I can't sleep. I can't—I need this. I need *you*."

She looked down for dramatic effect.

Then she flicked her eyes up, hoping to see some change in Lou's expression. "You'll *enjoy* hunting him. I promise."

Blair shifted nervously in her periphery, but Diana held her smile. It wasn't easy in the face of that cold stare. She'd never seen anything like it. It was wind blowing across the tundra, as if Lou was made of snow and ice herself.

At last Lou lowered the gun, but the cold fire didn't leave her eyes. "Tell me about him."

20

D ani shook on the apartment floor. Her matted hair was stuck to her face. She looked feverish, red-cheeked, eyes glassy. They'd covered her in King's comforter, stripped from his bed. But her teeth still chattered as if it were the dead of winter.

"What can we do for her?" Piper asked, pacing nervously. She wrung her hands.

"I'll be back." Mel rose from her crouch and left through the kitchen door.

King remained on the floor beside Dani, a mug of hot tea in one hand, a cup of water in the other. "You want something to drink?" he asked hopefully.

She didn't even look at him.

Piper ran her hand down her face again. She'd never seen Dani like this before. Her fears and anxieties would rise up suddenly, sure. Sometimes when they were in a club or a bar, she would get this look on her face, and Piper knew it was time to get some air. Or she'd move a little closer on the sofa during a movie. The movement wouldn't be tinged with sweetness or desire—there was a desperate need in it. And there were the dreams from which she woke up screaming.

But this...

She tried to remember the things she'd read about PTSD and what *not* to do.

"Baby," Piper said, trying to get those dark eyes to look into hers. They wouldn't. "Dani, listen."

Dani continued to shake.

"You've gone through this before and you can get through this again. And we're going to sit right here with you, me, King, and Mel, for as long as it takes."

Lady whined.

"And Lady. We're not going to leave you alone until it's over. You're safe. I promise."

Dani looked up, meeting Piper's eyes for the first time. But they were still unfocused.

Melandra appeared with a prescription bottle, orange with a white plastic cap. "Here."

She opened the bottle and shook a round blue pill out onto her hand. "Dani, open up."

"Are you just going to give her a Valium?" Piper asked. "Is this consensual?"

"If we take her to the hospital, they will sedate her with or without her permission. I don't see how this is different."

Cursing inwardly, Piper held the water glass, flinching against the way Dani automatically drank it down.

Someone could take her onto the balcony and tell her to jump and she would. Piper didn't like this checked-out version of Dani.

She's somewhere else. She's somewhere very, very far away.

Come back, baby.

"Did any of you try to contact Lou while Dennard had us?" King asked suddenly. He stretched his neck to one side but didn't try to get up.

Piper loved him for that. She knew that sitting on the floor must be really hard for his old bones, but he stayed right beside Dani like he'd said he would.

"I did," Piper said. "A million times."

"Me too," Melandra said.

"But she didn't come right away," King said. "You know what that means?"

No, Piper didn't know what it meant. All of her attention was on Dani. She wondered how long it would take the Valium to kick in.

"She can't hear us when she's in La Loon," he said.

"What is your point?" Piper said, chewing on her thumb.

"Lou has her limitations. Her shoulder was the first warning. Tonight was another."

"It's hard to forget she's human sometimes," Melandra admitted, pushing Dani's hair back from her face so she could rub her forehead and neck with a warm cloth.

"But she is," King said. "And she won't always be able to step in and handle a situation. We need to get serious about our own security."

The light returned to Dani's eyes. She looked up and sighed. She stopped trembling.

"That's better," Melandra said, encouraging. "You like the hot cloth? I'll make you another."

Mel's knees popped as she rose. At the sink, she rewarmed the rag with the running faucet.

"Let's move her to the sofa so she can lay down," King said. Piper lifted her torso and King grabbed her legs. They moved in tandem, placing her limp body on the red leather. King put a pillow under her head and repositioned the blanket.

Lady looked up at King imploringly.

"All right," he said. "Just this once."

Lady hopped up onto the sofa and draped herself over Dani. She laid her head on the girl's stomach.

Mel placed the warm rag on Dani's forehead. "Her breathing is better."

"Yeah," Piper said, noting the same. "Is she going to be okay?"

"She'll be okay," Mel assured her with a squeeze. "She just needs some time."

"Are we going to talk about why you have a prescription for Valium?"

Mel gave a crooked smile. "Dani isn't the only one who gets panicky."

The pressure between Piper's ears intensified. Lady's ears flicked and her tail began to thump against the sofa.

Piper turned and found Lou emerging from King's darkened bedroom. Her hair was still wet, her cheeks red. She had a gun in her right hand and Piper was pretty sure that was blood splattered on her face.

Mel made a small sound of surprise, her eyes roving Lou's body. "I'll make another rag."

"Tell me that psycho is dead," Piper said.

"Dennard's alive."

"*Why?*" Piper hissed.

"Shhh," King said, raising his hand and waving at them. "She's finally dropped off to sleep."

Piper looked down at Dani, her dark hair framing her face. Her eyes were closed and her breathing a slow, steady rhythm.

Restraining her voice to a whisper, she said, "*Why* is she alive?"

"She wants to destroy a pedophile."

"Who cares what she wants?" Piper raised her fingers and pressed them into her temple. "Do you have any idea what she put Dani through tonight?"

Lou's brow creased. She looked the sleeping girl over. "She hurt her?"

"Not physically, but Dani had a freaking panic attack because some *psycho* kidnapped her, and you're just going to give her a pass for that?"

"Back up," King said. "Tell me about the guy she's hunting."

"Goes by Winter. He runs a child pornography ring on the internet. She doesn't know he's a man, but she assumes."

King shrugged. "I've never heard of a woman running child pornography rings, but maybe. Is it just him?"

"No, he finds and recruits abusers through the internet and pays them to live stream the attacks."

"Why live stream? Why not pictures and video?"

"Harder to trace. No agency can track it. Once the feed is terminated, it's gone."

"Sounds smart." King rubbed the back of his neck. "I prefer my criminals stupid."

"I want to get the children first."

King snorted in disbelief. "There are thousands of kids being raped every day. I'm not saying it's a good thing, but you're not going to be able to move them all in a night."

Lou's eyes darkened. "I'll start with the ones Winter broadcasts. Then I'll take out the abusers and move the kids."

Piper put her hands on her hips. "Okay, fine. There's a worthy cause here and we can help. But then what?"

"Then I'll kill Winter," Lou said.

"And *then*?" Piper pressed.

When Lou didn't seem to understand, King said, "She wants you to kill Dennard."

"Why?"

"Why?" Piper squeezed the bridge of her nose. *Because she kidnapped us. Because she slapped me. Because I took one look at that woman and realized how crazy and how dangerous she is. And if we don't shake her she's going to hurt us,* really *hurt us.*

Did Lou really have no sense of self-preservation? Couldn't she tell when there was someone in the room that you didn't screw with?

Maybe not, if you usually are that person.

Piper exhaled. "Because she's not our friend, Louie! She's not a good guy."

"She wants to destroy a pedophile. Why should I stop her?"

"Easy now," King said, raising his hands. "Everyone take a breath. Piper..."

Piper's jaw was clenching and unclenching, but she managed to roll her eyes up to meet King's.

He leveled her with a soft look. "What happened to Dani scared us, but she's going to be okay. And so are we."

Piper shook her head. "We can't be buddy-buddy with this woman. We can't have another psychopath hanging around. One is enough."

She hadn't meant to say that. She was angry, and tired, and Dani's condition *had* scared her. It'd scared the *hell* out of her.

Piper looked at Lou. She saw nothing. No recognition. No reaction to her words. Her heart plummeted into her stomach.

"No psychopaths," Lou said coldly. "Got it."

And disappeared.

21

L ou wasn't entirely sure where she was going when she stepped from the dark of King's apartment into nothing. She welcomed the compression, the escape.

She shouldn't have been surprised it was Konstantine's apartment that formed around her, his living room with its uneven clay-tiled floor and a large desk set off to one side. An archway showcased the open kitchen.

His desk lamp was on and he was typing away at his laptop with a steaming mug of something within arm's reach.

He looked up and frowned. "You have blood on your face."

"Do I?" she asked. She could smell his shampoo and cologne from where she stood. His hair was still wet from a shower.

His frown deepened. "Is it yours?"

She wiped her face. "I don't think so."

Something in him relaxed. "The others?"

"Everyone's alive."

Here his lips twitched with a smile. "The blood on your face says otherwise."

"King, Piper, Melandra, and Dani are alive," she amended. She shrugged out of her leather coat, but had a hard time doing it.

He hissed when he saw her bare shoulder. "That is swollen. Badly."

"It hurts," she admitted.

He raised an eyebrow, rising from his seat and crossing to her. He inspected it without touching it. His frown only deepened. "It must be nearly unbearable for you to say that. It looks really bad. Come on."

He led her up the stairs to his bedroom above. He stepped into the bathroom and turned on the shower. On a hook, he hung a fresh towel.

"I don't need you to take care of me," she said.

"We've already established this." He gave her a forced smile. "Can you indulge me?"

She stepped out of her pants easily enough, but when it came to pulling the shirt over her head, she found her arm wouldn't move.

Konstantine was frowning again. "Did this happen in the fight with Diana?"

"It was already...irritated."

"How?"

She didn't want to talk about Jiri, about the hunt in Prague. She only rolled her eyes up to his, daring him to press her on it.

He didn't. "You must have compounded the injury. I have something you can take, after your shower, if you want it."

"Something legal?"

He laughed. "Yes."

She gave a slight nod.

"May I cut this?" he asked, pulling scissors from the vanity.

Lou didn't care. The shirt was already ruined with the blood caked into its fibers. So she let him cut it from her body so that her arm didn't have to move. Then she stepped into the steaming stream and closed the glass door behind her.

Konstantine gathered up her clothes and disappeared. She was left with only her thoughts.

Traitorously, they ran on a loop.

Piper's angry face. Dani, sweaty and panting on King's sofa. Even Lady's look of admonishment. Who knew a dog could scold with her eyes?

Lou felt like she'd done something wrong. And she couldn't recall the last time she'd had this feeling. When her aunt Lucy was sick, dying, maybe. There'd been a hint of this feeling, of *not okay*, that had permeated everything then as well.

But that look in Piper's eyes.

Piper. *Yelling* at her.

Had Piper ever yelled at her before? No. Piper was a cheerful person. Lou had seen her cry a few times, usually when it came to her drug-addicted mother, but those unhappy feelings had never been directed at Lou before.

She'd never looked at Lou as if somehow Lou had *betrayed* her.

Lou exhaled and scrubbed her face with a cloth. She washed her hair and body and made slow work of it, given her one able arm.

After she stepped out and wrapped herself in the soft towel, she found a comb in Konstantine's medicine cabinet.

In the bedroom, he'd laid out a pair of his black sweats and a large, loose white shirt.

She put them on and sat on the edge of the bed to brush out her hair.

When she heard a noise, she turned and found him standing there, a glass of water in one hand and a small sauce cup with two pills in the other. He was watching her with a strange expression.

"What is it?" she asked.

He started as if remembering himself. "My mother used to sit on the end of my bed and brush out her hair."

"This bed?"

"No," he said, his smile widening. "It was a long time ago. Here."

He handed her the water first. She had to set down the comb so she could take it with her good hand. Her bad shoulder felt better after being pummeled by the hot water, but it still throbbed. She'd done too much too soon, and that was painfully clear now as the night was moving in on her, as the adrenaline was leaving her and her muscles were stiffening.

"What is this?" she asked, opening her hand for the pills.

"It's your Vicodin, which you stopped taking." His voice held a hint of playful challenge. It reminded her of Lucy's *I told you* voice.

She remembered leaving the hospital with a prescription for it after she was shot. She'd taken it for a week, when the pain was at its worst, and mostly slept because she was so tired. But after that she hadn't liked feeling dull in her mind or in her body. She hadn't realized Konstantine had kept the rest of the pills.

"I doubt I can convince you to see a doctor. I'll settle for immobilizing the arm and treating it until the swelling goes down. And if you *rest*, your shoulder should feel okay in a few days."

"We're going to go after Winter," she said.

He stood and placed the water on a small desk against the wall. "Of course you are. And who is Winter?"

"It's a fake internet name."

He gave her a patient smile. "Yes, I know what a handle is. What do you know about him?"

Lou did her best to recount what Diana had told her.

He positioned himself against the headboard. "I'll see what I can find out. I hate those who prey on children. When are you moving against him?"

"That hasn't been decided. But King is on board."

After a pause, he said, "I heard that Jiri Svoboda went missing tonight. Any chance you've been in Prague?"

She met his gaze. "Was he one of yours?"

He laughed. "Yes. Would you have spared him if you'd known? Did you know?"

"No," she said. It was a blanket answer to both questions.

He smiled. "I didn't think so. He can be replaced. But you do love causing trouble for me—and yourself—don't you?"

He was so beautiful there, relaxed, his hair framing his deep green eyes.

She kissed him. She hadn't known she was going to do it until her lips were pressed against his.

"Hello," he said, a laugh in his voice, as she settled her weight against his lap. "*Buonasera.*"

When she began to rock her hips, just slightly, he stopped her.

"As tempting as you are," he said, his face flushed. "Do you want to make your shoulder worse than it already is?"

Piper's face flashed in her mind again. Why? Why did it keep haunting her like that? When was the last time anything had haunted her?

"What's wrong?" Konstantine asked. When she didn't answer, he said, "If you really want—"

"No." She sat up.

"Was it something I said?"

"I was thinking about Piper."

His brow arched. "Do you often think of lesbians when you are in bed with me?"

His joke fell flat. Lou was too far away, deep in the recesses of her mind. "She's mad at me."

"For what?"

"I don't know."

He snorted, settling back against his pillows. "It is true I am not an expert on women, but what I do know is that they're usually only mad at you if you've done something wrong."

Wrong.

There it was again, that feeling of *not okay*. It made her itch under the collar. It made her want to hold a gun.

"What did she say?" he asked.

We can't have another psychopath hanging around. One is enough.

"She doesn't want me to work with Diana."

"But you agreed to anyway."

"Yes."

"Why?"

When she met his eyes, he flinched. "I'm not questioning your judgment. I'm only asking your reason."

"They're hurting children."

"Okay. But do you need to work with her to save them?"

Lou turned the question over in her mind, but it blurred out, grew fuzzy. She felt her eyes fluttering.

"The Vicodin is working. You should sleep." He patted the bed beside him. "All of this can wait."

He said it as if she had a choice.

But even as the darkness reached out to take her into its arms, it was still Piper's hard, accusing face that she carried with her into the deep.

———

22

King wasn't sure Lou would come. He sat at his desk sipping coffee, his eyes straying to the door labeled *Ms. Thorne* every few seconds. He'd even made the coffee himself, using the small coffeemaker in the office, lest he should miss her by going down to the café.

He was trying to get some work done, but it wasn't easy. He kept thinking of the night before, of Dani's panic attack, of Piper's anger. He'd known about Mel sometimes taking Valium. She'd turned down his offer to smoke weed once or twice because of it.

"You're too late," she'd said. "I already took a pill. I don't chase my downers with downers."

And drama aside, there was something irresistible about Diana's offer. It was a great case, busting a large pornography ring.

But he wanted to go over the plans for the move against Winter. And he wanted to make it absolutely clear to Lou what she had to risk by working with someone like Dennard.

Only one concern plagued him. When Lou had left, she'd

been too quiet. *More* quiet, he thought. It was the sort of silence that unsettled him. It usually meant that Lou was about to do something he wouldn't like.

He glanced at the closed door, leaning back in his chair. He wondered if he could step out for lunch, albeit quickly. He was getting hungry again.

That morning, during a tech blackout, King—with Konstantine's assistance—had been able to find and remove the cameras and bugs.

"We have an uneasy truce with Diana," he said to the urn on his desk. "We'll see where this gets us."

His heart ached. He missed his wife. Not just her smile, and her laugh. He also missed her brain. She would know what to do about Dennard—about Lou.

You forget I came to you for help, her distant voice reminded him.

His eyes flicked to the closed door again. Nothing.

Come on, come on, he urged. This time he even sent a page, hoping it would be picked up by the GPS watch Lou often wore.

Piper's door was also closed, but the girl wasn't home. King and Mel had both given her the day off so she could stay with Dani. King had offered to let Dani keep Lady until she felt better, but there was something about a cat named... Taffy? Tabby? He hadn't caught that part.

Lady stayed with Mel.

The door creaked suddenly and King jolted.

Lou stepped into the office, complete with leather jacket and mirrored shades. Her hair was pulled back in a low pony-tail today, but a few dark strands hung around the sides of her face.

"Hey," King breathed, wondering if his relief was too obvious. He held back from saying, *You came.*

"I got your page." Her eyes fell on Piper's empty seat and her shoulders sagged.

"She's off today," King said. "It's just us."

Was that relief he saw flicker across her face?

"You okay?" he ventured.

The stiffness returned.

"Never mind," he said. "Let's talk about Winter. Do you know anything about him?"

"Not yet. Konstantine's searching."

King decided to go for sunny and see where that got him. "That's okay. We'll learn what we need to know."

She hadn't lifted her shades yet, so King couldn't see her eyes. Not a good sign.

"I placed a call to Sampson this morning and he's going to see if Winter is in the system at all. But before we get to that, we need to talk about you."

Lou scowled. "Me?"

"How are you going to protect yourself from Dennard?"

"With a gun."

King laughed. "I mean your abilities. It's one thing to have Konstantine wipe footage or destroy cameras. He's not going to be able to do a damn thing if Diana sees you in action with her own eyes."

"I'll be careful."

Like you were last night? He thought of the room going dark.

"I don't think that'll be enough," King said. "Not for someone like her. People like Dennard are observant, meticulous. She's going to try to figure you out. Hell, she's already trying."

He worried he was veering toward a lecture. Nothing would send Lou running like a lecture. He ran a hand through his hair.

"I'm just saying she can't be trusted with that information. If you're not going to kill her."

"Why should I?" Lou asked.

The genuineness of the question surprised him. It was as if she was looking for a legitimate reason.

"When that reporter from *The Herald* tracked you down, you shot him, didn't you?" It was a rhetorical question. "And if she finds out, would you kill her too?"

"I've revealed my gifts to people without killing them before. Women," she amended.

So it's about the fact that she's a woman.

Damn. King had hoped that wasn't the case. He understood that one day they would find Lou's weakness, whatever it was. He knew she wouldn't hurt children, but children rarely hunt you down and try to shoot you.

This Dennard woman was a different problem. She wasn't like the women Lou was used to saving. If Lou didn't wrap her head around that, she might end up dead for it.

"She doesn't have your abilities," King began, looking for an opening, "but Dennard is very dangerous. Would you shoot preemptively, if someone like you was on your trail?"

She didn't have an answer.

King sighed. He was beginning to feel old again. The feeling was coming on more and more frequently these days, making his mind ache as badly as his body.

"All I'm saying is that we need a plan. It's too dangerous to let her know what you can do."

"She might have already put it together," Lou said.

"Because of last night? I doubt it. She probably thinks you've got tricks. Escape rooms or tunnels in every French Quarter building. I guarantee by the end of the day she'll have convinced herself that you came through a trap door or something. You'd be surprised the bullshit people peddle to themselves when they can't understand something. In the 1700s, they'd had no problem believing in witchcraft. Today? No way. People are too *sensible*. It'll be worse for someone like Dennard, who prides herself on her sensibility."

Lou watched his face for a long moment. Finally, she pulled up the chair to the other side of King's desk. "How do we take down Winter without letting Dennard know what I can do?"

His excitement spiked. He couldn't help it. His love of a good challenge had driven him toward law enforcement in the beginning. Playing by the rules and still winning the game —that was something he understood.

"First, we need to know her plan. She must have one if she's been obsessing about this guy for a while. Once we talk to her and see where she's at, we can build our sham operation around hers. It'll be brilliant, actually."

Famous last words, he thought, glancing at the urn.

He wanted it to work. He wanted to keep his promise to his dead wife, Louie's aunt, that he would keep Lou safe.

"How do we build a sham operation?" she asked. "There's only six of us. And you're not a cop anymore."

A knot loosened in his chest. "I've got a plan."

Diana stepped into the house expecting...something else.

When they'd brought the detective, the shopkeeper, and those two whimpering fools in, the townhouse had been pristine. Now it looked like a Halloween attraction.

She stretched on the latex gloves, scowling at the blood pooled on the kitchen floor. Bending down to inspect the damage, she wrinkled her nose.

The smell of it was heady, fruity to the point of intoxication, and it made her skin crawl.

Diana had selected the building because the bottom level

was protected by a secluded garden. This meant that neighbors and passersby couldn't see the entrance or what happened past the townhome's high gate. It had helped that it was only a block from King's office. It had made it easy to bring them in without arousing suspicion.

But it might not have been only to her advantage.

Had Lou relied on this entrance?

Diana had done a headcount that morning and could account for only five of their original crew—including Spencer, Blair, and herself. That either meant Lou killed fifteen people or some of them ran off.

Steph and Sarah Zink—Diana's favorites—had stayed. But everyone else was gone.

Maybe after meeting Lou's gaze down the barrel of her gun, she should be running too. But here she was, mopping blood off the floor.

The stairs creaked and Diana stood, looking into the hallway.

It was Blair, with a knit brow and her own pair of black nitrite gloves. "No bodies. Where the hell are all the bodies?"

"Maybe Lou has a cleanup crew."

Blair snorted, stepping into the kitchen. "Shitty cleanup crew. There's blood everywhere."

"Any idea on how many she shot?"

"If each of the big puddles counts as a body, then fourteen."

Maybe she took them all. Somehow that was better. Diana hated nothing more than cowards.

"But maybe someone ran off," Blair offered. "Can you blame them?"

Diana scowled at her. "Don't tell me you're a chickenshit too."

"I'm just saying, the woman dropped fourteen people in less than a minute. She was in and out of this building and took four people with her before we could get the lights back on. If you aren't concerned, then you're stupid."

"Stupid? No." Diana wasn't stupid. Diana was pissed.

She wanted to know how Lou did it. How did she get in and out so quickly? How did she kill so quickly? *How, how, how?*

The admiration only carried so far. Then it soured, hardening into envy.

There was much more to Louie Thorne—she *knew* it. She only had to crack her code.

"She's dangerous," Blair said, stepping over a puddle of blood. "*Too* dangerous, frankly."

Diana gestured at the room, at the house. "Look at what she can do. Think of what *we* could do with her help."

Diana thought herself magnanimous for the use of *we*. In truth, it was an *I* that framed her fantasies.

I'm *going to kill Winter. This time* I'll *pull it off.*

"What we're doing is fine," Blair insisted. "You don't need her to bring down Winter. You don't."

"You don't understand."

"I do!" Blair exclaimed. "You're the one who can't get your head out of your ass and see what you're doing. Take the blinders off, Dee!"

Diana's face hardened. "If you're scared, you can leave."

Her irritation chewed at the back of her neck, nipped at her earlobes. Blair never broke rank with her. Why would she do it now, at such an important moment, when they were so close?

Lou had agreed to help them, hadn't she?

Winter was within her reach.

But if you're being honest with yourself, it's not only about Winter anymore, is it?

"I'm not leaving. I promised that I'd see this to the end

with you and I'll do it," Blair said, her jaw tight and face red. "I just want you to tell me where the end is."

"I don't need your doom and gloom today, Blair."

Her sister took a deep breath. "What *do* you need then?"

"Manpower."

23

"Here you go," Piper said, bringing the hot tea to Dani's bedside and placing it on the end table. "And a little saucer for you to put the tea bag in so it doesn't oversteep. I know you hate that."

"Thanks." Dani's voice was gruff. Her face was still puffy and her eyes red. She'd slept for almost twelve hours, but she looked far from refreshed.

Dani caught her staring. "Do I look that bad?"

"You're beautiful," Piper said without pause.

Dani gave her a weak smile. "My chest hurts."

"I think that's from the panic attack." While Dani had slept and Piper had kept watch over her, she'd read what felt like a thousand articles about PTSD on her phone. It was common for people who had had a panic attack to feel sore the next day from the barrage of contracting muscles.

A Valium hangover could also leave someone feeling subdued, tired, and out of it. Between the two, Piper had a good sense of what Dani might feel like right now.

Meow.

Piper glanced at her leg and saw Octavia, Dani's cat, rubbing against her legs.

"You're trying to kill me," Piper said.

"She knows you're allergic," Dani said, lifting the mug and blowing the steam. "She wants you to love her anyway."

"I do," Piper said, sniffing and rubbing her nose. The fluffy Russian Blue was beautiful and mostly sweet, though Piper had seen her sassy side a few times in their months together.

Oh god, her eyes were already starting to water. "But I still can't pick her up and put her by my face if I want to keep breathing."

When Piper looked up, smiling, she saw Dani was nearly in tears.

"What? What is it?" Alarm shivered through her. "Babe, I love Tavi."

"No, it's not that," she said, her lip trembling. "I hate you seeing me like this. I can't believe—"

"Hey, *no*." Piper rushed to the side of the bed and sat down in the small space between the edge and Dani's covered legs. "Don't do that. Don't beat yourself up. What happened was bullshit. It shouldn't have happened. But we're fine. We got out of there. You're okay. I'm okay. Everyone's okay. Except Lou, who is out of her damn mind, but I'm hoping that will pass."

Dani's gaze was a million miles away, but at least the tears were holding off. Piper hated it when girls cried. It never failed to leave her feeling helpless and inadequate.

"I suppose I asked for this," Dani whispered, sniffling.

"What? No."

"I'm the one who keeps insisting that I be an investigative reporter. I'm the one who keeps asking King for cases even though things like this are going to keep happening. I knew it'd be dangerous and that I'm not as—not as *together* as I used to be, but I keep doing it. What's wrong with me?"

"We could always quit our jobs and open a cat café. Everyone loves cats and coffee. We'd be billionaires. Except, you know, I'd die of anaphylactic shock."

Dani didn't laugh. She pressed the heels of her hands against her eyes.

"Hey," Piper said, taking her hands. "Listen to me."

When Dani looked up her eyes were rimmed red.

"Something terrible happened to you. Some absolute *bullshit*, and instead of giving up on your dream, you're still chasing it. That's *amazing*. Seriously, do you have any idea how incredible that is? You're not backing down, you're not quitting. You're going to have bad days, but you keep getting up and kicking ass and that's what matters. Daniella Allendale, you're *incredible*."

"There were a lot of compliments in there."

"Yeah, well, how many do you need before you believe me?"

"A billion," Dani replied, and then she smiled.

Tavi jumped up onto the bed.

"Hey, not mine!" Piper cried, taking the pillows on her side of the bed and pushing them under the blankets. "Seriously, your cat has it in for me."

"She just likes women who play hard to get."

"Am I playing hard to get?" Piper asked with a smile. She leaned in, putting her lips in range for a kiss.

Dani grinned, an honest-to-goodness grin. "No. Not really."

Dani's lips were warm and swollen, sticky to the touch, but Piper didn't mind. She'd take any kiss from this girl, however it came. She reached her hand into Dani's hair and pulled her closer.

"You're okay," Piper said, pressing her forehead to Dani's. "You can do this."

"What happened?" Dani asked, her breath warm on Piper's mouth. "After I passed out."

Piper gave her the rundown of Lou's rescue and the aftermath in King's apartment. The only part Dani remembered was Lady comforting her. Piper didn't mention that Diana had slapped her. She wasn't sure that Lou even realized it had happened. She thought she might have appeared a second after the fact.

If she told Lou that it happened, what would she do? Would she finally kill Diana on the spot or shrug it off? And if she shrugged it off...

Piper's heart clenched. "I don't get why she doesn't just finish her off. She's a bad guy. She kills bad guys. Period. Full stop."

"Didn't she tell us once she'd never killed a woman?"

"Who gives a shit if she's a woman? Women can be evil too."

Dani sipped her tea. "Maybe she's just curious."

"What do you mean, curious? About *what*?"

"About someone like her. There's another woman out there, hunting and killing these guys, and I don't think she's ever encountered that before. She's got to be curious. It's like finally seeing her own kind or something."

"Diana is not her kind."

We can't have another psychopath hanging around. One is enough.

Piper flinched. "Though I might have implied that she was."

Dani lowered the mug, her face pinched in confusion. "What do you mean?"

Piper replayed the conversation, embarrassment heating her cheeks.

When she finished, Dani squeezed her hand. "You were upset. You didn't mean it."

Piper ran both hands down her face. "I still shouldn't have said it. I practically pushed her into the woman's arms."

Way to prove you're not disaster friends, she thought bitterly.

"What do you want to do about it?" Dani asked.

Piper pulled herself out of her thoughts. "What?"

"We have a psychopath on our hands. What are we going to do about it?"

"I don't know. I'm used to Lou being the one who handles the psycho parts."

"That's our problem," Dani interjected. "We rely too much on Lou's abilities. And in times like this, when she makes the wrong call or when she's hurt, what are we supposed to do?"

Piper saw the color returning to Dani's face. Her eyes were clearer, brighter. She didn't think it was the tea working that magic. It was action. Dani was always at her best when there was something that had to be done.

"We're a team," Dani said. "Me, you, Lou, King, Mel. That Italian guy."

"Konstantine."

"We need to work together. If one of us is out of commission, or has a bad day, the rest of us need to step in and pull our weight. We have to stop thinking that Lou is invincible and is just going to solve all our problems. She's *human*. An exceptionally talented, ruthless human, but she's human."

"King said something like that," Piper recalled. "He said we need to get serious about protecting ourselves."

"Not just protecting ourselves," Dani said. "We need to be in control of the situation. If you're not someone who makes the things happen, then the things will happen *to* you."

"I thought today was supposed to be one of your bad

days," Piper said. "You're supposed to be the one resting and I'm the one pulling the weight, right?"

Dani didn't seem to hear. She chewed her lip, her eyes cast down in concentration.

"It'll take me a minute to find my Diana Dennard story. Do I want to expose her? Get her arrested or just force her underground? I'll need to think about it. But that's my plan." Dani put the mug on the side table and lay back against the pillows. "That still leaves you."

Piper crawled under the covers, pressing herself into Dani's side. "Me?"

"Yeah, what are you going to do about her? Lou is curious, so she's playing with fire. King is going to be too seduced by the idea of busting a child pornographer to bow out. Melandra has a shop to run and is dealing with her ex's trial. And Konstantine is probably trying to get Lou to chill out and rest like you are with me right now, but he'll offer her whatever she asks for. That leaves you, baby. What's your move?"

That leaves me, Piper thought. She saw Diana's face, the twisted rage in it when she'd brought her hand across Piper's face.

My move, she thought. *What's my move?*

"She's funding her operation with credit card scams," Piper said thoughtfully. "What if we outed her for that? I can make some calls, talk to the local PD."

Dani cupped her cheek. "Sounds like a good place to start."

24

L ou crossed and uncrossed her legs, staring out at the bustling square. It was getting hot under her leather jacket. The coffee on the table in front of her was growing cold. It was King's idea to meet Diana at Café du Monde. He was insistent that Lou guarded the extent of her gift as closely as possible.

Lou thought that was pointless. People either believed in the supernatural or they didn't. If Diana was the sort of woman to rewrite the universe around her to suit her world view, she could have seen a ghost on one of the infamous New Orleans tours and talked herself out of it.

The chair opposite her scraped against the concrete loudly, making Lou's teeth vibrate.

Diana settled into the metal chair with a hint of a smile.

"You like coffee?" she asked, eyeing the Styrofoam cup. "You ordered it at the diner too."

"When you took my coffee cup," Lou said. "I remember. Was it the money or the cup that you pulled DNA from?"

Diana's face smoothed out, removing itself of emotion.

"I'll tell you if you tell me what happened in Julia Street station."

"I was shot," Lou said simply.

Diana's lips quirked. "Does that happen to you a lot?"

"More than average."

Diana snorted. "Is that what's wrong with your shoulder?"

Lou waited. She was used to playing the staring game. It was why she liked to wear her mirrored sunglasses. People found it harder to look at themselves. As expected, Diana looked away first.

"I used both. The money and the mug. I like to be sure." She ran her fingers through her ponytail. "Winter is in Springfield."

"Illinois?"

"Missouri." Diana shifted in her seat, her excitement showing. "He has a fourth-floor apartment in a commercial district. Red brick, flat roof. With a coordinated attack we can get him on all sides. There's no way he'll escape that building alive."

She must be expecting me to bring this manpower, Lou thought. She'd shot nearly everyone Diana had brought to the townhouse with her. "Do you want Winter alive?"

"Yes," Diana said with a smirk. "I don't need to tell you why, do I?"

No, Lou thought. Sometimes it was fun to vent a bit of steam.

"Are the children in Springfield?" Lou asked, trying not to rotate her shoulder. It was throbbing again. The eight hundred milligrams of ibuprofen she took that morning were wearing off. But having strapped her arm to the side of her body had helped.

"No," Diana said, twisting a paper napkin between her fingers. "He finds and recruits his rapists online, pays them online too. They're located all over. But I expect that some are on-site."

She said this as if annoyed by the interruption. Something about it unsettled Lou, made the muscles along her spine itch.

"How soon can you get to Springfield?" Diana asked. "He's been there for two weeks already. He's never in a place long, so I don't want to wait."

Now, Lou thought. *I could be there right now. I could close my eyes and just—*

"Three days," she said.

Diana frowned. "Three days?"

Lou couldn't tell if Diana thought three days was too short or too long of a wait.

"It's...far away," Lou said, forgetting what King had told her to say. "We need to get everyone in place."

These words were strange on her tongue. She should've asked King for a script. How long did it normally take to mobilize large groups?

"How many can you spare for this operation?" Diana asked.

Lou looked out over the square. "Enough."

King's voice sprang to mind. *Ask misleading questions so she doesn't get a sense of how you work or what you can do.*

"Do you know what he looks like? Do you have a photo?"

"No photo," Diana said. "He's been careful to keep his face hidden. I only know where he is by his internet trails, and I can only establish those while he live streams."

Lou didn't need a photo. Even now, her compass was searching the dark.

Where are you...the one she wants.

Something clicked inside her. On the other side of the darkness, a man took shape. And Lou could feel that it was a man now. He smelled like cologne, something cheap and alcoholic, and body odor. The hiss of a grill was nearby. For some reason, Lou had the impression he was in a restaurant. A small one where the patrons sat quite close together. She pushed further, she caught the smell of fried potatoes and meat.

She supposed even monsters had to eat.

"What?" Diana asked.

Lou blinked.

"Where'd you go just now? You looked like you were a million miles away."

"I was in Springfield with Winter."

Diana laughed, mistaking this for a joke.

"I'll bring manpower. What will you bring?"

"I can offer technical support and a bit of muscle, but I'll be relying on you to surround the buildings and take Winter down. After you extract him, he's mine. Are we clear on that?"

"I want the children," Lou said honestly. "I don't care what you do with Winter."

Diana smirked as if amused by the answer.

Was that what it was like, Lou wondered. When one had to rely on large coordinated efforts to achieve an aim. Lou thought their small operation of six was cumbersome at times. She wasn't sure she could work with more people than that, not when she preferred being alone.

"You don't have anything to say to me? No 'I'm sorry I lost my temper and killed your entire team'?" Diana pressed. When Lou said nothing, she harrumphed. "Yeah, okay. I guess I deserve that. I kidnapped your pets. And you're going to make it up to me anyway. Give me Winter and we'll be more than square."

Lou wondered why talking had to be a part of this. Conversations were taxing on the best of days, but like this, when it felt more like a dance, an exchange of double-edged blows and parries, it was particularly exhausting.

Diana rubbed her nose. "I have to say, when it came to your crew I expected a little more steel."

The hair on the back of Lou's neck rose.

"The cop and the black woman, they're stone cold. I like them. I'd recruit them if I thought they'd ditch you. But the two girls...*whew*. Where did you find those crybabies?"

Lou found her hand opening and closing under the table. It itched for a gun.

"You must be more lenient than I am." Diana wrinkled her nose as if she disapproved. "I don't tolerate any weakness on my team. If I'd heard even one *second* of that sniveling, I would've dismissed her. Or put a bullet in her head."

She must've seen something in Lou's face that frightened her. The sneer evaporated. In its place, there were only wide eyes.

"Don't give me that look. We're partners now. I won't touch your people," Diana said, though her grin had too many teeth. "What's good for you is good for me."

Is that right? Lou wondered. *We're about to find out.*

25

Konstantine stood and took a turn around his living room again. He regarded the sofa pressed against one cream wall. The large red rug on the stone floor. The desk, the painting, the pristine kitchen that he'd spent an hour cleaning. The smell of espresso in the air. He glanced at the stairs but knew that was ridiculous. They wouldn't come through his bedroom. The living room was largest. She'd bring them here, to the heart of his home.

"Close the drapes," Lou had told him. "Make the room as dark as you can."

He pulled the curtains together and stood in the dim light, trying to decide what to do with his own body. Did he want to be behind his desk or on the sofa when they arrived?

He decided to sit at the desk, affecting a pose that didn't convey the unease in his stomach.

He caught himself drumming against the arm of the chair and forced himself to stop.

The pressure rose between his ears suddenly and popped. Then his living room wasn't so empty.

In the center of the room stood four figures that hadn't been there a second before.

Lou was the first to meet his gaze. The others seemed to just be getting their bearings.

He found his voice quickly. "Can I offer you something to drink? Coffee? Water?"

"Whoa," Piper said, breaking ranks first, stepping away from the huddle and toward Konstantine's desk. "This is where you live? God, what smells so good?"

He wasn't sure what question to address first. "Espresso. Would you like one?"

"*Yes.*" She looked around, appraising the apartment. "Nice place."

"Can I offer you a seat?" he said, motioning to the sofa. Only then did he realize that it would only seat three of them comfortably, and he had no other chairs in the room but his own.

It was clear now that he never entertained here. Stefano had been to his apartment, and little Matteo, who often followed Konstantine around with a dog-like reverence.

He motioned toward his seat as he stepped into the kitchen to make a fresh espresso. Lou waved him off, crossing instead to the window. She pulled apart the drapes, letting light fill the room again.

As he made the coffee, he took her measure.

Her left arm was still strapped to her chest, immobilizing that shoulder. He wasn't sure if this was a good sign, that perhaps she was finally taking her self-care seriously, or if it warned of a greater vulnerability.

"Where is the other one?" he asked, tamping down the grounds. "Mel?"

He didn't even attempt to say her full name. Just the nickname felt strange on his tongue.

King answered, looking relaxed as he reclined on one end

of the sofa. "She's with Lady, the dog. They're running the shop. Truth be told, she's preoccupied with her husband's trial. The court date is in a couple weeks, so she has enough to be getting on with."

"She won't be involved in this operation?" Konstantine asked as the moka began to burble.

"Operation," Piper snickered. "You sound like King."

Piper's spirits seemed high at first glance, but now Konstantine saw the puffiness under her eyes. She wore makeup to hide it, but the swelling was still noticeable.

But it was the other who looked truly pained. Dark circles sank deep beneath her eyes. Her skin was sallow. Konstantine wondered if she'd slept in days.

He caught Lou watching him. She arched a brow.

He smiled, bringing his focus to the detective. He'd begun speaking again.

"Our objective here is to hide Lou's abilities from Diana. I think we can do that," King said, tapping his knee. "What do you think?"

He was speaking to Konstantine.

"Aren't you worried that by helping this crazy person at all, we'll never get rid of her?" Piper asked. She sat between Dani and King. "What if she shows up every time she needs help with something? Is this the sort of behavior we actually want to *encourage*?"

"No," Konstantine and King said in unison.

Konstantine handed her the espresso in its little cup. "Would you like sugar?"

"No, thank you." She sipped it and scowled. "Oh, it's *bitter*. Maybe I should've said yes to the sugar."

"Give it to me," the other one said. She downed it in a single go.

"Have you considered killing her?" Konstantine asked. He was watching Lou. She stood at the window, watching the courtyard outside, her arms crossed. He wondered how her shoulder was feeling. She wore dark cargo pants and a tight black tank top.

"She hunts predators," she replied without looking away from the window. "Why should I stop her?"

Konstantine saw movement in the corner of his eye and turned his head ever so slightly to better track it. Piper was taking the other girl's hand in hers. Her jaw was furiously working. The emptied espresso cup was placed on the table beside the sofa.

"And if she hurts someone? One of us, for example?" Konstantine asked.

"Then I'll kill her."

She said this plainly. And perhaps anyone else listening to this statement would believe it. Lou's ice-cold exterior was terrifying. It made such declarations easy to believe.

But Konstantine heard the slight drop in her voice. He saw the miniscule shift in her body weight. She might kill Diana if the woman crossed her in some way, but she didn't *want* to.

How interesting.

"This man that Dennard wants to find—"

"Winter," the dark girl interjected.

There was a bit more light in her eyes now. Konstantine wondered if he should offer her another espresso.

"Correct. If they wanted to arrest a man like this, what's the lawful protocol?"

They were looking at King.

"I assume that you mean without all the red tape. Because when someone does a sting like this legally, it's all about warrants and probable cause. Bureaucracy prevails."

"And we don't want this man to be put on trial?" Konstantine asked him.

"I always try to get the families justice if I can. Peace of mind is priceless, you know? But in cases like this, I'm not sure it matters," King said. "Sometimes the families are the pimps themselves. Or if they aren't, an arrest doesn't undo what happened to the kids."

"I can take him," Lou said calmly. There was no boast in it.

Konstantine knew better than to point out the obvious, but he did so anyway. "Your shoulder isn't a hundred percent, *amore mio*."

King almost looked relieved. *Better you than me*, that face said.

This amused Konstantine, the idea that he wasn't the only one trying—and failing—to take care of Louie Thorne.

"I second that," Piper said. "You were supposed to rest for six months. I don't see how this is *resting*."

"I'm with Lou," Dani said. "I can't think about those kids enduring one more night of that."

King held his hands up when everyone's eyes fell on him. "I can't tell anyone what to do with their own bodies. But we should be sensible here."

Konstantine stepped forward. "Assume that the red tape has been cut and the operation to capture Winter was approved. What would a police force do? We can't pretend to be such an operation if we don't know what it looks like."

"That's the problem, isn't it?" King laughed. "We don't know what Dennard thinks we are. An off-grid organization of some kind?"

"We'll pretend to be whatever you think is most believable," Lou said.

King shrugged. "A privately funded enforcement agency?"

"And what would they do?"

"They'd go to his last-known location, surround the place. Extra points if he's home and apprehended, but they'll go in regardless to collect as much evidence as possible."

"And how many people are needed for such an operation?"

"A ten-person SWAT team is standard for a small city, but there's as many as sixty for an urban area like Chicago. If there were multiple locations, such as a home and a workplace, they would move on both at once. Usually there's a bit of a stakeout to see if he shows up, so that the likelihood of apprehension is higher."

"Diana wants to move against him once he gets online and starts a feed. She says she can confirm he'll be in the building if he starts streaming from it."

This is true, Konstantine knew. He knew it was possible to track a person's location in such a way, if they remained connected long enough. There were ways to disguise one's exact location as well. For a man such as Winter, Konstantine suspected he knew how to do that.

"We need to be prepared for the possibility of a second location," Konstantine said. "Or it is possible he will not be in the building. He can mask his location."

"Not from me," Lou said.

"True," he acquiesced. "But if you're at a raid location with Dennard and she is convinced he's there and you know he's not, how will you explain your knowledge? You cannot disappear. That's what we are trying to plan around."

"Why do some criminals have to be smart," Piper bemoaned. "Why can't they all be dumb?"

After brief eye contact, Piper's face reddened and she looked away.

"Could we put Lou on an earpiece so that Diana thinks she's there and involved, but that frees her up to move if necessary?" King asked. "It would also explain any information that comes in."

"That would be ideal," Konstantine said. "Perhaps a large team as well, a show of force, enough to give her pause in moving against Lou in the future, and then a second, smaller support team in case Lou needs to pivot."

"I'm fine," Lou said with a tone that brooked no argument.

"We know, babe," Piper said. "Everyone here is aware that you'd tear your own shoulder off rather than lose your new BFF."

Dani squeezed Piper's hand.

Lou frowned.

"Would it be possible for you to get fifty or sixty people together in two days?" King asked.

"Yes," Konstantine said plainly. "But you realize that I cannot hide what they are. They will not look or act like police officers. If you want Dennard to perceive you in a certain light—"

"I don't care how she views us," Lou said. But she was looking at King to see if he objected.

King only shrugged. "I don't think it's a bad thing if she thinks we run with rough people. I wouldn't mind instilling a bit of fear in her."

"Have you ever managed a coordinated operation like that before?" Konstantine asked, watching the detective pick something out from under his fingernails.

"With the DEA? Sure. We did drug busts all the time. I can figure out the schematics of the building, the entrances, exits, electricity, and all that. Who moves where and when. I just need a team who can follow directions and a good communication system. We can have a contingency plan for the presence of any children in the building versus if he's alone. What would be more impressive, though, is if we can coordinate a cross-country attack where all the streamers are taken down and arrested simultaneously. They busted a ring in South Korea and made over three hundred arrests all over the world. In the US, UK, Canada, and Saudi Arabia. That would really scare the shit out of her, if she thought we were everywhere."

"I'd need more than three days for that," Konstantine said. Did he have people everywhere? Yes. But well-executed plans still took time.

"You're right," King relented. "It would be cool, but unimportant at the moment. Let's just dispose of Winter, rescue the kids, and placate Diana. Then if Diana is stubborn enough to stick around, we'll deal with her too."

Piper was watching the other girl, whose name Konstantine finally remembered. Daniella Allendale. She was the newest addition to their inner circle, and what Konstantine had learned about her wasn't much except that she was an investigative reporter who helped expose the killers Lou had tracked down. Her mother's ancestors were rich sugar barons from Cuba who'd emigrated to the US when Castro seized their homeland. Somehow, they'd maintained their considerable wealth despite those first, uncertain years. But more interestingly, he knew that Dmitri had tortured her almost to death—yet here she was. She hadn't run.

She must be much stronger than she looks, he thought. Though she didn't look it today. Not with those dark circles and a face drained of color.

"Would anyone like gelato?" Konstantine asked.

"Hell yeah," Piper replied, leaping to her feet. "Babe. We have to get gelato. We're in Italy."

"Where is it?" Daniella asked, as if the idea of a walk troubled her.

Konstantine stood, crossed the living room to a window, and pulled back the shade. "Across the courtyard here, under that archway. The gelateria will be open for another hour. Stella makes delicious tiramisu and limoncello gelato."

"Stracciatella is my favorite," Piper said. She pulled Dani to her feet. "It's basically chocolate chip. Come on."

Konstantine didn't think this was the time to argue that American ice cream could never compare.

Dani wiped invisible dust from the front of her jeans. "But I don't have any Italian money."

"Tell Stella I sent you."

"No," Lou said, and fished her wallet out of her cargo pants pockets. She produced a wad of euros, handing them over. If Konstantine's eyes weren't deceiving him, that wasn't the only foreign currency she was carrying. At a glance, he also saw pounds and yen, tucked in beside the euros and American bills he recognized.

"Right," Piper said. "We don't want your gang people recognizing our faces, and if I walk up in there saying Konstantine said give me some gelato, that might send the wrong message."

Konstantine smiled. "The gelato will be worth it. I assure you."

The two girls were down the steps and halfway across the courtyard when Lou said, "I want to go with them."

"I'll wait here for you," King said. "Go on."

Lou seemed to need no other encouragement. She closed the apartment door behind her, leaving the two men alone.

King rubbed his chin. "Can you really assemble fifty or sixty trustworthy men in two days?"

"Yes," Konstantine said. He crossed to his kitchen and turned on the espresso maker. It was almost too late in the day for it, but he wanted it nonetheless. Just the smell of the ground coffee freshened his mind. "Can you really lead them with only a set of walkie-talkies?"

King laughed. "Yes. But to be honest, it's not the operation I'm worried about. I'm worried about Lou."

Konstantine refilled the moka, but didn't interrupt.

"It's not just her shoulder, it's Dennard."

"I haven't had the pleasure of meeting her," Konstantine said. "What's your assessment?"

"Like Lou on steroids. Determined, focused, doesn't know when to quit, but it's more than that. She's like a rabid dog. She doesn't have an ounce of Lou's self-possession or control. She isn't as hard to read as Lou, there's that. Her anger and coldness are all over her face, and there's..." He seemed to consider his next words carefully. "I don't know. There's an unsteadiness. An unpredictability. If I didn't know better I'd say she's crazy. Clinically out of her mind."

"That sounds like a very dangerous woman. But Lou can defeat her easily." And he believed it.

King laughed. "I don't think she wants to. That's what worries me."

Konstantine wondered if it was more than seeing a kindred spirit in Diana. What if Lou was unable to kill a woman? Women, children, animals—Konstantine had a sense that Lou never raised a gun against those weaker than herself. Perhaps it violated some unspoken inner code.

And what would she think of him if she knew the truth? That he held none of the qualms she did, if the end prevented unnecessary bloodshed in the future.

"We could take care of it," King said quietly. He pitched his voice low, as if he was afraid someone might overhear them. "There will be a lot of commotion. Something could just go wrong at the operation."

Konstantine smiled ruefully. "If I kill Diana for her, she'll be furious. At the very least, she will kill whatever man I gave the order to."

King was watching him with a strange expression, and Konstantine wondered if he'd gone too far. The relationship between the two of them was an odd one. King represented the law, having invested over thirty years in an organization that actively worked to disassemble the power of men like Konstantine.

Yet here they were, working on another case together and sharing a concern for the woman standing between them. Did it matter that King lived by and respected the law while Konstantine violated it at every turn?

"Lou is better about letting Piper help. Or was," King added, glancing out the window.

Konstantine felt a twinge of jealousy at that.

"Maybe because she's a woman. I don't know. But I think Lucy would support us in this."

Konstantine reluctantly pulled himself from his thoughts. "In what?"

"In protecting Lou from Diana. She might not want my help, but I promised to look after her. And Lou looks out for all of us. It's fair."

Fair, Konstantine mused, hearing Piper's voice in the courtyard and knowing the girls were almost back.

When was anything in this world fair?

26

Piper sat in her bed with her laptop open on her lap. Her purple comforter was pulled around her and the A/C clicked on in the living room. She stared at the blinking cursor.

Lou, Konstantine, and King had their plan for the Missouri operation. Every time Piper thought about it, bees buzzed in her temples. They were playing with fire—didn't they know it?

Diana couldn't be trusted, and if they weren't careful, that viper was going to bite them. She felt like they were already poisoned and she was the only one seeing it.

What are you going to do about it? Dani had asked.

She regarded Dani sleeping beside her, her dark hair spread over Piper's pillow. If she was honest with herself, she liked her there, in her bed, in her apartment. She liked that Dani's soap was in her shower and her makeup was on her sink. She liked that Dani could pull a mug down from her cabinet like it was the most natural thing in the world, that she had her preferred spot on the sofa.

It steadied something inside her.

Piper opened the new desktop folder labeled *DD*. It contained all the information they'd gathered on Diana as far back as March, when they'd first bumped into the woman while hunting Fish.

She scanned the data, opening and closing files at random. When nothing caught her eye, she went online to Diana's forum and began scrolling. Most of the posts were about missing women. Some were about abuse and asking for help in taking down an abuser because authorities had failed to take their complaints seriously.

There were *thousands* of complaints. Maybe even tens of thousands.

God, Piper thought. *Why is the world such a mess?*

A post snagged her attention. It was dated two days ago.

Want to make Earth a better, safer place for women? Ready to work hard for something that matters?

Piper wasn't sure if Diana had created the post herself or if she'd simply seized and repurposed it, but the forum seemed to be her hub for recruiting.

Yeah, you need new people, Piper thought. *After Lou laid waste to your ass.*

Piper took the name from the post and added it to her growing list. She'd added more names every time she found a new admin in the forum. While she couldn't be sure that every admin posting was Diana, she was sure that at least seven of them were her aliases.

"Sloppy," Piper said.

"What?" Dani asked, stirring beside her.

"Oh, sorry," Piper said, closing the laptop enough so that the light didn't fall on Dani's face. "I didn't mean to wake you."

"What time is it?"

Piper checked the computer screen. "Just past midnight. I'm almost done."

It was a lie to buy her time. Hopefully, Dani would drop back off to sleep and she could keep working.

But Dani didn't turn back over. Instead, she rolled toward Piper. "What are you working on?"

Piper closed the laptop rather guiltily. "Diana. I'm making a list of the names used on admin posts. Since it's her site, some of these might be her credit card aliases. Piper wrapped an arm around the girl. "Maybe we can get her arrested for her credit card scams. That's pretty illegal."

"Fraud only has a jail time of ten to fifteen years," Dani said.

"Yeah, but that's fifteen years we don't have to deal with her. She'd be in her fifties when she got out. Or maybe she'll get shivved in prison and save us all some trouble."

Dani gave her a sleepy laugh. "I don't think so. Ask Mel how this one goes."

Poor Mel. Her abusive, homicidal husband had been in prison for twenty-five years, and the first thing he did when released was show up on her doorstep and bully her for money.

Piper sighed. "Possible payback aside, this is the most solid option I've got."

"Why are you so worried about her?" Dani asked, her dark eyes on Piper.

"You mean except for the fact she kidnapped us and gave you a heart attack?"

Dani didn't answer.

"I don't like her. Having her around is screwing with Lou's head." These excuses sounded pathetic, even to her own ears. *I don't like her* wasn't a great reason for conspiring to send someone to prison or wishing them dead.

It was more than that.

To Piper, Diana felt dangerous. Dangerous in a way that Lou, and even Konstantine or any of her work for King, had never felt. Even when Dmitri Petrov was joking about cutting her finger off, she hadn't been this afraid.

Maybe I'm an idiot for that, she thought, but she didn't think so.

She said, "The sooner she's away from us, the better."

"I can help with the research," Dani offered, rubbing at her eyes. "I'm doing it anyway with my story. We'll need someone to officially open a case and charge her. If we can make her a national fugitive, put her face everywhere, that would be a bonus. Journalism can only take us so far. We've got to get someone else involved. Preferably someone with connections to the law."

"Konstantine might help," Piper said hopefully. "He knows good and bad cops."

"Yeah," Dani yawned. "Maybe."

"I could call Sampson, but he's going to want to know why I'm calling him instead of King."

Dani smiled. "Your mind is really working this over."

"I don't like her," she said again. *What am I, five years old?*

Dani snuggled closer. "So you've said. But I've never known you to hate anyone apart from Mel's husband."

Piper shrugged. "She slapped me."

Dani pulled back, mouth open. "When?"

"When I was yelling at her to let you go." Piper felt the heat rise in her face. "It didn't hurt."

A lie.

"But it pissed me off."

Dani came up onto her elbows. "Does Lou know that she slapped you?"

"No. I think she appeared a second or two after that."

"You could just tell Lou that she slapped you, and that'd probably solve all your problems."

What if it doesn't? What if Lou straight up sides with a psycho over me?

Dani's brow scrunched. "You *do* know that Lou would kill her for touching you, right?"

"Hmm. Would she?"

Dani sighed, collapsing back against the pillow. "You don't know. That's why you haven't said something. Piper, what's going on? Ever since the road trip you've been weird about Lou."

The shift in her voice made Piper look at her.

"Spit it out."

Piper tried to articulate this feeling choking her. Nothing came. If she couldn't say *what* was wrong, she'd start with *when*. "I think it started when she hurt her shoulder."

"What started?"

"This feeling." She saw Dani's face and shook her head. "I don't know what to say."

"Walk me through it," Dani said, adjusting the pillow under her head.

Piper sighed, searching an invisible point on the wall. "Maybe this isn't the right way to enter it, but it's the moment that keeps coming to mind."

When Piper didn't go on right away, Dani added, "I'm listening."

"It's like...King was an agent for *decades*. He's got a million cool skills. You're only a year older than me and you're this amazing journalist with a college degree. I don't even have thirty credits yet. I can't fight. I'm not a ninja. I don't have powers like Lou and I don't own half the world like Konstantine. I don't even have my own thing like Mel. I'm just...I'm just me. All I can do is be her friend, but we're not even friends. Not really. We're *disaster* friends."

"What are you talking about?" Dani laughed, disbelieving. "Are you serious?"

"When we first met, you even targeted me as the weakest link for your story. You thought I could get you close to Lou. You picked me because there's nothing about me—"

"Whoa, *wait*. First of all, that was a stupid mistake on my part, and says way more about me than about you. You're not a weak link. I'm sure King, Lou, and Mel would all say that you are very important to them. Everyone relies on you, baby. You're essential."

"I barfed on a Russian guy trying to crawl up the fire escape. That's not what I would call *essential*. There's nothing that I do that makes me critical to this team. You guys could replace me with anyone."

"Piper," Dani interjected. "The work you do for King *literally* puts criminals in jail. Secondly, how many times have you helped me through my attacks on my bad days? My own mother would've thrown me in the loony bin if she'd seen me like that. Mel wouldn't be able to keep her shop open without you. You're in there every day, keeping the shop running, and I see the way she looks at you. You're practically her daughter. And how about the fact that it *doesn't matter* what you do? You're a lovely person to be around. Period. Your very existence makes people happy. It's not about how useful you are to them or what degrees you have or don't have. It's about how you make people feel."

Piper's face must've conveyed her disbelief.

Dani wrapped her arms around Piper's neck. "I guarantee that Lou hangs out with you because of how you make her feel. Not because she needs you to dig up bodies in the dead of night. She had the bodies thing covered long before you showed up. As hard as it might be to believe, she asks for your company because she *likes* it."

"Then why does she have to act like she's got more in common with a complete psychopath than with me?"

"I would tell you to talk to her, but I don't know if Lou is self-aware enough to clarify this for you."

Silence stretched out between them. Piper was listening for Dani's breath to change, to drop off into peaceful sleep, so she could get back on her laptop, though she wasn't sure how she was going to open it without waking the girl nestled into her neck.

But into the darkness, Dani said, "I hate her too."

"Lou?"

"Dennard."

"You didn't hate her before?" Piper asked, sincerely surprised.

"No, it felt like my own fault that I had a panic attack. But now that I know she put her hands on you, *ugh*." Dani growled. "I want to take her down."

Piper grinned, opening her laptop again. "Let's see what we can do about that."

27

King found Mel's apartment door open. He stopped at the entryway regardless, raising his fist and rapping on the wooden frame. "Anybody home?"

Lady appeared first, her tail swishing back and forth as her nails clicked across the tiled floor. King took this as a good sign. If something was wrong and Mel's door was ajar for some nefarious reason, surely the dog's behavior would reflect that.

He inhaled, smelling popcorn.

"Come on in," Mel called from somewhere deep in the apartment.

He entered and hesitated. "We expecting anyone else or can I close the door?"

"Close the door."

King shut it behind him. Mel's apartment was a mirror of his own. They had the same counters, appliances, and tile. They both entered through the kitchen and beneath an arch, a spacious living room spread out beyond that. Both their living rooms ended in a door leading to a balcony. Both connected to a single bedroom and bath.

There were some differences, of course. Mel's furnishings were lighter, pale lavenders and pinks. Instead of a large armoire doubling as a TV cabinet, she had a simple TV on a stand opposite her sofa. By the balcony door, where King had his record player, she had two armchairs and a potted plant that fanned out against the wall almost like feathers. In the small corner between the kitchen wall and bedroom door, she had an antique rattan chair with a peacock back. King's mother had had one of those chairs. But that one didn't have the bright orange pillow that Mel's had.

Mel came out of the dark bedroom and closed the door behind her.

She checked her watch then crossed to the television. "We've got five minutes. Will you grab the popcorn off the counter? And your soda is in the fridge."

He did as he was told, grabbing two cans of Coke with one hand and the large bowl of popcorn with the other.

They settled onto the lavender sofa together, the bowl between them. He handed her one of the Cokes.

"Who do you think will be eliminated this week?" King asked.

"It's hard to tell," she said. "I think it should be the one who rapped. She should've been eliminated last week."

King laughed. "What do you have against rappers?"

"Nothing," Mel said, bringing a handful of popcorn to her mouth. "When they can actually rap."

"I think the rabbit might go."

"Kalynda Kicks?" Mel asked, surprised. "I thought she was pretty good with the song she sang."

"Me too," King said. "But the judges have been giving her a hard time for three weeks now. I think they're going to toss her soon."

"Or they're building us up for a comeback story."

King shrugged, shoving another fistful of popcorn in his mouth.

"How's the Diana bullshit going?" Mel asked.

King snorted. It always amused him when Mel swore, because it was such a rare occurrence.

"Still mad at her for tying you up in the dead of night, huh?"

Mel harrumphed. "She didn't even buy me dinner first."

Coke went into King's nose as he sucked in air to laugh. "See what you made me do?"

He rose, went to the kitchen, and grabbed a napkin. He dabbed at his jeans, which had taken the worst of it, and a small spot on his shirt. Lady lifted her head from her paws to watch the show, before deeming him boring and putting her head on her paws again.

As he settled back down beside Mel, the program started. They watched it without speaking. It was an unspoken agreement between them.

But once the first commercial break aired, encouraging them to switch insurance companies, King turned to her.

"Are you sick of us?" he asked, his face serious.

She frowned at him. "What are you talking about?"

"You know what I'm talking about," he said, turning the Coke can on his knee. "First it was Chaz who broke in and put a gun to your head."

Just the idea of it made King's blood boil.

"Then it was Petrov and now Diana. Aren't you sick of it? Aren't you afraid one night it's going to end in you getting shot?"

Mel looked at her hands for a moment, as if considering each of her gold rings carefully. Then she met his eyes and said, "If I get shot, I'll know I had it coming."

"Lou didn't die."

"I still shot her," she said. She sighed, letting the silence rest between them. "When Terry was still around, I used to have a lot of trouble sleeping. I was scared he would come home, knowing if he did, he'd hurt me. And scared that he wouldn't and what might happen to me if he didn't. I know what it feels like when your home isn't safe. That's not what we've got here. You, me, Piper, even Lou and Dani. It feels right. It feels like we're supposed to be together, all five of us, here, in this place. It's why I haven't hired another person to run the shop. It's not that we couldn't use the help. And I've got the money put back for it now if I change my mind, but no. It's because we're all here now. Do you understand? We're all here."

King took her hand and squeezed it.

She squeezed back. "If some bastard comes up in here and makes trouble once in a while, fine. Let 'em. But we're together and that's how it's supposed to be. I feel it deep inside. That this is how it's supposed to be."

When Terry was still around, King thought, remembering the lean man in the bone choker and denim, the crow feather sticking out of his hat.

"When's the court date?" he asked.

"The twenty-first," she said. "I've already gone over my testimony with my lawyer several times. I feel like I could testify in my sleep at this point."

"Nothing wrong with being prepared," King said, watching her face carefully. He saw the strain there, the worry. "They're going to put him away."

She turned and gave him a weak smile. "I know. And I can't wait to see it."

28

When Lou appeared in Konstantine's apartment, he was standing at his bedroom window. The window's high arch was laid bare, the shutters pulled open to reveal an unfettered view of the Arno River. He stood there with his back to her, and her eyes traced the planes of his shoulders, his bare neck. The back of his exposed arms and the tattoo peeking out from under his sleeve.

Beyond him, the river glittered as the light from the lamps shone on its surface. Laughter carried up from the street below as a warm breeze pushed past him.

His heady, dark scent washed over her.

"What are you thinking about?" she asked.

Something in his back relaxed. "I was thinking about your world. *La Loon.* It's very different from ours."

"Miss it already?"

He laughed, turning to face her. "No. But it would be nice to get out of the city. Even if only for a night."

In the soft light from the lamps outside, she could see the dark circles under his eyes. This gave her pause.

Bad day? she thought. She didn't ask.

She suspected running one of the largest criminal organizations in the world had its fair share of stress. And this was the thin line they walked. She the destroyer of the criminal world. He its benevolent manager.

Lou stepped toward him, wrapping her arms around his waist. Before his hands could fully envelop her in return, everything shifted. His sensuous touch tightened in reflex.

When all resettled, the scent of a forest swelled around them. Thick green pine sap and packed earth.

"Wish granted," she whispered.

They were at the edge of a clearing, the tall grass connecting the woods at their back with those on the other edge of the circle.

At the far end, something moved through the trees. Moose? Wolves?

"It's beautiful," he said, stepping forward to behold the moon.

Though not as quiet, she thought, noting the swell of crickets, frogs, katydids, beetles, and all the other voices vying for their part of the night.

She shrugged her shoulders in her leather jacket. It was too warm for it. It made her long for fall and winter, her preferred seasons. Summer was always too bright, too hot. But it was almost over. She could taste it on nights like this, that first crisp shift in the wind.

Soon the nights would run long again.

"How does your shoulder feel tonight?" he asked.

"Fine." She would have said this even if it was torn in half and hanging limp from her body.

He smiled as if he knew this, the moonlight collecting in his teeth and the whites of his eyes. "Of course it is."

Lou didn't want any more questions about her shoulder or

whether or not she felt well. Instead, she shrugged out of her leather jacket and laid it on the ground.

"You can sit if you want," she said.

He laughed. "How chivalrous of you. But what about your jacket?"

"I'll wipe it down later."

He looked reluctant to sit on the packed earth even with the jacket.

Lou suppressed a laugh. He was fussy about clothes. It wasn't only that she often caught him wearing expensive brands that hung off models on the runway, but also how he cared for them. Her own wardrobe was much less luxurious. When every other night ended with her covered in someone's blood—not to mention the sweat—it didn't pay to waste money on nice clothes.

Lou got most of her t-shirts and jeans from thrift shops. She had only a few items she really cherished: her father's two flannels and his bulletproof vest. She didn't wear those when she hunted. She also loved her leather jacket, but it was far from irreplaceable. She could have another one if she wanted it.

"Are you thinking about tomorrow?" Konstantine asked, looking up at her from the ground. "Everything has been prepared. My men will meet King at the rendezvous point he's chosen."

"I was thinking about your clothes," Lou said.

This surprised a laugh out of him. "Why?"

"I was wondering if I could take them off without you objecting."

"Yes," he said, too quickly.

She knelt in front of him, bringing her eyes to his level. "Are you sure? Because they might touch the ground."

He laughed harder. "I'll make the sacrifice."

"Lay back."

He did, his eyes roving her body.

"You're very beautiful," he said. "Do you know it?"

Did she? Sometimes. When she caught her reflection in the mirror, there was nothing there that pleased her, but there'd been hints in the way others regarded her. The way their eyes lingered on her face or her body. It was something she noted, distantly and only in context.

She didn't answer the question. "Is that what you're thinking about when you look at me like that?"

"I'm thinking about a lot of things," he said, his eyes sparkling with starlight. "About you. Tomorrow. Diana. The yakuza. My mind often rehearses before the actual event."

"And you're rehearsing for tomorrow?"

"Yes," he said. "Do you wish you could read my mind?"

She hesitated.

"Would you trade your ability to be anywhere at any time to know what people are thinking?"

Lou considered this, placing her hands on his chest. "No. I don't think I want to know what people are thinking all the time."

"Will you lie beside me?" he asked.

He sounded small. Sad.

"Why?"

"I want you closer."

She lay down beside him. The earth was cold despite the warmth of the day. They were in Tennessee, quite close to the eastern mountains, and it had been nearly a hundred degrees all day. Yet the earth was cool on her bare arms.

He turned to face her. "What are *you* thinking about?"

"The weather," she said. "You."

He smiled. "What about me?"

"Do you know that you're beautiful?" she asked with a mischievous grin.

He took her hand and pressed her index finger to his cheek. "Even with this?"

He forced her to trace the rough ridge of his scar. It was long and vertical, bisecting most of his cheek.

Lou remembered Nico pressing the blade into his flesh, the way the cheek had hung open, bleeding, a mask of blood covering half his face.

He'd had at least two surgeries to improve the scar's appearance and to repair the muscles cut beneath. While they had returned the muscle function, it hadn't been enough to completely remove the surface damage.

"I like you better with this," she said, and meant it.

It surprised another laugh out of him. "Really?"

"You were too pretty before."

"I am more attractive to you now, with the scar?" he asked, his voice deepening.

"Yes."

He rolled onto her then, holding his body above hers, careful not to add any weight. That heady scent pressed against her.

"I should thank Nico then," he said.

She slid her fingers around the back of his neck and into his hair and pulled him down into a kiss, forcing his body against hers. Her muscles rolled instinctively, and his body tightened in response.

She deepened the kiss, forcing her tongue past his lips and holding him in place. He didn't object. He relaxed into her, opening his mouth wider, meeting her tongue with his.

It was easy to slip her free hand, the one not wrapped up in his dark hair, under his shirt. She lifted the fabric and he broke the kiss just long enough to let her pull the shirt over his head.

His skin pricked with goosebumps as she put the shirt on her jacket for safekeeping.

Her fingers traced the tattoo from his shoulder to his elbow.

"Do you like it?" he asked. "Some women do not like tattoos."

Lou arched an eyebrow. "No woman has ever told you she didn't like this tattoo."

"No," he admitted. "But I'm asking you."

"I like it."

"What else do you like?" he ventured. He was smiling down at her.

"You want me to inventory the things I like about you?" she asked. It made her think of Piper suddenly. Hadn't she asked similar questions?

Lou hadn't known how to answer her, any more than she knew how to answer Konstantine now. What did she like about him?

Physically? His green eyes. His thick dark hair and its tendency to curl. The scar and the tattoos, but also his stillness. Every move he made seemed deliberate. He was very comfortable in his skin.

She liked the look that filled his eyes when he regarded her. The way his voice dropped, softened, when he spoke to her.

"Why do people need assurances from me?" Lou asked softly.

Konstantine pulled back, looking into her face. "For me, because you're difficult to read. Who else?"

"Piper."

He didn't look surprised by this answer. After a while he said, "You have nothing else you like about me, besides the tattoo and the scar?"

"Your eyes," she said. "Your voice."

She thought harder.

"The way you smell."

She came up onto her elbows and placed her face into the crook of his neck. She ran her mouth along the line of his throat up to his jaw. She had an urge to bite his throat, so she did, pressing her teeth into his skin until he shivered.

"The way you taste."

When she released him, pressing her back to the ground again, she saw his eyes were heavy with desire.

She grinned and reached beneath him, unclasping the button on his pants and sliding her hand between his legs.

KONSTANTINE SAW THE LOOK IN HER EYES EVEN BEFORE HE felt her hand tug at his pants. He knew what was coming. He supported his weight on one side, thinking, always, of her shoulder and the dangerous day they had ahead of them.

When her fingers found him, cupped him, sliding over his skin warm and smooth, he hardened. His desire, which had already begun to form as soon as she'd removed his shirt, mounted to an uncomfortable high.

He found himself squirming, pressing harder into her palm.

He couldn't decide if he would accept this, if it was enough just to be in her hands now that he knew what she felt like.

He wanted to be inside her, buried to the hilt. His face and neck felt like they were on fire, and the throbbing between his legs had grown unbearable. He rose up suddenly and began tugging off his pants. He freed one leg, then the other, until he was completely naked on top of her.

He waited, looking for any objection, but she was unhooking her own pants and lifting her hips to remove them.

He helped, tugging the fabric down to reveal long,

muscular legs. He wanted to remove her shirt, but she was already reaching for him, pulling him back down onto her.

He settled for pushing it up enough that their bare stomachs touched.

Skin on skin.

He probed her first with his fingers, found her soaked. He moaned into the hollow of her throat.

"We didn't use a condom in La Loon," he said. "And I don't have one now."

"I'm clean."

So was he. "But there's still the matter of *bambini*."

"I take birth control," she said, her hand already on him, guiding him in.

He sank into her, enjoying that first rush of warm, wet sensation. She wrapped her legs around him, locking him into place, making it hard to pull out more than a couple of inches before driving in again.

When she moaned, his whole body shivered, something in him relaxing.

His mouth was on her throat, at her ear.

I love you, he thought.

Don't say it.

I love you.

Don't say it. Don't say it.

He remembered their conversation in the hospital. He'd replayed it in his mind many times since. She'd woken from her brief coma. She'd said, "I didn't want you to fall in love with me."

He confessed, "I'm already in love with you."

"Don't. People in love want to get married, they want kids. I don't want any of that."

It had hurt to hear her say it, to hear all his desires laid bare and dismissed. But he was also prepared to love her on her own terms. To respect her own desires. He had dreams, as many as any man. But what he wanted most of all was her.

If this was all he could have, moments like this, losing himself in the feel of her, he would take it.

She came first, and he was grateful because he followed a second after. He moved to pull out of her, but she wouldn't let him go. The heels of her feet pressed into his lower back.

"Not yet," she panted in his ear. She was shivering.

For a terrible moment, he worried he'd hurt her shoulder.

"I'm not finished," she said, as if anticipating his question.

She rolled him onto his back and began to slowly rock against his hips.

After a minute, maybe more, she shivered again, collapsing onto her good side.

He lay on his back, looking up at the stars. Something bright and streaking crossed the sky. Konstantine tried to remember what it was like three years ago. Five. Ten.

When he'd wished for this woman in his arms, when he'd longed for her so badly that it left a raw and burning cavern within him.

And here she was.

After so much dreaming, here was her weight against him, her breath hanging in the silence of their collected pleasure.

"Will it always be like this?" he asked into her hair.

She stiffened.

Don't ruin it with romance, he thought.

"Outside. On the ground," he said with a forced smile. "Do you have something against beds?"

She relaxed against him. "You said you wanted out of the city. You didn't say anything about a bed."

29

D ani, Piper, King, and Lou stood in the middle of The Crescent City Detective Agency. King thought they looked like a rather somber bunch despite the sunny summer day pressing through the front windows.

"Don't die," Piper said, frowning at them. Her arms were crossed over her chest as she looked from Lou to King and back to Lou again. "You look too relaxed. Take this seriously, okay? Diana is crazy. Be on your guard."

"Sure you want to sit this one out?" King asked. It wasn't like Piper to insist she stay behind during the action.

"I'm sure," Piper said. She glanced in Dani's direction. It was such a quick micro movement, King wasn't sure she realized she'd done it. But it told King a lot. Maybe Piper was staying behind for Dani's sake. Maybe because Dani didn't want another encounter with Diana.

"We've got plenty of work to do," Dani said, taking Piper's hand. "But you guys be safe and let us know as soon as it's over."

Piper was watching Lou closely.

King wondered if it was the guns. Lou had a shoulder holster with two Browning pistols and a hip holster with two Berettas. Her arms were covered with Kevlar sleeves. The body armor on her chest made her look battle ready. That and the fact her hair had been pulled back from her face, in a ponytail.

"Be careful," Piper said, stepping forward. She looked like she wanted to give Lou a hug but wasn't sure how to manage it with all the guns.

To King, Lou said, "Let's go."

Piper's face fell.

They haven't made up.

"Sure." He stepped into Lou's office, the broom closet with her name on the door, and she followed him in. She closed the door, leaving them in pitch darkness.

"Did Konstantine tell you where he assembled the men?" King asked into the dark.

"There was an empty office building across the street from Winter's apartment. That's our first stop."

Before King could ask more, the room shifted around him. The darkness rolled over him, squeezing him, and the floor dropped out. His stomach turned, and then the gravity shifted again and he was on his feet in the middle of a large lobby.

King would never get used to it, the feeling of being compressed, pinched, and stretched out in turn.

"Shit." The man closest to his left elbow jumped, bumping into a dusty plant. A cloud puffed into the air.

King took this moment to right himself and take the room's measure. The men were spread around the dusty, forgotten place, standing in small huddles or leaning against the sheet-covered furniture. The buzz of conversation died upon their arrival.

Silence stretched out between them.

The man they'd startled hung over one of the sheet-covered armchairs as if ready to throw himself over its back and run if necessary.

"Damn. He wasn't joking," someone said. "It's her."

All eyes were on them now. No, not *them*. Lou.

They tracked her movements with keen interest—and perhaps more than a little fear.

Her shades were down, her weapons in full view.

No one wanted to move closer. When her mirrored shades passed over them, their gazes flicked away.

This gave King ample room to make his own assessment.

At first glance, they didn't look like gangsters.

A few had tattoos across their exposed hands, but that didn't mean anything. One had some writing sticking out from under his shirt collar. But mostly, they looked the part of operatives. Head to toe in black, bulletproof vests, earpieces, and guns.

"Good evening," King said, finding his voice at last, despite the nausea from Lou's slip lingered. "Before we get started—"

"He said we answer to her," one of the men said, motioning toward Lou. "Not some cop."

No need to ask who *he* was.

"Sure," King said. He was a little miffed that despite his hard work over the years, he still emitted a cop vibe. He thought he'd done a pretty good job of eliminating it, *thankyouverymuch*. "Do you have anything you'd like to tell them?"

A few stiffened, their backs straightening.

"Listen to him," Lou said. She grinned. "Or we're finished here."

More than one shifted nervously at the implied threat. Someone muttered, "Fuck," as if only just realizing what they'd gotten themselves into.

"Any other questions?" King asked, eyebrows raised.

No one spoke.

He hated his hard-ass voice. He hadn't had to use it in years, rarely since he'd trained recruits at Quantico. But it was a necessary evil tonight. These men had to follow his lead if they hoped to fool Diana and take down Winter.

I'm the only one here that knows what an operation is supposed to even look like.

"Good. Now we're going to split into two teams of twenty, and a third team of ten." When no one moved, he added, "Now."

The men separated into two groups. King made a few adjustments, asking men to switch sides until he had an even mix.

"Okay, Team A, that's you." King pointed at the cluster on his left. "We're going to position you on the ground, surrounding the building. Team B, we're sending you into the building. Do any of you Team B-ers have experience clearing a room?"

Most indicated they had.

"Team C, you'll stay close to—" He'd almost said Lou's name. "Her."

"She's here," Lou said, her eyes fixed on the parking lot.

King turned and saw two black cars swinging into the cement lot. Diana stepped out from behind the driver's wheel into the gloomy day. Her entourage exited the two cars and came toward the office building's entrance and its two glass doors.

"And now," King said as Diana reached for the door handle, "pretend we've known each other forever."

LOU BARELY LISTENED TO KING AS HE PRATTLED ON ABOUT the instructions for the raid. Even after Diana entered the building and explained how her team would be overseeing the technology and monitoring of the operation, Lou couldn't hold her interest.

Her eyes kept straying to the apartment complex across the street. Its faded brick exterior seemed watchful, as if it was waiting for this moment as much as she was. But it was also what she was feeling.

Or *wasn't*.

She reached out for Winter again, trying to get a lock on his location.

Close, she thought. But it wasn't fixating on either of the two apartment buildings. The compass kept circling.

Lou tried to remember the last time her compass had done that, been unsure of a target's location. Even if they were in cars or airplanes, somehow their bodies in motion, it was still enough.

"We good?" King asked her suddenly.

She turned and saw that most of the eyes were on her. Not just King, who was waiting for an answer, but Diana, the silent, leather-clad woman beside her, and the short man with the hobbled gait. Lou noted the bruising on his neck.

All of the others too, watching her carefully as if waiting for her to say something.

Lou motioned King close.

His brow furrowed. "What's wrong?"

"I can't get a lock on Winter," she whispered, keeping her voice too low for the others to hear.

King was careful to keep his voice low too. "You don't think he's in that building?"

"He's close," she said. "But I can't get an exact lock."

King rubbed his jaw. "Has this ever happened before?"

"No."

King shook his head. "We'll work with what we've got."

"Anything you want to share with the class?" Diana called. This earned a few snickers from her own people.

Those who belonged to Konstantine said nothing.

What stories did they hear about me? she wondered. She understood that she had some notoriety in the underworld. She'd killed too many of them to not loom in their imaginations larger than life.

"What are we waiting for?" Diana asked, her arms crossed.

"Dark," Lou said, and the men around her stiffened, reacting to her voice.

Someone murmured the word *vampira*, but Lou didn't catch the source. She considered smiling mischievously, fueling their fear, but her eyes kept sliding toward the buildings across the street.

"Sundown is in twelve minutes. We'll need another thirty minutes after that for full dark," the woman in leather said.

She must be the sister. Lou watched how close she stood to Diana, almost protective.

Her eyes fixed on Lou and didn't waver. Unlike Diana, who often dismissed the people around her, this one paid attention. No detail seemed to escape her notice.

"Plenty of time to get ready," King said. "Now let's run through the plan again. I want to go through the scenarios. Scenario one, if there are children in the building..."

Lou only distantly noted King's instructions as he drilled the men again and again about the situations they might encounter.

When Diana began to issue her own orders, Lou learned some names. The woman in the leather pants was Blair. The hobbled man with the fresh bruises on his throat was Spencer. From the corner of her eye, she watched Diana affix technology she didn't recognize to their clothes.

Sitting on a sheet-covered sofa, Diana opened her laptop.

"He's streaming," she announced. "Just give me a couple of minutes to confirm his location."

Which is more than I can do, Lou thought, her insides tensing.

The streetlights grew brighter, the night darker, and Lou began to see lights in the building across the street. She focused on each one, wondering which one might be Winter, but again her compass only swirled and swirled.

Was she concentrating too hard on the building?

Lou felt the moment the sun slid behind the horizon. The itchy heat in her body cooled instantly.

Sometimes it was like that. The second the shadows took control of the world, she felt a surge of energy, something inside her waking up.

"He's there," Diana said, speaking up, her face lit with excitement. "The building on the right."

She was vibrating like a tuning fork.

King motioned toward the glass. "All right. Into positions. Remember, we're surrounding the building on all sides first. He might try to bolt the second he sees us setting up formation, so be prepared for that. Let's go."

Everyone followed him out of the building into the cooling night.

Lou considered slipping from the dusty office building straight into Winter's room, but since this whole charade was to fool Diana into thinking Lou was a normal woman with abundant resources and nothing more, she restrained herself.

It surprised her how quickly they had the building surrounded.

Those who weren't part of the raid, including Lou, King, Diana, Blair, and Spencer, stood under the row of manicured trees expertly arranged along the side of the road opposite the apartment complex.

Diana didn't like being in the proverbial backseat. Every time King issued an order she looked ready to speak over him and rewrite his command.

Somehow she held herself back. Perhaps it was because these were not her men, and she had no guarantee that her order would be heeded anyway.

Whatever it was, Lou watched her struggle with amusement, aware that while she watched Diana almost everyone else watched her.

Konstantine's men stole sly glances, as did Diana's remaining team. The sister in particular seemed to be reconciling something in her mind.

Meanwhile Lou's attention kept returning to the apartments.

No, she thought. She wasn't drawn to *both* of the buildings. It was the façade on the left that drew her. The twin to the building now surrounded.

Are you in there? she wondered, tracing the windows with her eyes. *Have we chosen the wrong one?*

"Go!" King said.

Men pushed through the doors on all sides. On Diana's monitor, Lou could see them moving silently, snakelike through the bowels of the place. They filled all the stairs, corridors, and doorways.

"Come on, come on, come on," Diana said, urging them on.

"Any change in the signal?" King asked.

"No," Diana said. "It's good that your people are going in quiet. He probably doesn't realize we're in."

Then Lou realized that King was looking at her, not Diana. The question, *any change*, was about her inability to get a lock.

"I need to check something," Lou said, retreating across the parking lot and into the office building as if she'd left something inside.

When she turned back, looking through the glass front,

she saw that Blair had followed her halfway across the parking lot, standing beneath the orange lamplight.

Lou couldn't worry about that now.

She stepped into a hallway off the main lobby. It was more than dark enough in this space. Already she felt the thin gossamer curtain of the world shifting around her, threatening to pitch her through.

Winter, she thought. *Winter, where are you?*

Again, she got only a strange doubling in her mind that seemed unable to settle upon a single place.

The one Diana wants, she thought. *Come on. The one she wants.*

At last the dial shifted, her focus sharpened. The dusty office building around her fell away. In its place, a hallway with scuffed red carpet materialized.

Near the end of the hallway, a child was crying. Lou walked toward the sound.

"Shut up and put on your coat," a gruff voice said.

Then a door was opening, and the child was shoved out into the hallway, her feet tangling beneath her. But she didn't get far.

It was a little girl, seven or eight years old. She had on a pink coat that was dirty at the elbows with a smear of something at the throat. Her hair hadn't been brushed in a few days at least. Both cheeks were tear-stained.

A squat man with a bald head stepped out after her, yanking the door shut behind him.

"Stop crying. We have to get out of here. In five minutes *here* won't even exist."

As soon as the girl saw Lou, her eyes doubled in size. Lou pressed a finger to her lips, urging the girl to stay silent as she crept forward.

But even the smallest invitation of salvation was too

much. The girl took off at a run, bolting for Lou as if she were the gates of heaven.

"Hey!" the man screamed, releasing the door handle and turning until he came face to face with Lou.

His eyes roved her body, took in the leather and the body armor, the guns.

That's when he pulled something from his pocket.

Without thinking, Lou grabbed the girl and stepped back into the shadows, the world falling away.

This new apartment was like a movie set, with lights and a camera set up over a stage.

"No," the girl murmured. "No, not here."

And on the stage, a child-size bed.

"Please, please," the little girl begged, her hands tightening around Lou's neck. An ice pick of pain ran down her left side. Lou sharply inhaled, but didn't let go.

"Please don't leave me here," the girl said.

"I won't," Lou said.

She wanted to kill that man. She wanted to tear him apart and handfeed what was left of him to Jabbers.

But Lou couldn't fight with a kid hanging from her neck.

"Okay," she said. "It's okay. I've got you."

Lou listened to the feet on the stairs, noting their growing distance. Instead of giving chase, she stepped away from the shining movie set and back into the dark.

When the dusty office building sprang up around them, Lou carried the girl out of the building into the night.

"King!" she shouted, trying to cross the parking lot as quickly as she could. He turned, pulling the headphones off his head.

"We've got the guy!" King said, his face lit up and bright. Then his eyes fell on the kid.

"No, you don't," Lou said. "Get everyone out of the buildings and back up. They're about to blow."

His face fell. "What?"

"They wired them to explode. Get everyone out."

"There are kids in there," King said, panic growing on his face.

Lou tried to pry the little girl off her neck and the girl squealed. She didn't want to be handed over to King.

"I'll take her," a voice said. Lou looked up to see Blair, hands open.

The girl finally released Lou.

"Go," Blair said, eyebrows arched, and Lou had the distinct impression Blair meant *go. Slip.*

"Go on," King echoed. Then, into his headset, "There's a bomb in the building. Both buildings," he amended. "Clear out now. Pronto, chop-chop! Back to the admin building!"

Lou glanced toward Diana and saw that she was poring over her laptop footage, cursing to herself.

"Where is he?" she hissed, scrolling furiously. "Where is he?"

Lou ran toward the apartment building. Once she was around the side, in the shadows thrown by the trees, she slipped.

Kids, she thought. *I want the kids.*

Lou materialized in a dingy room and immediately realized the problem. A boy was shackled to the floor. A thick iron chain was latched to the floor, connecting to the collar around his throat.

He was crying and naked, trying to cover himself.

"We can't get it open," one of Konstantine's men said, real panic in his voice. His eyes were round, his jaw working.

The apartment door burst open. "I've got them!"

The incoming man stuttered when he saw Lou, the bolt cutters coming in front of him like a shield.

Lou snatched them and put the chain between the blades.

She snapped the handles together. The fire in her shoulder intensified, but she pushed past it.

The chain broke and the freed boy collapsed with relief.

"How many kids are in the building?" Lou asked, scooping him up.

"Six," he said. "That we know of."

Lou threw her mind out, searching the dark.

"There's a bomb in the building. Get out of here," she said, and with that scooped the boy into her arms and disappeared.

It was the night that formed around them again. An alarmed bird startled in the tree above her.

"You see those people?" Lou asked, putting the boy on his feet. She pointed at King. "Run to them. Go on. Get away from this building."

She pushed the boy forward and he ran on unsteady legs.

Lou reached out for the next child and found her on the second floor. Another snap of the bolt cutters and Lou pulled her through the dark.

Each child that she delivered to the patch of darkness took off over the uneven grass as if their life depended on it.

"Over here!" King called, waving them forward. "Hurry!"

Lou had just managed to get the seventh kid out of the building when King screamed, "Forty seconds!"

They must've found the bomb, she thought. Either on video or while still canvassing the building. Lou dematerialized again. The room that reformed around her was a nightmare.

Two men with their pants around their ankles lay face down in their own blood. A girl no more than twelve years old stood over them. Lou didn't recognize the men as either Konstantine's or Diana's.

The girl was naked from the waist down, with a dark crust

of blood spread on her inner thigh. Her hair was matted to her face with sweat, her chest heaving.

Lou didn't know where she'd gotten the gun, if it was given to her by one of Konstantine's men or if she'd taken it in the commotion.

But she stood there heaving, crying, unable to move. Unable to lower the gun. Her whole body trembled.

When she saw Lou, she raised the gun instinctively and fired. Lou shifted through the dark and felt the bullet graze her good arm, ripping a hole through her leather jacket, a second before she reappeared behind the girl and grabbed her.

She thrashed in Lou's arms, screaming, crying beneath the large evergreen above them.

"It's over," Lou said into her ear. Her voice was strained with the pain of her shoulder. "It's over."

The girl went soft in Lou's arms, and Lou scooped her up.

She was in the parking lot when the building blew behind them.

30

There were seven men and two women cuffed face down in the grass median between the admin building parking lot and the street in front of the apartment buildings—or what was *left* of the apartment buildings.

Sirens wailed in the distance.

"Go on," King said, waving the men away. Konstantine's men cast one look at Lou as if to make sure she wasn't going to follow them into the night.

"Go," she said.

They fled like kitchen-fed cockroaches when the light comes on. They dispersed in any and all directions, across parking lots, into the trees, down the streets.

Diana rolled one man onto his back. "I don't understand."

"Get out of my face, bitch," the guy said. He was thin and mean, his face etched with deep scars.

Diana yanked up the sleeve of his jean jacket and scowled. "Give me a light."

Blair produced her phone's flashlight, which Diana used to inspect the man's bare arm.

"No," she screamed, shoving him back down. "No!"

"What's going on?" King asked, leaning toward her.

"There were two men," Lou said.

"No, I saw them on the feed before she shot them. They weren't him."

"I'm not talking about the men in the building." Lou could feel the heat wafting from the burning buildings from here. Sweat beaded at her temples. "There were two men using the handle Winter. The man you actually wanted and this one. They ran the operation together."

Lou toed the lean, mean bastard with her boot. "You're Winter, aren't you?"

"Who's asking?"

"No, he's not," Diana said, kicking the man in the gut.

King's eyes lit with recognition.

"And you saw him, the other guy?" Diana asked, chest heaving. "He was here tonight?"

"He left."

"Damn it!" She kicked the man a second time. "Where's your buddy, asshole?"

"Long gone," the man cackled.

Diana brought a foot down on his face, splitting the nose.

"We're going to have to explain any damage to the authorities," King said.

"The hell we are. Spencer, get him in the car." Diana hauled the guy to his feet and thrust him toward the man with the hobbled walk.

Spencer managed to get Winter across the parking lot and into one of Diana's cars.

Then she pulled her gun.

"Hey!" King said.

But Diana was already firing. One bullet into the back of every head lying in the grass median. Those toward the end of the line, realizing what was happening, began to scream, to rise up. The children also began to scream, huddled behind Lou as if she could protect them.

Brains splattered across Lou's boots.

When Diana's gun clicked empty, she met Lou's gaze, her chest heaving.

"A lot of help you were!" Diana shouted, shoving the emptied gun into her waistband. "You let the bastard get away!"

"He can't escape me," Lou said, and now he couldn't.

Not now that she understood why the strange doubling had happened, when her compass had warred with itself to reconcile the difference between the man named Winter and the one Diana was really hunting.

"He wasn't for you! He was for *me*!" Diana said, throwing herself off the curb. "We're leaving!"

Her team broke and ran for the vehicles. In one movement, Blair dropped the girl she was holding and snatched up the computer.

The girl let out a small, startled cry.

Lou pulled her close, and the girl rested her head against Lou's thigh.

"Shit," King said, watching them go. "That wasn't how we were supposed to wrap this up."

Red and blue lights illuminated the trees at the end of the street. Any second, the police would turn onto the road and see the devastation.

A bunch of dead bodies, two blown-out and burning buildings. And the children.

"We have to go," King said. "*Now.*"

"What about them?" Lou asked, pointing at the children sitting huddled together on the grass.

King bent down to talk to the kids. They shrank away from him.

"I'm not going to hurt you," King said tenderly. "I want

you to stay right here until the police arrive. When they get here, I want you to give them your names, okay? And they'll make sure you get home to your parents."

One boy visibly flinched at the word *parents*. He looked past Lou to the man lying face down in his own blood.

"Was that your dad?" Lou asked, her insides boiling.

The boy nodded.

She reached out to him and he climbed into her arms. Even in the orange streetlights, she could see the bruises along the side of his face.

Her anger rose so intense it obliterated all thoughts in her head.

"You're okay," Lou said into his ear as he tucked his face into her shoulder. She wasn't sure if she was speaking to the boy or herself. "You're okay."

"What about us?" the little girl squealed, the one Lou had rescued from the hallway, from the real Winter Diana sought.

"What're your names?" King asked.

"Mitchel."

"Katie-Jo."

"Raelara."

"Jean," said the one who had first run into Lou's arms.

"Zoe."

"Lea Reynolds. And this is my brother, Lane Reynolds."

"And what about you?" Lou asked, noticing that one hadn't spoken.

A silent girl reluctantly rolled her eyes up to Lou. "Danielle."

"Pretty name." Lou smiled. "I want you guys to stay here and stay together."

"But!" The outcry was immediate.

"Stay here," Lou insisted, "and those officers will make sure you get home."

They could see the police now, the cars zooming into view.

Before the headlights got too close, Lou reached out and grabbed King's elbow, and the three of them disappeared through the dark.

"HOW CAN YOU DO IT?" THE LITTLE BOY ASKED WHEN THEY stepped out of the storage closet in The Crescent City Detective Agency. "Are you magic? Are you an angel?"

"No," Lou said. When she tried to untangle his arms from her neck, he only tightened them. She relented. "Can I shift you to the other side, please?"

Her shoulder was throbbing and each pulse made red flash behind her eyes.

The boy loosened his grip enough to let Lou adjust his weight.

"What's your name, buddy?" King asked.

The boy didn't answer.

"It's okay," Lou said into his ear. "He's a good guy."

"Shai. With an *i*."

"How old are you, Shai?" King asked, coming around his desk and settling into the chair. He unlocked the drawer with a key from his wallet and fished out his laptop.

"Six," the boy said.

King booted up the computer. "You got a last name?"

"Wilson."

King began punching at the computer furiously. Lou crossed to Piper's empty chair and sank into it.

"Tampa, Florida," King said. "He was reported missing by his mother eight months ago."

"Eight months is a long time," Lou said, and she and King shared a knowing look.

A door creaked open and Piper stepped into the office. "I thought I heard you guys. How'd it go?"

Then her eyes fell on the kid.

"Oh, hey." Tears sprang to her eyes. "Oh gosh. Um, I'm Piper."

"Shai Wilson."

She held out her hand, swallowing hard. "Nice to meet you, Shai."

"I'll take him to his mom," Lou said. To Shai, "Do you want to see your mom? Is she..."

Lou couldn't figure out how to finish the sentence.

"Has she ever hurt you?" she managed.

"Mommy is nice. But she doesn't like it when I leave my trucks on the floor."

"Sounds reasonable," King said. To Lou, "I don't suppose you need the address."

Shai's stomach rumbled loudly. The boy looked embarrassed.

"Sorry," he whispered.

"Don't be sorry," King said.

"I have stuff to make a sandwich," Piper said. To the boy, "Are you a ham and cheese guy or a peanut butter and jelly guy?"

"Peanut butter, no jelly," he said. Then he looked afraid.

"Crust or no crust?"

"Mommy cuts off my crusts."

Piper looked ready to cry. "No crust, no jelly it is. Be right back."

She started up the stairs two at a time. Overhead, Lou heard a cabinet snap shut. A drawer slid open, then closed.

Lou reached out with her compass. She searched the darkness, looking for the mother first. She found her, sensing that she was in a very dark room. Maybe the only light was the television droning on somewhere in the background.

Safe? Lou wondered. *Will he be safe with you?*

Piper reappeared with a sandwich with no crusts tucked into a paper towel.

Shai took an enormous bite, like a dog lunging into a food bowl.

"How'd I do?" Piper asked. "Enough peanut butter? 'Cause I got more."

Shai spared her another smile. "It's good."

"*You're* good, you know that?" Piper said.

The kid was getting breadcrumbs on Lou's jacket.

"We're going," Lou announced. To Shai, "Are you ready?"

"Where?" he asked, squeezing his sandwich so hard that the bread flattened out in his fist.

"To your mom. Is that okay?"

"Can't I stay with you?"

Lou shook her head dolefully. "You can finish your sandwich first."

What commenced was the slowest consumption of a sandwich that any of them had ever seen. And when there was nothing left but the barest sliver of bread, Piper took the paper towel and wiped the peanut butter and crumbs off his face.

"It was nice to meet you, Shai. Be safe."

"Thank you," he said.

Lou placed one hand on his back. "Ready?"

"No."

Lou stepped back into a pocket of shadow in the corner office.

"Come back when you're done," King said. "I need to—"

That was all Lou heard before the darkness rolled over them, pulling them through.

The office was replaced by a small house with its porchlight on. The bungalow sat on a street with many identical houses, and an identical concrete walk linking them.

Lou stood outside the soft circle of the porchlight, regarding the house. "Is this your mom's house?"

"Yeah," he said, sliding out of her arms for the first time.

She wanted to believe it. She **wanted to believe** that he would be safe here with his mother.

"Mom!" Shai called, running up the walkway. "Mommy!"

Lou walked up the sidewalk, casting glances up and down the quiet street. A black cat sat at the end of a driveway, watching them with interest, its tail flicking against the warm concrete.

A breeze rubbed the palm trees, the large fronds lifting.

"Mommy! Mommy!"

The door opened. "Shai?"

The woman looked dazed, as if half dreaming. Lou wondered if this was the first time she'd opened her door calling her child's name.

"Shai?"

"Mommy, it's me!"

Recognition dawned in her eyes the moment she put her hands on the boy's shoulders.

"Shai! Oh my god, Shai!"

She cupped his face and cried out, "Oh my god, baby. My baby! What happened to you?"

She fingered the collar of his shirt, yanking it down to reveal his slender, bruised throat.

"Oh god, oh god, oh my god."

She crushed Shai against her, collapsing into her sobs.

Then her eyes fell on Lou. On the body armor, on the guns. "You! Did you do this? Did you hurt him?"

She launched herself at Lou, fingers hooked into claws as she swiped at her face.

Lou sidestepped easily, catching her wrist and twisting it.

The woman screeched.

"It wasn't me," Lou said calmly, ignoring the pulsing pain in her shoulder.

"She's an angel, Mommy! She saved me!"

The woman yanked her hand away.

Lou turned, intending to walk to the trees across the street and disappear in the shadows between the two palms.

"Don't go!" Shai seized her leg. "Please don't go. *Please.*"

Lou turned. "I can't stay." She cut her eyes up to the mother.

"What if I need you?" Shai said. "What if—"

Lou placed a hand on his chest. "I'll be around. If you need me."

"Can I pray to you?" he asked. "If I pray like this, will you hear me?"

Shai closed his eyes, pinching them tightly shut.

Lou felt her compass spin inside her, responding to it. It reminded her of Piper, who also used calls of help to get Lou's attention.

"You can do that," Lou said. "But only if you're really in trouble. Don't waste your prayers."

In this life, we learn how to save ourselves.

The boy nodded solemnly.

"Who are you?" the mother asked, pulling Shai back as if Lou were the dangerous one. And between the three of them, Lou supposed it was true.

"No one."

"She's my angel," Shai said. "She saved me."

"An angel?" the woman asked, frowning down at her son. "Is that..."

Her question died on her lips. When she looked up, Lou was gone.

31

I t wasn't hard to find Diana. Lou simply had to think about her and the compass did the work. It spun around in the dark, orienting itself in time and space, before locking in on her.

Stalks swayed in the breeze. The smell of corn silk hung in the air. As the stalks parted, Lou saw a barn, with a single light in the darkness.

Lou moved through the corn, her boots crunching on fallen stalks.

"How the *hell* did you find us?" a woman cursed.

Lou turned and found Blair standing, legs apart, gun cupped in her hand. She aimed at Lou's head.

"I knew you were a freak." Blair laughed, but there was no humor in it. "I told her to believe what we saw, but *no*. My sister has to be the rational one."

"Lower your gun," Lou said. She thought she was being rather polite about it.

"No, thanks. I know what you can do."

If you already know... Lou thought. She sidestepped through the shadows, reappearing behind Blair. She took in the woman's long, slender neck before bringing her elbow down hard on the back of it.

Blair collapsed, falling face down onto the dirt. This was when Lou heard the others, moving through the corn, drawn to the sound of the commotion. The hobbled man would be here, of course, with the others who served Dennard.

Get me closer, she thought, and the swaying stalks and stench of packed mud and corn silk fell away.

Then she was at the back of a barn, a rough red door under her hand.

She pushed it open.

In the doorway, Lou hesitated. She smelled hay, but also something electric and burning.

Winter was tied to a wooden chair in the center of the room. Three utility lights were strung overhead, beating down on the man. Cinderblocks were latched to the bottom of each chair leg as if to hold it in place.

His chest was bloody from throat to bellybutton. The light hair covering most of his stomach was matted. Lou suspected the source was the three thick gashes along his collarbones and chest.

His white-gray hair was mostly untouched except for a crust of blood on the right side, the side facing Lou.

The scene reminded her of her early hunting days. How she would find one of the Martinellis and string him up, hurt him until something inside her, a long-festering sore, broke open and oozed. In this letting, she'd find a momentary relief from that unquenchable ache within her.

Had she looked like Diana did now? Her sleeves rolled up, a knife twisting in her fist, her face all business and fury.

"Has he told you where he is yet?" Lou called from the doorway.

Diana looked up, her eyes still glazed.

"He will," she said. "If he knows what's good for him."

"You're going to kill me either way," the man said, turning his head and spitting blood on the ground. "Just fucking do it already."

"No," Diana said, pressing her boot onto the ground. The man convulsed, twitching wildly in his chair.

At this distance, it looked like Diana was stepping onto a block. Lou edged closer and saw it was a peddle connected to wiring wrapped around the chair.

Pushing the peddle down ignited an electrical charge which then coursed up the wires and into Winter's body.

Diana was watching her face instead of the convulsing man. "It doesn't bother you?"

What should bother her? The smell of burning hair? The pitiful mewling? She'd seen—caused—worse. "No."

"You are *cold*." Diana smiled. "But you still fucked up tonight."

"Because the other one got away?"

"He's not the *other* one," Diana hissed, pulling her boot off the switch and wiping the bloody knife on her pants. It left a smear across the top of her right thigh. "He was *the one*."

"Why?" Lou asked, leaning against the doorway, arms crossed.

She tried to piece together Diana's story. She remembered most of it from the diner, the night they spoke for the first time.

Her father's friend had picked her up from school and taken her home to his house, locking her in a soundproof shed. She hadn't gone into detail about what had happened in the shed in the weeks he'd held her captive, but Lou could guess. When she'd escaped, she came back with a gun and shot the guy. If the one who'd hurt her was dead, who were these two men to her?

Where did they fit into her story? Lou was ready to believe that there was more than one villain.

For her, there hadn't been just one either. Not really.

Her *one* had been Angelo Martinelli, because he'd pulled the trigger. But there'd also been Gus Johnson, her father's partner, who'd given the Martinellis their address in exchange for sparing his own life. There'd been Chaz Brasso, King's old partner, who'd sold out Jack and Gus as the ones who'd busted Benito Martinelli for drugs.

There'd been Senator Ryanson, who'd been lining Brasso's pockets for years and who'd given the order to take her meddlesome father out of the picture once he'd gotten too close to the source of the corruption. Not to mention Angelo's father and brothers, who'd executed the ambush of her childhood home and the murder of her parents.

No, not one man. It was rarely *one* man responsible for a woman's accumulated pain. Lou understood that.

"Who is he to you? Really?" she asked, blinking past the irritation of her shoulder. She needed another Vicodin, but it could wait.

It didn't look like Diana would answer. Then she surprised Lou.

"Do you know that these photos and videos that end up on the internet stay on there forever? *Forever.* Unless someone actually takes them all down, but even then, sometimes copies will resurface."

She wiped her nose on her sleeve.

"The internet was a new thing when I was taken," Diana said. "It had only been around a few years, but it was sophisticated enough. My rapist didn't just screw me. He filmed himself doing it. Never his own face, but my face? *Sure.* My face was everywhere. You see, these sick perverts get off on the crying as much as the raping."

Lou waited. She knew the story was only getting started.

"What you don't realize is that people can *recognize* you. Once you're in the system, once a hundred or a thousand assholes have jerked off to your crying face, they *remember* you. Remember this, you piece of shit."

Diana stepped on the switch again and the man resumed convulsing. It wasn't until he slumped unconscious that she took her foot off the pedal.

"One night, when I was fifteen, a couple of years after that nightmare in the shed, I'm walking home from the library with one of my friends. I notice that a guy is following me. I can't get a good look at him, but I'm ready for any bull-shit. After what I did to Daniel, I stayed ready."

Lou assumed Daniel was her original kidnapper. She wasn't about to interrupt the story to ask.

"This guy waits until my friends and I split up, and of course he follows me. He follows me three blocks, and I know he's looking for the right time to grab me. So I make it easy for him. I cut across the playground. It wasn't a nice playground. It had a busted swing and the grass was over-grown, and it sat between two abandoned houses. I thought about going into the houses, but I wanted someone to hear me scream if my plan didn't work out."

Lou shifted against the door.

"He grabbed me by the back fence, before I could get to the gate. When he threw me on the ground, you know what he said to me?"

Lou didn't answer.

"He said, 'I *knew* it was you. Look at you, my good girl. My good little slut.' That's what Daniel was always saying, 'my good little slut.' He kept saying it while getting his hand under my skirt. He kept saying it until I cut half his fucking arm off."

She slammed her foot down on the switch but nothing happened. The man's muscles twitched but he remained unconscious. White foam bubbled at the side of his mouth.

"You were looking for a scar," Lou said, remembering the

way Diana had yanked Winter's sleeve up. "Of where you stabbed him."

"That's what they do," Diana said, more to herself than anyone else. "These sick bastards. They come back."

She met Lou's gaze at last, and Lou knew the look in her eyes. She'd seen it in her own.

"Don't wear yourself out," Lou said, taking a step back into the darkness. "You've got one more coming."

32

L ou's wrist buzzed.

Are you okay? the message read.

Lou sat up in bed, trying to shake the sleep off. She'd needed it, and the pill she'd taken after Diana's raid had given her long, uninterrupted hours of it.

Even with two days of rest behind her, her body ached. She wasn't sure which act had actually exacerbated her shoulder, but it was still speaking to her in low, threatening tones.

Two days and two nights in her apartment, alone, sleeping and eating and standing under the pounding stream of hot water. All of it had helped, but it hadn't erased her discomfort entirely.

Amore mio?

Lou looked at the watch face and sent a simple return text. *I'm fine.*

All other explanations would have to wait. She had a date with a man with a scar.

She might need more rest, but two days was the most she could manage before her restlessness overcame her again.

She rose, kicked off her comforter, and stretched. She

particularly stretched her shoulder, until it moved without hitching in its socket.

She ate the second half of a burger she'd procured the night before. She'd only eaten half of it before the Vicodin had kicked in and her desire to sleep outweighed her desire to keep eating. But now the hunger was in full swing. She chased the burger with two apples and a banana from the glass fruit bowl on her kitchen island.

She washed it all down with water, wishing instead for about half a gallon of coffee.

She settled for a pot of it, which she drank as she stood by her large picture window overlooking the Mississippi river.

Her eyes were on the shimmering waters, the way they sparked with the fading embers of the lowering sun. Outwardly she was relaxed, ready. Inwardly, her compass churned. It whirled, searching the darkness that connected every point in the world for her target.

She didn't use the word *Winter* now, since it hadn't been accurate. She used the face, the one she'd seen in the hallway as he stepped out to lock the door behind himself.

That was what she locked in on. That was the face her compass searched the dark for.

And found.

Something inside her clicked, jerked into place, and she felt a slight tug forward, like river water pushing at the backs of her knees.

As she drained the last of the cup, the sun descended, tucking itself beneath the horizon for the night. And with each passing moment, Lou's limbs grew stronger. Her hands steadier.

Good.

She'd need her strength.

. . .

MICKI JAMES STAYED ON THE MOVE. SINCE SPRINGFIELD two nights ago, when Murf got himself caught, Micki had known better than to stop his car for more than a few hours. He gassed up, grabbed a cold sandwich from a case beside the soda fountain, and got back on the road.

This car smelled like cigarettes whenever he rolled up the window, so he kept it cracked while he drove. The breeze hit his eyes, encouraging them to stay peeled.

He took speed from those little packets found on gas station counters and named after insects—wasps, bees, whatever—that kept him awake long after his brain begged for sleep.

He understood why the drugs were named this way now. After four pills, it was definitely like bees were in his brain, buzzing, bouncing off the insides of his skull.

He thought of Murf again. They'd been partners a long time—Micki and Murf. They'd had a good thing going. But he'd known this day was coming. What did his mama use to say? All good things come to an end?

And where had she heard that? From her Sunday morning preachers over the radio or the old biddies with whom she crocheted sweaters for the war veterans?

It didn't matter. His mother had been dead for twenty years.

And now Murf—*Winter*—was dead too.

You got caught 'cause you're careless, his mother said from the backseat.

There she sat in her curlers, a cigarette hanging from between her lips, her Coke-bottle glasses so thick he couldn't actually see the eyes behind them. *You've always been a careless boy*.

"Shut up, Mama," he said, and his voice, gruff, echoed in the car.

That cigarette smoke smell made his stomach hurt. He rolled down the window more.

Micki realized he was tired, maybe too tired to be driving, if he was having conversations with his dead mother.

But he couldn't stop, not now, when it felt like someone was still following him.

Welcome to California.

He turned in his seat, following the sign as far as his eyes would allow.

He planned to stop in San Diego, maybe Tijuana. Yes, Tijuana was better. That's where he'd regroup, assess his situation. That's where he'd get some sleep. When he woke with a clear head, he'd figure out who had found him and where he'd gone wrong. He had plenty of cash on hand and more stashed away in a few accounts, and even two computers locked in the trunk.

He'd be up and running in no time.

He reached into his plastic cup holder and fished out another packet of speed. He tore it open with his teeth, his sweaty fingers sliding off the steering wheel as he grabbed for his drink. He tore off the red cap and downed it in several deep gulps.

The car hummed, groaning as it slipped over the rumble strip on the side of the road.

He pulled the wheel left, getting back into the lane.

He threw the drink back into the cup holder with a sudden rage. He was pissed about losing the girl. She was such a sweet little cherry. Just the thought of her little hands on him was enough to get him hard.

That bitch with the guns and the mirrored shades. He'd make her sorry for taking away his girl.

Bees bounced off the inside of Micki's skull, lulling him with their rhythm. The Coke in the back of his throat stopped burning and the white line in the middle of the road swayed, seeming to be playing a song. A bass line.

Da dum da dum da dum.

You were always a careless boy, his mother said again from the backseat. *Remember when you fell off that little wooden bridge into the river. You weren't watching where you stepped and you got your nice shoes, your best Sunday shoes, all wet. Tore a hole in the seat of your pants, too, if I remember.*

"Shut up, Mama," he said again, wishing he'd grabbed a bag of chips or something he could have mindlessly shoved into his mouth. Something for his hands to do.

He turned on the radio, but a touch too loud, and it made his head hurt. He turned it off and opened the window, all the way down now, and angled his head out into the fresh air.

That was better, as the frigid cold pulled tears from his eyes. The sleepiness receded.

With his head back in the car, he blinked away the tears and saw a woman in the backseat.

"Go away, Mama," he said. "I told you to shut up."

"I'm not your mama," a voice said.

His bleary eyes snapped to the rearview mirror again.

She was right. It wasn't his momma in her Coke-bottle glasses and tight gray curls. There was no cigarette smoke rising thin and blue toward the car's roof.

It was the shades he remembered.

The woman in the hallway, the one who'd taken his little cherry pie. She leaned forward and grabbed the steering wheel. She yanked it hard, veering his car off the road, over the rumble strip and into the grass.

Here Micki thought to hit the brakes, but at first attempt his foot slipped off the pedal. The second attempt sent the vehicle into a slide but didn't actually slow it much. He was going too fast, the pillar was too close.

He began to scream.

The concrete barrier rose in his vision, doubling, tripling in size until all else was blotted out.

His heart hammered, beating furiously as he waited for the impact that never came.

LATER, AS THE EMERGENCY CREWS HOSED DOWN THE flaming car, they'd wonder where the driver was, and if he—or she—had taken off on foot. All agreed that whoever the driver had been, they must've rolled from the vehicle before it slammed into the overpass barrier.

They sent a search party to look for the driver. If they'd survived, they might be hurt, disoriented. But after three hours and no sign of life except the coyotes hunting rabbits under the large moon, they called it a night.

They believed the driver would turn up eventually.

Cars didn't drive themselves.

33

Diana emptied her Smith & Wesson .45 into the wooden target at the far end of the dirt path. Once the gun clicked empty and the trees lining the path stopped their rustling, an optimistic cardinal let out a shrill chirp. However, Diana was just getting started. She reloaded and went for another round.

Again, her mind railed. *He escaped again. How could it keep happening? How?*

There was nothing special or gifted about Winter. He should've folded like a house of cards under all her efforts by now.

A tap resounded against her shoulder. Blair held a folded piece of paper between two fingers.

"I told you not to bother me," Diana said, turning toward the target again and raising the gun.

"Spencer's gone. I think Lou killed him."

"No, she didn't." Diana gestured to the heap of dirt beneath a nearby sycamore. "He's over there."

She managed to empty the gun before her sister recovered from the news.

"*You* killed him?"

"I thought you hated him," Diana said, unable to hide her irritation.

In truth, Diana hadn't meant to do it. She'd said *the word*, giving Spencer permission to plunge himself inside her after roughly four weeks of refusal. Before she'd had a chance to orgasm, he came, abruptly ending her rhythm and her pleasure. The next thing she knew she had her hands around his throat, squeezing, grinding her hips into his, until an orgasm finally shivered through her.

She'd thought he'd liked it, the squeezing, since he'd resumed thrusting. It wasn't until she unzipped the leather mask and saw how blue his face was—she would never forget the bulge of his eyes—that she'd fully realized what she'd done.

I didn't mean to do it, she told herself.

Are you sure about that? a colder voice asked. *Or did you know exactly what you were doing? Will that be your next craving? Find a guy, enslave his cock, and kill him once you get bored? Sounds promising.*

"It had to be done," she said simply. "He wanted to go to the police. I couldn't let him do that."

Blair gawked at her, unblinking. "You're lying. He did everything for you. He was—he was the best—"

"Don't exaggerate." Diana wanted to change the subject. "Why did you think Lou killed him?"

Blair produced the folded piece of paper she'd first waved to get her attention. "She left this taped to the bathroom mirror. She was *in* our house. Surprise, surprise, it didn't even trip the alarm."

With a huff, Diana applied the safety to the gun and slipped it into her waistband. The warm metal bit into her flesh, chafing the bones beneath.

She unfolded the note. There were jotted coordinates, and then below them, *Get there before he wakes up.*

Diana's heart skipped a beat. "Have you checked it out?"

"I don't like it, Dee. She's shown up at our house *twice*. And in the cornfield, she just slipped past me like I was nothing. One second she was there, and—"

Diana was sick of these ghost stories. She raised her voice. "Did you check it out?"

Blair shifted. "Yes. You'll want to see for yourself."

Diana took off for the waiting truck at a steady jog. At the end of the dirt path and adjacent lot, her beat-up truck sat parked in the shade of an old-growth maple tree. She hauled herself up into the beast.

Hanging from the window, she called to her sister, "Coming or not?"

Blair climbed into the passenger seat, her jaw tight and working. Dust swirled around them as the truck reversed and sped out of the lot. It was almost a mile of packed dirt before concrete finally rose up to meet them.

The coordinates on the note were a short drive from Diana's worn farmhouse in Kansas. She was trying not to be bothered by the fact that Louie had found her so easily. The land and farmhouse and its two barns had been her hidden sanctuary for over six years. It was off grid and buffered by wild, overgrown land on all sides. The idea that Louie could find it only hours after they parted made her mind run wild with possibility. Had she put trackers on their cars? On her, somehow?

The coordinates took them to a service road marked only by a number. Diana drove the beat-up truck down it slowly, letting the oversized tires gently roll through the dips, creaking.

It seemed like an hour before they found a small, leaning shack at the edge of a dirt field.

Diana pulled the truck around back into the heart of the thicket so that it couldn't be seen from the road, and the two women hopped down into the long-overgrown weeds.

Someone was crying inside the shack.

The deep, rolling sobs could barely be heard over the rushing water of the river coursing behind them.

Diana pulled her gun from her waistband, removed the safety, and inched toward the shack.

"You won't need it," Blair said.

Diana paid her no mind. The door was rough under her hand and felt wet.

It's rotting, she noted. One more good rain or storm and this shack would go down. She wondered if this was what was left of a garage, perhaps the house long obliterated by the elements. Or perhaps a boathouse for the river behind them.

A man lay in the middle of the concrete floor. Naked and shackled.

Not just shackled, but in the way the children were often chained in his videos, with iron-like collars clamped over their throats and thick, unyielding chains drilled and hooked into the floor.

He was pulling on the chain, but it wouldn't give.

When their boots hit the concrete, the scuffs muffled by the wooden walls, he jumped. His cries escalated into panicked yips.

Then he seemed to see Diana.

"Please," he said. He shuffled toward her on his knees. "Please help me. Get me out of here before she comes back."

Diana knelt down and took his arm, turning it in the light to see the scar.

"Wha-what are you doing? What are you looking for?"

It was an old scar, at least twenty years since she'd carved it, but she'd recognize the hooked mark of her savage blade anywhere.

This was her man.

This was her Winter.

"Please," he begged, his face red and covered in snot. "Please, before it gets dark. She moves in the dark."

"I'm not here to help you," Diana said, dropping his arm.

The shack stank of his body odor and sweat. She thought he'd probably pissed himself too.

Even so, her pleasure uncoiled inside her. Her excitement doubled, then tripled, until her chest felt ready to explode with it.

"I'm here to *hurt* you."

The wind blew and the wooden sides of the shed groaned. He flinched, his eyes darting toward the blackened corners pressing in on them.

"Please," he cried, inching toward her. "*Please*, before it gets dark. Sh-she could come back."

Diana yanked hard on the collar.

His hands shot out instinctively to catch himself. Seeing him on all fours reminded her of Spencer. "Did you hear me?"

"He can't hear anything. He's scared out of his mind," Blair said. There was a sound in her voice Diana didn't like. Awe? Fear? Or some unnamable emotion halfway between the two?

And Winter *was* scared out of his mind, that much was clear.

But he wasn't scared of her. He barely registered Diana's presence at all.

No, she thought. Her fist tightened on the chain. *No, he should be afraid of* me.

She *deserved* that much from him.

His eyes kept darting to the corners of the shack every time the wind rolled along its delicate sides. Each creak and moan intensified his fear. Diana could almost taste it, like battery acid on the tongue.

He made himself smaller and smaller. He folded and compressed himself in the medallion of sunlight shining from the hole in the roof above, as if the light was his last chance at salvation.

He's terrified, but not of me.

34

"Questions loom around the suspected raid in Springfield, Missouri. Police have identified two of the men as registered sex offenders connected to an internet pornography website known as—"

"Turn that up!" Piper stepped out of the bedroom with her toothbrush in her mouth and pointed at the television.

"In the eight hundred apartment block of Henderson Street..."

Dani, wrapped up in a thin summer blanket on Piper's sofa, reached for the remote. She turned up the volume with a mash of her thumb.

"We've found evidence in the building behind me that this was a shooting location for child pornography videos," a man was saying. He stood in the camera's spotlight with the smoldering building behind him. Even though the firefighters had been working on the building for days, it seemed the smoke wouldn't quit.

"Several children, all identified and returned to their families, were rescued from the scene. The only bodies present were the suspected pornographers, shot execution style in the back of their heads."

Piper spit into the bathroom sink. "Can they say that? Can a cop just say that on television?"

"I think he's in shock," Dani said. "Look at his face. Maybe he's not thinking about what he's saying."

Piper wiped her mouth and turned off the bathroom light behind her. The man on the television did look shocked. His eyes were too wide, the visible white nearly eclipsing the color. His mouth had a slack look to it, as if it were incapable of fully closing.

Piper suspected that if he took his hands off his hips, there would be a tremble to them.

A rough knock on the door made both girls jump. Dani pulled the blanket close. Piper reached across the counter and pulled a knife from the butcher's block.

"Who is it?" she called, her voice an octave too shrill.

"It's me." King's gruff voice was muffled by the door.

The tension in the room evaporated.

"Come in."

King entered with a cardboard box in one hand, the other on the knob he was turning. "I'm heading out for the night. I thought I'd see if you guys wanted the other half of this pizza. I'm not going to eat it."

Stepping into the living room, King stopped. When he saw the knife in Piper's hand he frowned. "Did I miss something?"

"No," she said, sliding the knife back into the block.

His gaze flicked from Piper to Dani. "You okay?"

"I'm good, thanks," Dani said automatically.

"Sure," he said with a snide laugh, as if he didn't believe anything either of them was saying. He lifted the cardboard box to show his half-devoured sausage pizza. "Do you want this?"

"What do you think, babe? Pizza?"

Dani smiled a bit too brightly. "Sounds good. Thanks, Robert."

"My pleasure." He placed the box on the island cabinet and headed back toward the door. "I'll lock up on my way out."

He hesitated when his eyes caught the news report.

"Is that—"

"Yeah," Piper interjected as she slid a slice from the box. "It looks like a mess."

"It was," King said as the story faded to black and the next tragedy cued. "Diana made a real mess of it. Trigger happy, that one."

"Authorities are searching for a woman by the name of Diana Dennard. The suspect, white, female, thirty-eight years old—"

King, who'd been turning toward the stairs, froze and whirled back. "What did she say?"

"Oh yeah." Piper spoke around the pizza in her mouth "Here we go."

Diana's picture appeared, covering half of the screen while the report prattled on.

"—responsible for at least thirty fraudulent scams across the US. Credit card bills exceeding two million dollars have been attributed to her seven known aliases..."

"Shit." With his hands on his hips and mouth ajar he looked like the police officer who'd reported on the raid. He turned to Dani. "Did you do this?"

Dani pursed her lips, ready to speak.

"It was me." Piper sucked in a deep breath. "Before you get mad, let me explain."

She took another slice of pizza from the box in case King decided to rescind his gift.

"What'd you do? Why in the world would you provoke

her?" King ran a hand through his hair, clearly trying to compose himself.

"Aren't you tired of it?" Piper threw up her hands. "Bad guys are always coming after us, kidnapping us, telling us what the rules of the game are."

"If we were confrontation adverse, we would find new jobs," he said.

"I don't want a new job. But I'm not going to be the prey either. *Nope.* No more waiting around to be rescued while Lou does all the badassery. I'm taking control, damn it. Those jerks are going to start worrying about *me*."

"Huzzah." Dani was smiling as she took her slice from the box and began picking off the sausage. "That's the spirit, baby."

King, however, looked far from optimistic.

DIANA WAS SCRAPING THE DIRT AND BLOOD OUT FROM under her fingernails with a metal pick when she saw someone step into her periphery. She met their eyes in the mirror, finding Blair, her body tense and face drawn.

Diana wanted a shower. She wanted to fuck Spencer and sleep for two days. Maybe then the dull ache in her over-worked shoulders and back would go away.

You killed Spencer, she reminded herself. *I suppose you could dig up his corpse and fuck that. And when you're done with him, why not Winter too?*

Diana sighed. She thought she'd feel better. Energized. Overwhelmed with triumph or at least relief.

But she didn't. Winter was dead and she felt—nothing. It was an anti-climactic end to a long and arduous search, and what did she have to show for it?

You're just tired. You need to rest, and then you'll feel it.

What she didn't need was whatever lecture Blair was mentally rehearsing behind those sullen eyes.

Diana sighed. "Before you ask, *yes*, I buried him deep. No coyotes are going to drag him out like the—"

"We have another problem," Blair said. Her tone was flat, nearly devoid of emotion. When Diana only continued to wash the dirt from her hands, Blair added, "A *big* problem."

"Don't be so dramatic." When she looked up, Blair was gone, her lithe form halfway down the narrow hallway connecting the bathroom and living room.

Wringing her hands with a towel, Diana followed her deeper into the converted farmhouse. It wasn't luxurious. She'd spent little money on renovating it. Only enough to get water into the pipes and electricity into the wires and a furnace strong enough to beat back the long fingers of a Kansas winter. Even so, wind blew through the place as if there were holes in the walls.

In the living room, a small television sat on an overturned milkcrate. A battered futon rested in its view with a strip of silver duct tape keeping the stuffing inside.

Blair pointed at the screen, turning the knob to increase the volume.

The blown-out and smoldering buildings filled the screen as a team of firefighters combated the flames. They struggled with the large hoses, looking small and comical in their raincoats.

"They found the bodies." Diana shrugged. "So what?"

"Keep watching," Blair insisted. "They've played this story on a loop for an hour."

"Diana Dennard"—her heart stuttered in her chest, plummeting into her stomach, and her arms and legs felt suddenly weak—"has run credit card scams for over two million dollars across the US."

The world shifted on a tilt as her face appeared, blotting out the rest of the screen.

"What we know about Diana Dennard results from an alleged kidnapping over twenty years ago. She has only one living relative, a sister. The whereabouts of her sister remain unknown, but seven known aliases have been uncovered in an attempt to—"

"Do you think Lou did this?" Blair asked, her hands cupping her elbows.

"No," Diana said. Lou couldn't be bothered with such a menial task.

Her mind sprang back to the night in New Orleans, to the bait lying on the floor of her townhouse.

Diana had dug deep into all of Lou's associates and had learned that Daniella Allendale, the simpering, pathetic girl who had fallen apart over a little zip tie, was a reporter.

Not just any reporter. An *investigative* reporter from a rich and well-connected family. No doubt an entitled and spoiled brat who thought she was above everyone and everything.

No, Diana didn't need to wonder how her story had been thrown to the press.

Was this payback? Had the little bitch decided to grow teeth?

"Wanted in connection with at least thirty-five cases of fraud," the television droned on. Diana's own face continued to look back at her accusingly.

Her face. Her face everywhere. And now her financial backing was compromised along with her anonymity.

Her freedom. Everything. Gone.

And it was a terrible picture of her.

Anger unfurled in Diana, so rich and full-bodied she was nearly drunk on it.

Lou. How could you do it?

Lou might not have pulled the trigger on this betrayal,

but she must've known it would happen. And did she stop it? Did she defend Diana?

No. She let her take the bullet.

"What are we going to do?" Blair asked.

Diana wrung the towel in her fist. "Kill her."

35

L ou was perched on the edge of her sofa, lacing her boots, when her watch buzzed. She rotated the digital face, turning it in the light to better read it. It was King.

911

She'd told Konstantine she'd be there tonight. She could feel his restlessness like a tight wire in her gut. It set her own teeth on edge.

The watch buzzed again.

911

"Coming," she grumbled. *Konstantine will have to wait.*

She stood and crossed to the island, grabbing her Browning pistol off the countertop. It was still light outside, so she stepped into the linen closet and shut the door behind her, the most complete darkness she could offer herself at this time of day.

The shadows rubbed against her body like a cat against a leg. Cool and needy. Her internal compass spun in the dark, seeking out King on the other side. When it clicked into place, she let go of her hold on this part of the world and slipped through the thin veil separating the two points of their respective space.

She'd expected the office, or maybe King's loft apartment. Either way he was more than likely poring over papers. He was a chronic workaholic, not unlike her.

What she found was something else altogether.

She was in a concrete bunker. Overhead, honky-tonk music blared and the rhythmic thumping against the ceiling conjured the image of line dancing and leather fringe. She could smell grease, maybe fried pickles, and the sharp tang of alcohol.

Lou raised her gun.

"It's just me," King said, stepping into the spotlight of a low-hanging bulb.

Lou lowered the gun. A chill ran up the back of her spine. It was cold down here. Where were they? A basement? "What's the emergency?"

"Did you see the Dennard story?"

"What Dennard story?"

He rubbed his forehead with his fist. "Christ. Don't you have a television?"

"No. You can get me one for Christmas," she said, her tone light. "If it bothers you so much."

His lack of reaction made her stomach harden.

"Spit it out," she said.

"Piper dug up some charges on Dennard. Her credit card scams, her disappearance, the sister, all of it. Then she sold it."

"What do you mean, sold it?"

"To some of Dani's connections, to some of mine. Names I had floating around the office. She broke Dennard's story wide open. Diana's face is all over the news. Her cover is blown."

Lou was having a hard time understanding. "Why?"

What did she have to gain by going after Dennard?

"That's what I asked," King said with a bark of surprised laughter. "Now that Dennard had her man, I was hoping she'd slink off into the sunset."

Lou had thought the same. She hadn't expected to see Diana again, at least not for a long time.

"She said Dennard had it coming. That she didn't want her thinking she could do whatever she wanted with us."

Lou thought of Winter, the way he'd cried when she'd clamped the metal collar around his throat and welded the chain to the hook in the floor.

"Diana might not have seen the news yet." Lou holstered her gun. "She might still be working on Winter."

Or maybe not, a little voice said. *How long did you play with Angelo? Twenty minutes?*

Would Dennard be able to resist ripping the man apart, swiftly and brutally? And no matter how much the punisher may enjoy it, the human body can only withstand so much.

Her man would give out on her, sooner or later. Lou knew that better than most.

Then Diana will discover the worst of it. That her hunt had been a distraction, a lie. It had promised relief, complete satisfaction.

But nothing would satisfy again. Not really.

"You know she's going to retaliate, right?" King ran a hand through his hair. "She's going to think we did this, and she's going to come after us."

Lou wasn't sure what to do with the mild panic thrumming through him. He seemed to need some sort of reassurance from her.

"It'll be harder to get to New Orleans now," she offered. "If her face is all over the news, it's not like she can walk around in the open."

"Please," King laughed, clearly exasperated. "She's blond,

blue-eyed, clean cut. There are hundreds of her in the French Quarter alone. If she's careful, she'll blend in. And she wasn't working alone, remember? She has people she can trust. If she were a true loner, this would be easier. But she's not. She's a master manipulator. They're far worse."

King's irritation, his borderline hysteria, nipped at the back of her neck, made her shoulders inch toward her ears.

"What do you want me to do?" Lou asked. Because it was clear he wanted something.

It wasn't the secure location or the 911 page or even his tense body language. It was the look on his face, the desperate, pleading look that said, *Please. Please, Lou.*

But whatever the request was, she needed him to spit it out.

"I want you to take Piper, Dani, and Mel somewhere safe. Drop them on a deserted island for all I care, but don't leave them here."

Lou laughed.

"This isn't a joke."

"They aren't going to let me take them anywhere."

"Take Dani at least," King said. "Diana probably thinks she's the one who ratted her out. She must know she's a journalist and has the contacts to launch a story like this. If Dani goes, maybe Piper will too, but they need to disappear, you understand that? Diana *will* kill them."

The hair on Lou's arms rose.

"She won't stage another pretend kidnapping to get your attention. There's only one statement she'll want to make."

You were supposed to understand, Lou.

"Her rapist took something and she killed him. Winter took something and she hunted him for years, and now we took her freedom, her anonymity. She's going to feel especially betrayed by you. You move like she does, hunt like she does. You're supposed to understand. The only difference is that if she comes for you, you can handle yourself. Piper and Dani can't."

King ran his hands through his hair.

"You could take her out, end it before it begins. Give Dennard a one-way trip to La Loon."

Lou snorted.

"What's funny?"

"You make me jump through hoops to nab someone like Fish, and now Diana comes along and you just want me to 'take her out.'"

"She will retaliate," King insisted.

"When?" Lou asked. "Tomorrow? In six years? Mel, Dani, and Piper have lives. You can't ask them to go into hiding forever. And it's impossible to know when she'll make her move."

And what about me, King? Will you try to eliminate me one day? Will I cross some unseen line and suddenly be too much of a liability to you? Will you be asking someone to "take me out"?

"I'm just saying it'll be easier if you kill her."

"No," Lou said, jaw clenched. "You can't sell me on this idea that the system matters, that the process matters, and then ditch it the first time someone scares you. Either I kill whoever I want, whenever I want"—*And I will anyway*, she thought darkly—"or we play by the rules. Which is it?"

King clasped the back of his neck.

Lou didn't want to point out the obvious. Holding Diana accountable for her work seemed hypocritical. Why should Lou hunt as she pleased while Diana must be restrained?

"I don't want any of you to get hurt." King rubbed his fist across his forehead. "But you're right. I can't tell you to back off on Fish then ask you to go hard on Dennard. That's..."

Wrong.

"Inconsistent," he said with a grimace. "But she's dangerous and she's going to blame us for the exposure.

Because it *was* us. It could only be us. I don't think anyone else knows who she is."

The music overhead renewed and the pounding feet changed their rhythm, increasing the tempo.

"What about moving the girls?" King asked, still hopeful. "Maybe Konstantine knows somewhere they'll be safe."

"I'll ask," Lou said. But she already knew Piper's answer.

"WHAT? NO." PIPER SCOWLED AT HER OVER A BAG OF tortilla chips. She took a handful, put them on a plate, and covered them with cheese. Then she put the plate in the microwave for thirty seconds. "I'm not scared of that psycho."

Maybe you should be, Lou thought.

"King wants us to leave?" Piper asked incredulously. "Or are you just mad that you can't hang out with your friend anymore?"

Lou noted her irritation distantly. *What now?*

"Listen to her," Dani said, sitting on the stool at her kitchen island. She took a chip from the bag.

Lou liked the color in her cheeks and the steadiness in her eyes. She was doing better.

A cat meowed at Lou's feet, rubbing its head against her boot. It reminded her of Jabbers.

Lou bent down and scooped up the feline, scratching her ears. The cat began to purr, cradled against Lou's chest.

Piper moved around Dani's kitchen as if it were her own. She knew where all the plates and utensils were. Where the ingredients were stored.

Piper opened the bag of shredded cheese wider. "Why should we run? Diana can't do anything. The French Quarter is full of cops. It's not like she can walk up to the shop or King's without someone seeing her."

Dani spread her hand on the countertop. "She could wear a disguise. Or she could send someone else after us."

Lou noted her bouncing knee and the way she pulled her lip into her mouth and pinned it there with her teeth.

Piper rolled her eyes. "She was dumb enough to walk into King's office and pretend to be Lou's sister. We're light years ahead of her, babe."

"She kidnapped us and zip-tied us. Like hogs."

Lou watched this exchange with a growing sense of unease.

The microwave beeped. Piper lifted a pan from the stove and scraped veggies onto the chips. On top of this, she spooned out generous dollops of sour cream, avocado, and salsa before pushing the plate toward Dani.

"Thanks," she said, but didn't touch the nachos.

Piper forked raw hamburger into the pan and continued. "That was before Lou killed like ninety percent of her men. She's not stupid enough to come at us empty-handed. She's a survivor. Survivors don't make futile moves."

I've made plenty of them, Lou thought. In the heat of a hunt, when led forward more by her hunger than a self-regard for her own life, she'd been more than careless.

Piper must've seen the disagreement on her face. "Do you want nachos or not?"

Lou sank onto a bar stool, still holding the cat. "Yes."

"Beef like mine or vegetarian like hers?"

"Beef."

Piper began arranging another plate. Once it was in the microwave, she said, "Even if she wants to come after us, and she scrounges up enough people to do it, *and* she's dumb enough to risk being murdered or arrested, there's still the question of *when*. We have no idea when this will happen. We can't just drop our lives and go into hiding indefinitely."

Here she turned to Dani, giving her a questioning look.

Dani took her first tentative bite of the nachos, and audibly swooned.

"You can't take any more time off work," Piper said. "And my semester starts in ten days. I need to be buying my books, not packing my bags."

Dani traced shapes on the countertop and sighed. "My job performance hasn't been a hundred percent lately."

The microwave beeped and Piper pulled the steaming plate from the machine. "We can't screw up our lives because of one crazy person. Not when we've worked so hard to rebuild it."

"What about you?" Lou asked Dani. She placed the cat on the floor. "Do you want to leave?"

Dani didn't speak. She eyed her nachos, fingering the edge of a cheese-covered chip.

Piper added sour cream and salsa to her own plate. "Babe, if you want to go, go. I'm not telling you to stay. I just don't think Dennard will risk getting caught."

Dani dragged a chip through a dollop of sour cream thoughtfully. "I *really* can't miss any more work."

Piper cut open and destoned a second avocado. After spooning the green mush onto the plate, she slid it across the island to Lou. "The beef will need ten minutes."

Seeing Dani's expression, Piper frowned. "Hey."

Dani looked up, and Piper reached her hand across the island. Reluctantly, Dani took it.

"Don't worry about this. Diana doesn't deserve an ounce of your stress and worry." Piper squeezed her hand. "We've got this."

Lou thought of Angelo Martinelli bursting through the back gate of her parents' home, a leather-clad nightmare of rage, and the white-flash pop of his gun going off. The sound of a wine glass shattering and her back hitting the surface of the family's moonlit pool.

"This comes with the territory. But we're tough. We can survive anything."

It came with the territory, yes.

But Lou didn't think Piper understood what that meant. Not yet.

36
─────────

She found Konstantine in his bedroom, his legs stretched out in front of him and a book open in his lap. His ankles were crossed as he sipped from a glass of red wine.

He looked up from his book, touching his ear as if it hurt.

"I felt you," he said, placing the wine glass on the bedside table.

"Did you?" She crossed to the bed and sat on its edge.

"Sometimes I can," he said, pulling his ear lobes. "It's like a popping in my ears."

"Dani says that too." Lou wasn't sure if she should take off her boots and leather jacket. Was she going to stay? He looked cozy and occupied. She pushed her sunglasses up onto her head as if in question.

"I was starting to think you wouldn't come," he said.

"King pulled an emergency call."

Konstantine nodded. "He must've seen the news."

"I'm guessing you did, too."

He took a bookmark from the back of the book and slid

it between the open pages. Then he snapped the book shut. "I am well versed in the news. Published and unpublished."

She was sure that was true, and how much news there must be in the world that never reaches the filtered content packaged prettily for public consumption.

"And something interesting happened," he said, laying the book face down and open on the bed.

"What?" Lou asked, reading the cover of the book.

Buonanotte. The author's name was Liane Carmi.

"Is this a romance novel?" Lou asked, surprised. The cover definitely looked romantic.

"I like romance novels," Konstantine said with a wicked grin. "They have happy endings."

She picked up the book, unbothered by the fact she couldn't read the words. Some of them looked familiar, like they might be words borrowed into the English language, but she knew enough about foreign languages to understand that false cognates were common.

"Someone has been trying to expose you," Konstantine said, taking up the wine again.

She put down the book. "What do you mean?"

"Your name and picture have popped up on a few websites. Two news outlets that I own published stories about you. I made a few phone calls and they were taken down. George, one of the editors, says that it was a young woman in leather pants who sold him the story. Maybe the sister?"

"King said they would retaliate," Lou said. "Clearly they're trying to." And in truth, she didn't mind. She would rather Diana blame her for the exposure than Dani or Piper. It felt safer, with herself as the target.

"Are you worried?" Konstantine asked, placing a hand on her thigh. His thumb traced the crease in her jeans.

"I think Diana is more dangerous than Piper realizes."

Lou stood, shrugged out of her leather jacket, and tossed it across the foot of Konstantine's bed.

Then she bent down and undid the laces on her boots. He seemed pleased by this and moved over to make space for her. He even peeled back the covers in a more obvious invitation.

"I must admit, I am surprised you haven't killed her yet," Konstantine said. "But I understand why you haven't."

Lou snorted, sliding in beside him. "Do you?"

"You don't believe you can hunt and kill every monster in this world. Here is another woman who can help. You also value your freedom above all else. You can't imagine stopping someone with the same drive."

Lou wondered if that was it. She had a feeling it might be something more. She searched Konstantine's face. "Are you afraid of her?"

"No," he said, finishing the wine and returning the glass to the opposite table. "She is no match for you."

"You'll jinx me." She pressed herself into his side as he used both his free hands to envelop her. She liked his scent, heady and all-encompassing.

"That's the danger, isn't it?" He retrieved his book and opened it to the bookmarked page. "Even beginners get lucky."

She put her head on his chest, listening to him turn the page every so often, his fingers playing absently in her hair while he read.

Lou was almost asleep when something occurred to her.

"The editor you spoke to, where was he?"

"Hmm?" Konstantine asked, looking up from his book. She felt his warm breath on her face. "The one who spoke to Diana's sister?"

"Yes. Where was that?"

"Oklahoma," Konstantine said. "Why?"

Oklahoma was south of Kansas, where Lou was fairly certain Diana's secret farm was hidden.

"Would you..." She didn't even know how to finish the request. She'd never directly asked anyone for help before.

"Anything," he said without pause. "What do you need?"

"Do you have someone you trust in New Orleans? Maybe four or five people that can follow Dani and Piper around until this is over. It wouldn't hurt to have eyes on Melandra and King, too."

Anyone to buy time, in case I'm too slow to reach them.

"When?"

"Now," she said, lifting up from her warm and comfortable position in the crook of his arm.

Konstantine put the book face down and retrieved his phone without another word.

She stretched out on the bed and watched him make the calls.

The compass inside her was spinning, trying to settle on a location that Lou couldn't yet see, only feel inside her.

Had Blair simply driven across the state line into Oklahoma? Had they hoped to sell the story and settle the score? Or were they already heading south, perhaps as far south as New Orleans?

37

Piper read her class schedule from her laptop while Dani turned a mug of tea in her hands. Piper was trying to decide if she wanted to make herself a cup of mint tea, too. Those nachos were turning in her stomach riotously. If she didn't take measures, it might be a long night of indigestion to look forward to.

"Since I have to go to campus for the lab class on Fridays, I was thinking I could stop by your work after class and we can do lunch before I head to the Quarter. What do you think?"

"A regular Friday lunch date?" Dani asked, taking a sip of tea. "I like it."

Piper got a whiff of the peppermint and her stomach turned.

"It's the only class I couldn't get online." Piper frowned. "But I like science, so I'm not too pissed about it. But a three-hour class every Friday, *gah*. It'll be nice to recharge with you."

She closed her laptop and pushed it onto the coffee table.

"How are you feeling?" she asked.

Dani smiled. "Better."

"Even though Diana is still out there."

Dani looked out over the living room as if it were a vast horizon. "Yeah. I think it's because I made my decision."

Dani snuggled closer, lifting her tea up as she settled in to make sure it wasn't bumped.

"I was having such a hard time because it felt like everything I was doing was losing. That I wasn't good enough. That I was failing to hold it together. But I've changed my mind about that."

Must be nice, Piper thought.

"All those feelings are still there, but I've decided they're bullshit. The only way I can really fail is if I let Petrov and Diana or whoever else comes along take away what I love. I love writing these stories. Uncovering the truth. That's my passion. And if I have to suffer nightmares or convulse on a floor once in a while to make it happen, then that's just how it'll be. But no one is going to take it away from me."

"I'm proud of you," Piper said. She thought this was the better thing to say, though part of her wondered if Dani was being masochistic by clinging so stubbornly to her dream.

"I'm proud of you, too," Dani said, tucked into Piper's side.

Uncomfortable heat spread up the side of Piper's neck. She laughed. "For what?"

"You work so hard. You have your two jobs and you're going to school. You're amazing."

Piper shook her head, as if this would volley the compliment away. Receiving compliments had never felt comfortable, but coming from Dani it was even worse. Part of her retracted, shrinking from the words as if they physically hurt. The other part, as thirsty as a desert plant, stretched forward.

She didn't like that part very much.

"If I'd stayed on track, I'd have a master's degree by now. Or I'd be studying for the bar instead of Biology 201."

"Everyone's life is different." Dani's voice was drowsy with sleep. "You've had a lot you needed to take care of. We're lucky to get a chance at education at all. In some countries—" Dani gasped, bolting upright. "Octavia! No!"

Piper craned her neck in time to see the cat squatting in the kitchen, pissing beside the potted fern.

"Oh geez." Piper took Dani's tea and guided it safely to the coaster on the coffee table, so Dani could leap up and assess the damage.

Dani unwound a wad of paper towels from their dispenser on the wall. "Her litter box is probably full. She's fussy about that."

She's fussy about a lot of things.

Piper was fairly certain Tavi refused to use her litter box if there was *one* turd in it.

"I'll change it." Piper threw back the light blanket and got up.

Dani was already on her hands and knees with the cleaner, spraying the floor and the side of the planter. "Would you? That would be a huge help. Everything is in the closet."

Piper found the pan liners, scooper, and fresh litter in the hall closet outside the bathroom. Not one for scraping or inhaling the scent of cat piss, she gathered up the whole pan liner and double bagged it closed. The pungent smell burned her nose, and she gagged before dumping the fresh litter into the pan, holding her breath throughout.

Octavia meowed from the bathroom door.

"All for you, you princess." She carried the bag past the cat to the front door. She slipped her feet into plastic flipflops, calling over her shoulder, "I'll run this out to the trash. Be right back."

"Thank you so much," Dani said, turning from the

kitchen sink, where she was washing her hands. "I'll have a big kiss for you when you get back."

Piper had more than a kiss in mind. She supposed her eyebrow wag said as much.

Dani's face turned red and a little nervous laugh escaped her. It brightened the dark mood that had hung over them most of the day. Something was weighing on Dani's mind. She hadn't brought it up to Piper yet, so they were in limbo.

In their six months together, Dani had sometimes gotten dark like this, discontent, unpleasable. Piper hadn't known her long enough to know if these moods were part of her natural temperament or if they were the result of her PTSD. Either way, there seemed no remedy for them except to let Dani share—or not—at her own pace.

I don't have much to offer, but I've got time, she thought.

And nothing said "I love you, you're going to be okay" like carrying a bag of cat shit to the dumpster outside.

When Piper stepped outside, she found the night hot and balmy. A sheen of moisture formed along her hairline and the back of her neck before she even reached the dumpster at the edge of the parking lot.

Damn, NOLA, she thought. *Why you gotta be so hot?*

She tossed the bag over her head and listened to it crash into the bin. Up and down the street, soft lamps burned.

She took her first big breath of air.

It smelled like sun-soaked trash, but it was still better than the piss-stained litter box.

Most of the houses in the Garden District had wrought-iron fences enclosing their yards. Half a block up the street, a woman—or man—paused to let their shih tzu piss on the iron rods.

The wind changed and she caught the scent of something sweet. Oleander, maybe.

On the other side of the street a trash can crashed and a

group of kids broke into laughter. A flash of metal sparked in the dark.

What were they swinging? An aluminum bat? A lead pipe?

Whatever it was, it struck the side of the can, spilling the trash. Their laughter rose as they ripped open the bags and kicked trash into the street.

She considered calling after them. *Punk asses.*

But since they had a weapon and she didn't, she decided it was better to go back inside and make out with her girlfriend.

Something slammed into her back. Her skull hit the pavement, ears ringing.

She rolled on her back, her hands going up to protect her head.

Her fear spiked. Her mind vacillated between screaming for Dani or calling out to Lou. Dani might be closer, but Lou would be of more use.

Someone grabbed the front of her shirt and hauled her to a sitting position.

The person wore a ski mask—in this weather, Piper marveled—and head-to-toe black on black.

"Show your face, coward." Piper spit gravel out of her mouth. She thought her lip was busted. She could taste blood as she dragged her tongue across her teeth. All were present and accounted for. "Tired of trash cans already?"

She thought she was talking to one of the kids. Street kids could turn like that. Anything for a laugh or to show off in front of their friends.

"Okay," a mature voice said, and the black ski mask was yanked up.

It wasn't one of the punk kids whacking trash cans. It was Diana. Her face was colder and more ruthless than those kids could ever manage.

"Tell Lou I'm waiting," she said, and slammed her fist into the side of Piper's face.

38

L ou woke to a buzzing sound. Then a light clicked on. Her eyes opened, squinting against the soft glow of the lamp. Konstantine sat on the edge of the bed, the phone pressed to his ear.

"I understand," he said. "Thank you for calling."

He terminated the call, tossing the phone onto the bed. He opened a drawer and pulled out dark jeans. "We need to go."

She sat up, her compass reaching out. But she felt nothing.

"What's happened?"

"Someone, presumably Diana, attacked Piper, and took Daniella."

Lou was out of the bed in a heartbeat. She laced up her boots and threw on her leather jacket.

Konstantine grabbed her arm. "Take me with you. I want to speak to my people."

"Your guys were there?"

"Dani's apartment building was blown up."

Lou's body iced.

"They found Piper unconscious in the parking lot outside. She is still unconscious, but alive."

"Dani?" Lou asked, her voice thick.

"I don't know."

"Your people in New Orleans called you?" She felt her mind trying to complete the scene, understand what was happening.

"No." He released her long enough to pull on pants and a black t-shirt. "There is a chain of command. I usually speak only to the boss of their boss."

Why can't I feel you? Lou thought of Dani. Her heart hammered in her chest. She had a sense of her location, but not her emotions. No fear. No need. She reached out to Piper and found the same.

She hoped they were both unconscious. Not dead.

"Okay. I have my wallet and—"

Lou was already pulling them both through the dark before he finished. She exchanged Italy for a hot, humid night in the New Orleans Garden District. The scent of flowers bloomed bright and instant, mixed with the smell of hot, putrefying garbage.

But both were overshadowed by the tremendous spike in heat.

She stepped away from the dumpster's deep shadows and was hit by a wall of it.

Piper was in the grass, between the street and parking lot. It made Lou instantly think of the pornographers that Diana executed during the raid.

A young girl, no older than sixteen, stood guard over her with an aluminum bat propped against her shoulder. Three guys jumped back when Konstantine stepped into the light.

"Whoa. Dude. Where'd you come from?"

Their eyes shifted to Lou instantly. "Shit."

But Lou didn't care about them. She wanted to see Piper with her own eyes.

She dropped to her knees and pulled Piper up to a sitting position. Her head lolled.

"Piper."

Her face was purple and swollen in two places. It looked like she'd been struck in the forehead and in the eye, which was swollen shut. And her lip was split and bloody.

Lou's anger began to well up inside her, threatening to overtake her senses.

"Piper. Wake up."

"I already tried that," the girl said, pulling a red lollipop out of her mouth. "I think they drugged her."

"What happened?" Lou asked. She saw unflinching eyes and a mischievous grin.

"We came by to check on things and saw this one"—she pointed the bat at Piper—"get jumped. But it was the other girl they wanted. Saw them carry her out and throw her in a truck before the building blew. The cat followed them out. Lucky cat."

Lou looked up and saw Octavia lingering near the dumpster. Meowing uncertainly, as if unsure she could come forward.

The girl snorted. "She's cute now, but don't be fooled. I tried to pick her up and she scratched me."

Konstantine was shoving money into the guys' hands.

"Don't you want to know what direction the truck went?" the girl asked, eyebrows arched. She ran the lollipop along the bottom of her lips.

"It doesn't matter," Lou said.

The girl laughed. "Sure. Whatever you say. Hey, is this girl important to you? I've seen her around the Quarter a lot. For the right price, I can keep an eye on her for you.

Make sure she doesn't run into trouble with psychos anymore."

Lou didn't answer.

"Alice," Konstantine said, and shoved a wad of cash twice as thick as the boys' into her hands. "Thank you."

"I go by Bane, actually," she said, flicking the sucker between her teeth. "As in 'bane of your existence.'"

Konstantine's smile twitched. "Bane."

She looked at the wadded-up bills in her fist again before flicking her eyes back up to Konstantine's. "Anytime, boss. Let's go, boys."

She took off across the street with the guys obediently in tow. She swung her bat one more time, knocking a trash can into the street. The boys behind rolled it for good measure.

"She won't wake up," Lou said. She heard the fear in her voice and hated it.

"She will," Konstantine said, kneeling beside her. "Let's get her somewhere safe."

Meow.

They turned to see the Russian Blue inching tentatively toward Piper.

Meow.

"Grab the cat. It's Dani's." Lou lifted Piper into her arms. Her shoulder protested, but she ignored it.

Konstantine crept toward the animal, speaking sweetly to it. "*Vieni qui, micia-gattina. Vieni.*"

ALICE BAINES STOOD IN THE DARKNESS, ROLLING THE lollipop in her mouth. She watched the woman pull the blonde into her arms while Konstantine coaxed the cat forward. And it *was* Konstantine. She didn't care what Micah said about the boss of all bosses being too important to mess with pissants like them.

He'd told the boys his name was Georgio. That he was just here to settle the account.

Bullshit.

Because it wasn't about them being pissants. It was about the woman, the boogeyman, the *strega* Bane had heard so much about. The Ravengers passed stories about her like they passed joints. And threaded through every story was the same theory: Konstantine and the woman were linked. Maybe she was the devil. Maybe he'd sold his soul for all the power and money he has. Whatever the reason, where you found one, you found the other. And Alice wanted to know if there was something to all those stories.

"Bane—" Micah began.

"Shhh. I told you, not a word."

"But—"

She shoved the head of the bat into his stomach. "*Shut it.*"

Silence.

Alice squinted harder, trying to keep the woman and Konstantine in clear view.

As soon as Konstantine's hand was on her shoulder, they disappeared.

One minute they were at the edge of the streetlight. The next, nada. The grass was bare.

No Konstantine. No mysterious woman in black. No blonde. Even the cat was gone. And it didn't matter what direction Alice searched, there was nothing to be found.

And it wasn't like there wasn't enough light. The burning building made it as bright as day. People from the adjacent houses were trailing out into the night to see what had happened.

A fire truck wailed in the distance, coming closer, drawn to the blown-out building like moths to a flame. And a burning building was all they'd find.

Not the woman who could disappear in the dark and be

anywhere she wanted with a simple thought. Woman. *Strega*. Devil.

"Badass," she whispered with a sigh.

She wished she could do shit like that. Some people had all the luck.

39

Piper was stretched long on her sofa, a blanket thrown over her legs. Lou sat on the floor beside her, staring at her as if this intense gaze would wake her up.

The Russian Blue wandered from room to room, meowing indignantly to anyone who'd listen. She was obviously displeased with the surroundings and the sudden displacement.

It looked like she was searching for Dani.

Dani.

Lou opened and closed her fists.

"I should go."

"They'll be expecting that," Konstantine said. He stood in Piper's kitchen, searching the cabinets for a mug. He found one to the left of the stove and filled it with fresh coffee. He placed this on the table for Lou. "She wants you to come unprepared."

Hold on, Lou thought. *Hold on, Dani.*

"Drink this." He put the mug in her hand.

"I thought this was for her," Lou said.

"Do you often pour beverages down the throats of unconscious women?" His lips quirked with a smile. "How strange Americans are."

"What if this is a coma?" Lou placed the untouched coffee on the table. "What if she's going to die from this?"

"Her heart rate and breathing are fine. She might have a concussion and an ugly black eye. But I don't think she will die from a punch in the face."

She didn't need to say the obvious. They'd probably hit Dani too. Knocking her unconscious would make sure they could get her out of the building without a fight.

If they'd left Piper conscious, she could've called Lou, alerted the authorities. Or possibly she could've gotten a plate number or vehicle description.

But why leave Piper alive at all?

A knock came at the door and Konstantine rose to answer it. Melandra and King entered the apartment.

"Me first," Melandra said, seeing Piper on the sofa. She elbowed her way past King.

"What is that?" Lou nodded toward the syringe in King's hand.

"Ask me no questions and I'll tell you no lies." He slipped the capped syringe back into his pocket.

"Adrenaline," Konstantine wagered. "By the look of it."

King shrugged, as if to say *maybe*.

Mel knelt in front of the girl and uncapped a small tube. She waved it under Piper's nose.

Piper's eyes fluttered, lazily. She groaned.

"Hey, baby. Welcome back." Mel touched Piper's cheek and cooed. "Ouch. Look at your face. I'm going to get some ice for that. Lou, open that window and get some air in here."

Lou opened the window as instructed.

Piper blinked, sitting up. She groaned, placing one hand over her eye and hissing. "Oh god. I'm going to puke."

Konstantine produced a trash can. White plastic with

blue birds painted on the side. Given the tissues inside, Lou suspected it came from the adjacent bathroom.

Piper locked eyes with Lou, holding the trash can but not using it.

"Would you rather have this?" She offered Piper the coffee, but she shook her head.

"I'm really dizzy. What happened?"

"What do you remember?" King asked.

Piper looked at her couch as if she'd never seen it. "I...I don't know. I paid for my classes. For the fall. I have a biology lab on Friday. It's three hours long."

"After that," King pressed on.

Piper searched Lou's face as if the answers were written there. Then, when those features told her nothing, she looked from Konstantine to King.

Mel reappeared with a towel-wrapped ice pack and held it against Piper's face. "That's going to hurt tomorrow."

"It hurts now," Piper mumbled through her fat lip.

Meow.

Piper twitched at the sound, seeing Octavia wander into the living room, tail flicking.

"Hey, Tavi," she said.

Then her face pinched.

"Wait. What is she doing here?" Piper's face screwed up with concentration again. "I took out the cat litter."

The ice fell from her hands. "Dani! Where's Dani?"

"Diana took her," Lou said plainly. There was no way to blunt this truth. "And I'm assuming she's the reason your face looks the way it does."

I'm going to kill her.

Piper stood on wobbly legs. She fell forward and Lou caught her by the arms.

"Is she, oh god is she—" Piper began.

"They took her. Presumably alive."

Piper seized her wrist. "Please, go. *Now.* You have to go get her."

Lou stepped back, ready to do just that.

Piper's hold tightened. "No, wait. Diana said something." Her face screwed up in concentration again. "She said...she said she'd be waiting for you."

"Of course she is." King was leaning into the kitchen island, jaw working. Lou saw and understood his fury.

"This is my fault," Piper said. "If I'd said yes to going into hiding, if I—"

King shook his head. "It's too late for that now."

"Robert." Melandra scowled at him. "Self-righteousness never helped anybody."

"Yeah, all right."

Piper held on to her like she was flotsam in a large and raging sea. With Konstantine's help, they got her back onto the sofa, but she wouldn't let go.

"It's not your fault," Lou said.

"Whose is it? Yours? You said you'd protect her."

"Blame won't help either." Melandra adjusted the towel and repositioned the ice pack on Piper's face. "We stick together. That's what we do."

Piper's gaze was fixed on Lou. "Get her back, Louie."

Tears sprang to her eyes. "*Please.* I'll forgive you for choosing that psychopath over me if you just get Dani back."

She finally released her, and Lou stepped back into the shadow-soaked corner of the room.

Konstantine caught her wrist before she could slip. "I won't ask to go. I know I will only distract you and slow you down, but she will be ready for you. She might have the building rigged to blow. Or she might place a sniper on an adjacent roof. You have to be ready for anything."

"I don't think she would blow up two buildings in one night."

"That is not a bet I would take," Konstantine whispered, his face drawn. "Be careful."

"Keep them safe," Lou said. "For all we know she planted explosives here before taking Dani."

Konstantine's lips quirked. "I've already checked."

"Post guards outside to watch the streets."

Konstantine's smile deepened.

"You already did that, too."

Then the smile was gone. "I'm not worried about them. I'm worried about you. It's you she wants, really."

"How can you know that?" Lou asked. It seemed to her that Dani was the target.

Konstantine sighed. "Because a woman like Diana, I can understand."

40

Once Piper's apartment bled away, Lou found herself in the hidden armory beneath her kitchen island. The smell of sawdust tickled her nose as she took stock of its shelves. She decided on a shoulder holster with twin Berettas and a hip holster with twin Brownings. She pulled Kevlar sleeves up onto her arms and fixed a bulletproof vest snug across her chest.

Not that that helped much last time, she thought. Being shot in Julia Street station had made her very aware of a vest's limitations.

Pulling on the jacket, her shoulder ached. A throbbing stab shot up her neck into the base of her skull. She considered taking a Vicodin, but immediately decided against it. She wanted her mind sharp for this fight.

Lou took a breath and pulled the string, extinguishing the overhead light.

The darkness pressed in against her as she exhaled, slowly, the sound of her breath filling her ears.

Then she was outside. The wind was cutting across her cheek and pulled tears from her eyes. When she blinked, she saw the city skyline. She gazed out over the lights, trying to place the view. She didn't recognize it.

"I knew you'd come," a voice drawled. At the edge of the darkness, a form shifted, stepping into the light. "Do you know where we are?"

"No," she admitted.

Diana inched forward, light cutting across her cheek, showing only the right side of her face. "We're on the Plaza building. Funny that your headquarters should be in New Orleans and yet you don't know this building. *Is* New Orleans really your headquarters?"

Lou said nothing. She was trying to find Dani. Her compass said she was here, that she was close, but Lou couldn't see her.

"Where is she?"

"It's dark up here, right?" Diana laughed. "I made it that way just in case Blair is right. I want to see what you can really do."

Lou searched the top of the building, but the dark was absolute. She saw no shapes, no shifting bodies. Only that bare sliver of concrete lit by the single lamp.

"Blair said that I'd be giving you the advantage," Diana whispered conspiratorially. "Because she believes you can move through the dark like it's a doorway. And I thought Spencer was the one with the imagination."

Diana snorted at her own joke.

"But you can't see in the dark, can you?"

Diana stepped back into the darkness, disappearing.

Lou froze on the spot, closing her eyes. There was no point in leaving them open if this was the game Diana wanted to play.

She searched the dark with her compass.

Dani, Dani, Dani, Daniella Allendale.

She felt the air shift on her right, knew the attack was

coming on that side, but it would be too slow. Lou was already releasing her hold on the darkness and sinking through.

The night disappeared for a moment, like passing behind a brick wall, a blessed reprieve, and then broke open again.

Diana laughed. "Oh, you're good."

Heat swelled on Lou's back and she turned at the last second, seeing the glint of a blade before the darkness swelled again.

This time icy fire sliced through her upper arm, drawing blood.

Another slash crossed her Kevlar sleeves. She took this opportunity to rotate her wrist and seize the hand holding it.

She yanked them forward, but it wasn't Diana. It was the leather-clad sister, Blair.

Her eyes were hidden behind night vision goggles, the mechanical eyes comically large and insectile.

Blair yanked herself out of Lou's grip and sidestepped into the dark.

Something slammed into her bulletproof vest, making her pivot her body. Fabric ripped. She reached out to grab the attacker but her hand swiped air.

Another cold flash of a blade sliced across the top of her thigh. An icy, electric fire preceded the warm welling of blood. She felt it gush up between the flesh and fabric, soaking her pants.

Diana laughed.

The laugh was too far away for her to be the one who'd cut her. There were at least three of them up here.

A foot slammed into Lou's torso, knocking the air from her. She went down to one knee.

"I'm disappointed in you," Diana said, her voice disembodied and echoing. "I thought you'd understand how important my work is. You were supposed to understand. You were supposed to *get* it."

Her shoulder was engulfed in pain. Lou struggled to draw a breath.

"And what's worse, I tried to expose you, yet somehow, every story I leaked, every picture I showed, just disappeared. Why?"

Lou managed to get to her feet again, but red crowded her vision.

"Why do you get to keep your name, your secrecy, but I can't have mine? Isn't the work I'm doing important too?"

"Yes," Lou said, thinking of the little boy who'd held so tight to her neck.

"Then how could you? Not one of them, King or those wannabe sleuths or my sister, or Spencer. None of them understand what our work means to us. No one but you. How could you?"

Diana stepped into the light, pushing her own night vision goggles up onto her head.

And she wasn't alone. She held Dani close to her chest, pinning her with one arm. But Dani's eyes were closed, her expression slack.

She's dead, Lou thought, fear ripping through her. "You killed her."

"No," Diana said, rolling her eyes. "She's just very, *very* sleepy. I didn't want her flailing around on the roof, you know? It wasn't safe."

She snorted, laughing at her joke. But it was cut short by an explosion of anger contorting her features.

"You let her expose me." Diana yanked on a fistful of Dani's hair. No reaction. "You did this."

Lou didn't bother to explain that she hadn't given the order. She didn't control her people—and now she realized, with fear banging at the base of her throat, they *were* her people—like Diana did.

Her leg was going numb. She was starting to wonder if the cut in the thigh might've gotten her femoral artery.

Diana's face fell. The anger folded into something saccharin. A parody of emotion. "I'm so disappointed, Lou. I was starting to think we could be really great, you and me."

Diana doesn't feel anything. Anger, maybe, she realized. *Frustration.*

But she had none of the fear clogging Lou's mind. She had no one she was ready to take a bullet for.

Diana seemed to read her mind and didn't like it. Her face screwed up with fresh irritation. "Let's find out if you can really do what my sister says. This building is forty-five stories high, five hundred and thirty feet tall. It's dark on this side of it. Look. Go ahead, look down the side. I won't push."

Lou didn't.

"I'm *not* going to push you. *I'm* the trustworthy one here."

Lou glanced over the side.

It was dark, but not completely. Lights from the city reflected off the many windows and ricocheted into the night.

"See, I didn't push you. Yet." She snorted, her delight returning. "Here's what's going to happen."

Lou shifted forward, wanting to put a hand on Dani—just a hand would be enough to get her off this roof and away from this dangerous game Diana wanted to play.

But Diana yanked her back, shoving a gun into Dani's forehead. "You're not faster than a bullet, are you?"

"No," Lou said. When in truth, she thought, *Sometimes.*

But she saw Piper's crestfallen face flash in her mind, and sometimes didn't feel good enough.

Diana trained the pistol on her instead. "Here's your choice. One: I put a bullet in her head and then one in yours.

Or two: I push her off the building and you jump off after her."

"You want to kill her."

"Hell *yes*." Diana laughed, high and hysterical. "Without a doubt. The only question I have is what to do about you. Do I toss her over, or shoot her, and then we fight it out on this roof? I already have two people with guns on you, by the way. Or would you like to go over the edge with her and save me the trouble?"

Lou saw a red dot scurry over her leg, abdomen, and chest. The fact she could no longer see it meant it must be higher. Probably trained at her head.

Diana's widening grin certainly suggested so. "No bullet-proof vests for a face, huh? Shame."

Lou's vision darkened at the corners again, another pulsing threat of unconsciousness.

I'm running out of time.

"What'll it be, Louie Thorne?"

Lou had never tried to shift while falling. She wasn't sure she could do it.

She wasn't even sure that the darkness could be collected and used in such a way. Where would it spit her out? Above another pavement?

If they died, if both she and Dani splattered on the concrete below, at least Piper would understand that she'd tried.

I tried to save her, she thought.

Because Lou knew she'd rather die trying to save Dani's life than look Piper in the eyes knowing she'd failed her so completely.

"I'll go over with her," she said.

Diana laughed like Lou had made the best joke in the world. She threw back her head and gave all of herself to it. "Will you?"

"Yes."

"You're serious right now." Diana laughed. "Oh god, Louie. It's a shame you're about to die. It really is. You're the most interesting person I've met in years. Possibly ever."

And if I survive this, I'll be the last person you ever meet, Lou thought. Because it couldn't end any other way. If Diana was alive, they'd never be safe.

Piper, Dani, King, or Mel.

A strange longing fluttered in her chest. She tried to find a word for it, but all that came was *affection*, and even that wasn't quite right.

Lou had known in theory that she'd liked her little crew. It was a dim acknowledgment that if they needed her she would come, without question. But now it was more than that. Diana had put them into sharp relief.

They weren't simply a way to pass the time.

They'd given her a reason to go on.

After Angelo. After all the hunting and longing and anger —they'd given her something to hold on to. The way she'd hung on to her father, his strength, as her growing power to slip threatened to tear her apart.

And here was some asshole trying to take it. *Again.*

That old, familiar ache rose up in her. The one she'd been waiting for.

Diana grinned as if she'd seen the shift herself. "Look at that smile. Are we about to have fun, you and me? You're starting to look fun."

Diana shoved Dani hard, the girl's body bowing as if punched. Her spine rolled over the concrete edge, tipping dangerously into the sky.

Without thinking, Lou shot her arm out. She grabbed a fistful of shirt and felt the fabric rip.

Instead of pulling her back onto the roof, to darkness and safety, they were pitched forward by Dani's weight.

Then hands shoved hard into Lou's back and over the side they went.

The wind was a force, tearing at their faces, their clothes. Lou managed to pull Dani against her, but that drop-sink feeling in her gut multiplied.

Come on, come on, come on, her mind begged. *Give us a soft landing. If we have to fall, give us somewhere soft.*

She knew she had six seconds at most, falling from this height. But she'd never believed herself fully in control of her trajectory. Now was a hell of a time to prove otherwise.

Five...four...

Please...

Three...two...

Oh oh...

One.

LOU EXPECTED DEATH. SHE EXPECTED HER BRAINS splattered on the business district sidewalk for some unfortunate soul in an ironed suit to find.

But she was slowing down.

Or at least, it felt like she was slowing down. The wind that had been terrorizing her a moment before lessened.

She opened her eyes to see the city of New Orleans was gone. The lights of the business district had been snuffed out. She was in the dark place. *Her* dark place.

In the world between worlds.

But slowing down wasn't the same as stopping, and after this heartbeat pause, the dark broke open again.

It wasn't concrete that slammed into Lou's back. It was water.

It was as if a horse had kicked her. The force was enough to knock the air out of her, even with her vest taking the brunt of the impact. Dani's body was cradled against the front of her torso and mostly spared.

Lou began to sink into dark depths.

She kicked for the surface in a circle, trying to get a sense of what body of water they were in.

Fresh. No salt.

She felt that pull at her leg, the membrane thinning again. An offer to sidestep this world into La Loon.

Lou broke the surface, checking to make sure Dani's head was above the water.

"No," she said, spitting water from her mouth and kicking her legs as if to free them. "Not now."

She paddled a circle, searching for shore.

And there it was. A familiar and welcoming sight. It was the shore of her lake, her place of eternal night.

"Dani, can you swim?"

No answer.

"Dani?" Lou turned the girl in the water, checked breathing and pulse. She was alive, but her eyes were closed and she remained unresponsive. Whatever Dani needed to wake up, she couldn't get it here.

One problem at a time.

Lou lifeguard-dragged Dani onto the muddy bank. This was the first time she'd pulled an unconscious body *out* of her lake, rather than into it.

On the shore, she panted, catching her breath. Her fingers sank into the mud, cold against her palms. A slight breeze chilled the droplets on her neck. Water dripped from her nose, splattering the side of Dani's cheek. Wind whispered through the trees.

She dragged her hand down her face, clearing it of water.

Then she laughed. A high, hysterical sound.

She couldn't stop until her throbbing shoulder made it impossible to draw a breath.

Her body was a buzzing tank of adrenaline—and she needed every drop of it to take on Diana.

Go now, she thought. *Right now, before she has a chance to understand what happened.*

PIPER PACED THE FLOOR, BACK AND FORTH, UNTIL IT threatened to leave a grooved trail in the hardwood. Her face hurt. Her body hurt. She wanted to skin Diana Dennard alive.

Every time the woman's face flashed across her mind, a murderous fury consumed her, heating her whole body. But she wasn't angry for herself. She was angry for Dani. The sick truth, she knew, was that if Diana had only hurt her, she wouldn't be mad at all. She'd be terrified.

And she was pissed about that too.

"They'll be okay," Melandra said. She turned over another tarot card on Piper's coffee table.

Piper didn't like that Five of Wands. "Is that what the cards say?" she asked with a derisive snort.

"That's what *I* say," Mel said.

"Lou is very capable," King added, opening the carton of pork lo mein in his hand and dumping it onto a plate. "Would you like some of this?"

Piper shook her head. She couldn't imagine doing something as simple and controlled as sitting down and eating right now. She felt like her skin was trying to crawl off her bones.

Her ears popped and she staggered.

Lou was on her hands and knees, crouching over Dani on the other side of King's coffee table. They were both soaked, Lou's hair sticking to her face.

Dani wasn't moving.

"Oh god, is she—"

"She's breathing," Lou said. "Just unconscious. Where's Konstantine?"

"He stepped outside to make some calls. What happened?" Piper demanded.

"Diana pushed us off a building."

"*What?*" Piper, Mel, and King asked in unison.

Mel left the room before appearing with three large towels. She offered one to Lou, who began to dab at her face and hair, shaking out her jacket.

King sat down on the couch. "Is Diana—"

"I'm going back," Lou said.

"To kill her?" Piper asked. To her surprise, she was suddenly afraid for Lou, her anger completely overshadowed. If Diana was capable of throwing Lou off a building—Lou, her invincible, faultless Lou—what else could that woman do?

Lou flicked her eyes up to meet Piper's.

Piper's stomach dropped.

"Yes," Lou said. "Like you wanted me to since day one."

Before Piper could say anything, apologize or explain, or even hug Lou, Lou was gone, leaving a mess of water in her wake.

"It's not just water." Mel turned the towel in the light, frowning. "There's blood. A lot of it."

They searched Dani but didn't find a scratch on her.

"It must be Lou," King said solemnly. "Something must've happened *before* they were thrown off the building."

Don't you die, Piper prayed. *Don't die and I swear to God, I'll apologize for everything. I'll stop being a whiny little ass and make it all up to you, Lou. I swear. Just don't you dare die.*

41

"What do you mean, she never came down?" Diana spat, whirling on the sidewalk.

The New Orleans humidity made the hair around her face curl. Sweat was beginning to bead in her body's creases, her elbows, knees, pits, and neck. She hated this place.

She searched the sidewalk stretching in either direction, disbelieving. But there were no bodies. There wasn't so much as a drop of blood. The sidewalk was unblemished, as long as one didn't count the crushed paper to-go cups in the gutter and the black gum ground into crevices by passing shoes.

There was absolutely no sign of two women hitting the pavement at all. And she'd had a lookout on the ground the whole time, so it wasn't a question of a cleanup crew. Lou might have a full support team, an organization capable of removing all evidence of her existence if it came to that, but they'd have at least *seen* the bodies being carried away.

People can't just disappear from the air, she thought. *Unless she can fly.*

"I told you," Blair hissed in her ear. "I know what I saw. Now you're fucked."

Blair punched Diana's chest hard enough to knock her back. Her boots stumbled along the pavement before she regained lost ground.

The fear climbing up the back of her neck bloomed to rage. She whirled, ready to throw her own punch until she saw the tears standing out in her sister's eyes.

"What's wrong with you?" Diana asked, deflating. "Pull yourself together."

"She's going to kill you," Blair said, lip trembling. "She's going to *kill* you."

Diana looped an arm around the girl's neck. "She can try."

Blair sobbed against her.

But her words were absent of their usual bravado. If Blair was right, if Lou could appear and disappear at will, then—

I want what she has.

Blair screamed, her shrill cry splitting Diana's ears, setting them to ringing. Her grip tightened on Diana but it made no difference.

She was torn from Diana's arms and thrown. She rolled, tumbling along the pavement before crashing into the side of the building. The wind from her rolling body scattered the trash in the gutter.

Diana already knew who she would see before the hand closed over her throat.

Murderous eyes the color of fire met hers.

Even in her periphery, she saw Blair pulling her gun, her crew lunging forward.

Too slow, she thought.

And they were.

The hot, rank streets of downtown New Orleans were replaced with resplendent pine. It reminded Diana of the Christmas tree farm their parents had taken them to as children each Thanksgiving weekend. Blair balling up a handful of snow and tossing it at her, laughing.

So long ago. Another life.

Diana's knees gave in the shift, the fluid in her ears trembling, contributing to her dizziness. But the hand on her throat held fast, keeping her on her feet before a punch slammed into the side of her face.

Pain bloomed red and fragrant across her cheek. She hit the earth like a rock. Her teeth cracked on stone. Mud filled her mouth.

She spat and held up a hand. "Wait!"

Lou's leg lifted, slamming down on Diana's knee. Something snapped and pain radiated down to her toes and up through her chest. Her heart stuttered and all the air left her.

Thought was obliterated from her mind.

There was no mind, only the body. Only pain.

Some aware, ever-awake part of her knew that the screaming animal in the distance was her.

Fists gathered up her shirt, hauling her limp body up to a sitting position. Any movement in the knee was enough to make her vision blur.

"Is this what you wanted?" Lou shook her until Diana's eyes fluttered open and she was forced to meet that black gaze. "You wanted me to prove what I was? Do you still want to see what I can do?"

Her voice was calm. There was no anger in it. No fury. The pure, impenetrable reserve was like a patina of ice, a tundra extending beneath an empty, starless sky.

Lou slammed her against the ground, once, twice. On the third time, Diana's head hit something hard and it felt like the back of her skull split open. On the fifth slam, she bit her tongue. Blood bloomed in her mouth, spilling over her lip and chin.

"How?" Diana asked, spitting blood. It was warm on her

skin. It was filling her mouth so fast she was forced to swallow it down or risk choking. "*How?*"

Her mind raced with possibilities. Government serum, some top-secret program that turned assassins into dangerous, obedient creatures. Fulfilling agendas on some political party's whim.

She suddenly, desperately, wanted to know who Konstantine was. Had he given her this gift?

"It runs in my family," Lou said.

Diana struggled to meet her gaze. But her eyes wouldn't focus. It was genetic?

No. No. "No."

Lou released her. "I thought you wanted to help the children, but this was about you."

The children? Who cared about children? Hurt kids grow up to hurt other kids. Didn't she know that very well? That boy Diana had seen in Lou's arms was just going to be another rapist, another pedophile.

And this bitch had the gall to suggest that Diana was the clueless one?

Diana laughed, a low, throaty sound. She turned and spit blood onto the ground. As she did, she thought she saw a tooth in the mud. A small fleck of enamel. One swipe of her tongue told her all of hers were accounted for.

Someone else's then. Was this a graveyard?

She looked around, saw the dark water and endless forest and what she didn't see. Any sign of civilization. No lights or smoke. No salvation.

She met Lou's eyes.

"Why should you have it?"

"I don't know. My aunt could do it too."

"Family heirlooms." Diana gave herself over to laughter. It sounded hysterical even to her. "If you want to kill me, kill me. Because I won't stop until I have what you have. If I have to slit your throat and drink all of your blood, I'll do it."

"I know," Lou said.

That was when the gun appeared, as if it had always been in Lou's right hand.

Diana had only a moment to register the cool muzzle pressing into the stretched skin of her forehead before even the dark forest blinked out.

42

Diana weighed nearly nothing. It was weird when that happened, when a body with so much weight to it one moment became a husk the next. Lou wondered if the soul, in fact, held all the gravity of a person. Or if humans were soulless, perhaps the weight came from the burden of living.

She walked out into the cold water slowly, Diana floating behind her until the depth was chest high. Her boots sank into the mud with each step. Her teeth were chattering. Her limbs weak.

Sleepiness pressed itself against the edge of her vision.

Almost done, she assured herself. *Just a little more.*

Still she dove, pulling the corpse under with her.

When the purple waters gave way to red and she found the embankment rising, she floated the body to shore. No sign of the reptilian orcas. In the distance, near the yellow mountains, she thought she saw the small cut of a fin. Perhaps that was their choice hunting location this evening.

Jabbers was already on the embankment, sitting on her haunches, chewing her webbed paw like a cat. She rolled those eyes up to Lou's as if expecting her. She was more than a little interested in the body she brought with her.

Jabbers' eyes tracked the corpse as Lou dumped it onto the shore, then turned to Lou. It was as if those eyes said, *This is new.*

Or maybe it was blood-drained Lou's imagination. Maybe she was projecting and Jabbers couldn't tell the difference between a female corpse and a male one.

"I know," Lou said with a tired laugh, walking backward into the water. Blair's and Spencer's faces flashed in her mind. "And there will be more."

WITH WHAT WAS LEFT OF HER STRENGTH, SHE SLIPPED through the shadow of a tall, proud evergreen and onto the bench seat of a moving truck.

Ahead of her, the yellow dash of the centerline ticked out the seconds, a headlight painting the black concrete bright. Blair was behind the wheel, one hand resting on it, the other on the stick shift protruding from the wide floorboard in front of the bench seat.

As soon as Lou appeared, her boot came down hard on the brake, pitching Lou forward into the dust-coated dashboard.

She was winded on impact, her chest connecting hard with the plastic casing of the dash. Slowly, she pushed herself back against the seat, but it was too late. Her hand was empty. The gun had fallen to the floorboard and her upper body was numb from the blow.

Breathe, she commanded. *Breathe.*

Her chest remained compressed and unforgiving.

Blair pointed a Glock at Lou's face, her pulse visibly jumping in her throat.

Lou still couldn't breathe. Her limbs were suddenly too

cold to move. And the deep shadows pressing in from the corners of her vision, overtaking her sight in undulating waves, were not the kind she could command.

Blood loss, she thought vaguely, her last thought before passing out.

Lou heard the beeping first. A slow, steady *beep beep beep*.

Something was up her nose and she pulled it out, detesting the feel of anything against her face. Plastic tubing came away in her hand. More, she soon realized, was affixed to her left arm.

The blurry lights cleared and her bed, the stiff hospital linens, and the low light came into view.

She thought maybe she'd slipped from the truck into Konstantine's apartment, as she'd done on the brink of death before.

But the nurses outside her room were speaking English. Perhaps it was King, then, who had hauled her to the blood supply she so desperately needed.

Then she saw her, still in her leather pants and studded boots. One leg was thrown over her knee as her unflinching eyes regarded her.

"We're still in Louisiana," Blair said. "If you're curious."

"You could've killed me and left me in a ditch." Lou's voice rasped, breaking at the ends. She needed water.

"I thought about it when you slumped over in my seat," Blair said with a flick of her eyebrow. "I'm still thinking about it."

Lou leaned back against the pillow and mashed the call button on her plastic bedrails. Blair must've seen her do it. If she was worried Lou might call for help, she showed no signs.

"But I don't think I can walk away without answers," she admitted. "And *boy* do I have questions."

"Like?" Lou prompted.

"Is Diana dead?"

"Yes."

"Did you do it?"

"Yes."

Blair didn't look surprised by this. She nodded once, a short jerk as if checking an unseen box.

"Were you planning to kill her from the beginning? Were you just fucking with us?"

"No." It hurt Lou's throat to speak. "She didn't leave me a choice."

Blair's eyes flicked down and to the side. It looked like she was having her own private consultation. "My sister is...*was* like that. She had a way of boxing people into corners they couldn't get out of."

A short black woman pushed open the door, knocking on it as she did. "Good morning, miss. Glad to see you're awake."

"Can I have some water? Please."

"Sure thing. And I'll tell the doctor that you're awake. He'll wanna have a chat with you about what happened. Your hero could only tell us so much."

When she closed the door, Lou arched a brow at Blair. "Hero?"

She shrugged. "I told them I found you on the side of the road."

She didn't speak again until the nurse left her with a Styrofoam cup of water, a straw, and assurances that someone would be back soon.

As the door clicked shut, Blair asked, "Can you really do what I think you can do?"

Lou continued to drink her water, her gaze steady over the rim of the cup.

"Right." Blair laughed, a tired, humorless sound. "You know, I don't think it was the questions or the curiosity that stopped me from killing you. I think it was the blonde."

The hair on the back of Lou's neck rose.

"What's her name? Your little sidekick? The squirrelly one?"

Lou said nothing.

"It was how she looks at you. I know that look. It's how I look—*used to look*—at my sister, before things got bad between us. I couldn't kill you knowing that someone loves you that much."

She rubbed the scrunched skin between her brows.

"When Dee disappeared, I was only eight. She was my world, you know? Everything she did was the coolest. When she started painting her nails, when she started dancing to MTV videos in the living room, mastering the choreo, when she would walk down to the gas station with her friends to buy soda and candy bars. I wanted to do everything with her. Then she didn't come home…"

Her voice trailed away.

"I mean, her body came back. *Someone* came back. My parents put her back in her room and called her Diana, but it wasn't my sister. Somehow she'd been replaced by this other creature. My sister had been funny and *fun* and kind, and the girl who replaced her…"

She searched for the words.

"It was like someone had taken Diana and scooped out her insides. Everything that was her was replaced by this insatiable hunger. And no matter what you said, or did, or gave her, it was never enough. Never."

Blair ran a hand along the back of her neck, massaging the muscles there.

"I think I was hoping that someday she would really be able to put it all behind her and we could build a life. Maybe that life would never be as great as what we started with, but it would be a life. But after she finished Winter, I realized how stupid I'd been. It was in her eyes. One look and I just knew. She'd finally gotten everything she wanted, but the hollowness was still there. And then she killed Spencer. *Spencer.* He'd been so loyal to her. If you can do that to someone who loves you so much—there's no coming back."

She looked up, finally meeting Lou's gaze.

"I guess I'm telling you all this because I want to understand, Lou. What the hell happened? Why couldn't she stop? *Why* didn't she come back?"

Lou looked at her blood-crusted knuckles and scarred arms. She thought of her own losses.

It had been one terrible night, but it'd been a clean break and she'd been saved from the worst of it when her father lifted her from their patio and threw her into the pool, knowing it would save her life. Angelo and his men could have—would have—done more, but they hadn't had the chance.

More than that, her landing had been soft. In the wake of her loss, she'd been folded into her aunt's arms. A kind, loving aunt who knew her and her abilities better than anyone. She'd been able to help her in ways that even her father hadn't managed.

Diana had been in the shed for weeks at the hands of the man who'd kidnapped her—and then Winter had come after her. The prolonged pain of what must've been done to her...

Lou licked her dry lips. "Maybe what happened to her was worse than what happened to me."

"How did you do it?" Blair asked. When Lou said nothing, she added, "How did you move on?"

"I haven't."

"But you have a life. You have people you love and who care about you. You don't push them away or use them as a means to an end. If someone comes for them, you blow them away. You might still go after assholes, but you do it for a reason that's not just about you, right?"

Lou was stuck on the phrase *people you love*.

"You might still be dealing with the shit that happened to you, but you built a life around all that darkness. How? *How?*"

The desperation in Blair's eyes hurt to look at.

Lou thought, *I don't know*. She said, "I'm sorry."

Blair sat back in her chair, tears in her eyes. "I forgive you."

Lou's throat squeezed.

"It was only a matter of time before she lost control and hurt a good person. *Spencer* was a good person. Hell, maybe she would've killed me. I guess I should be thanking you. But you probably want to make sure I'll never hurt your people either. I won't, but I understand if you need to be sure."

"No," Lou said.

Blair nodded, a tight, strangled sound slipping past her quivering lips. "It would've been easier if you just killed me. What comes next will be harder."

A rough knock rapped against the door and a black man in a white lab coat pushed it open. "Good afternoon, ladies. Mind if I come in for a chat?"

Blair stood, pushing back the chair. "I'm leaving, actually."

The doctor and nurse shuffled out of the way, clearing her path to the door.

"Blair," Lou called out to her. "What will you do now?"

With one hand on the door frame, Blair quirked a smile. "What I should've done a long time ago. What I kept begging my sister to do."

She tapped the doorway once, as if for luck.

"Move on."

43

P iper sniffed, rummaging through her dresser trying to find something for Dani to wear and finding it difficult. Her shirts were too small to accommodate Dani's ample chest and her pants too tight for her butt.

Meanwhile, voices warred in her head.

Maybe she can trade the Lexus for clothes. Or get her loaded parents to replenish her wardrobe.

Don't be like that. She just lost everything. Now is not the time to be petty.

At least all Piper had to worry about were the clothes and the cat. King, she knew, was working with the police department to create a decent cover story for the arson. With his connections, he was the most likely to throw suspicion off of Dani and onto Diana.

"We're sticking to the truth," he'd announced before leaving to meet up with Investigator Dick White.

What version of the truth did he plan to sell them, Piper wondered.

Good thing it's August, Piper thought glumly. *She'll just have to wear my night shirts and boxers.*

She wiped her running nose on her sleeve, and the pressure between her ears popped.

Still elbows deep in her dresser, she turned and found Lou standing in the dark corner of her bedroom. Her hair was wet and she smelled like soap.

"Is Dennard dead?" Piper asked.

Of all the things to say. How are you? Are you okay? I'm sorry I was an asshole. Thank you for saving Dani's life and jumping off a freaking building for her.

Lou looked paler than usual but her voice was steady. "Yes."

"Like you saw her *dead* dead? I don't want any of this villain-comes-back-in-the-eleventh-hour shit we get in the movies."

"I shot her and dragged her corpse into the lake. Last time I saw her, she was at Jabbers' feet."

Piper nodded. "Yeah, okay. That works for me."

Lou glanced at the half-packed bag on the bed. "Where are you going?"

"I'm making an overnight bag for Dani. Mel took her to the hospital. They think Diana dosed her with opioids or something. We just want to get her checked out to make sure there's no lasting damage. When she finds out she slept through a kidnapping and a base jump off a building, she's going to *freak*."

"Will she be okay?"

Piper sniffed again, her eyes beginning to itch. "She'll be okay."

Even though King and Mel had both assured her this was true, Piper had a hard time believing it. She wanted to see Dani's brown eyes open and lucid. Then she'd believe it.

Piper took her largest t-shirts from the top drawer, both of which she'd stolen from Henry, and slid them into the overnight bag. She'd have to pick up a package of underwear on the way. Dani had way more booty than she did. Oh, and socks. Dani's feet were always cold, no matter the season.

With the bag packed, there was only one thing left to do.

Piper crossed to Lou, stopping short of her. She wanted to cross her arms but didn't. She forced her back straight and met Lou's gaze.

"I'm sorry," she managed to spit out. "Lou, I'm very sorry for the things I said to you."

Lou shifted her weight to her other foot.

That's okay. No words is a valid response, she reassured herself. *Keep going. Finish the apology like you practiced.*

Piper cleared her throat, which was now itching more than her eyes. "It's my fault. I'm the one who pushed Diana out into the open by exposing her, and you had to clean up my mess. She came for Dani because of what I did, not what you did, but I put that on you. I've been so stupid lately. I've been suffocating you with this friendship stuff and you're clearly not into it. I get it. I'm...me, and you're this super-cool badass way above my pay grade. I should've never tried to—"

Lou's frown deepened. "What are you talking about?"

"The road trip and all that. I know you hated it."

"I didn't hate it."

"You were *super* bored, but I kept pushing it on you because I wanted you to have something normal in your life and I wanted to give you a reason to be my friend when all this is over."

"When it's all over," Lou repeated. Her eyebrows nearly touched.

"King is *old*. He's going to die or retire. And I have no idea what I'm doing in school, if I'll be a cop or a lawyer or whatever, but I can't expect you to hang around if my life goes off in a new direction and I get all suburban or something. I was trying to prove I had something to offer you, and all I did was drive you into the arms of a psychopath who understood you better. And I get why you liked her, I really do, but I want you to know I wasn't trying to change you. I wanted to give you more. You and Diana had more in common than you and me, but I care about you. I really, really care about you, and oh god please say something. Your scowl is terrifying."

Lou looked like someone had shoved a lemon in her mouth.

"*Please*," Piper prompted.

"I don't care if we're different."

"What?" Piper's itchy eyes began to water.

"I murder drug kings and mafia soldiers. Konstantine runs a gang of them. We're very different."

"Oh." Piper swiped at her nose with the bottom of her sleeve. "Oh, right. Wow, why didn't I think of that? But he's still living in that underworld with you. You guys have that. He's got resources and a decent level of badassery. He can hold his own with you."

And he's rich. Which I will never be.

"You hold your own," Lou said, searching her face.

"I mean, I can dig up a body and use a computer and I don't scare easy, but is that enough for you?"

Lou pulled her close. "More than enough."

Piper sniffed.

Lou's hair was cold and clammy, but Piper didn't care. She hugged Lou back.

"Are you sure?" Piper sniffed again. "It's just going to be bad TV and boring road trips and drag shows and pizza. And problems, oh *so* many problems."

Lou hugged her tighter. "It's enough, Piper. It really is."

An emotion so raw and coursing tore through her chest. The muscles in her back softened in Lou's arms and she sank into the embrace. It took her a while to gather enough air and control to speak again, but she managed a whisper.

"You're enough too. I don't ever want you to think I want you to be normal when I make you do normal things. Just because I...because I've never had a friend like you doesn't mean I want you to be like everyone else. You mean so much to me."

"I mean so much to you?" Lou repeated the words as if she didn't understand them.

Piper pulled back, wiping at her eyes. "Yes, damn it, you mean so much to me. You want me to say it again? Or tattoo it on my face, or what?"

"Is that why you're crying?"

"I'm not crying," Piper said, dabbing at the corners of her eyes with the collar of her t-shirt.

"You have tears running down your face. Your nose is red."

Piper was definitely crying, and not just crying but on the edge of a full-on ugly cry. Still, she stiffened her lip and affected a pose of mock offense.

"It's the cat. Don't look at me like that! It is. I'm really allergic and my apartment is so much smaller than Dani's and the air flow isn't as good. I think my allergies are worse because of it."

They regarded each other in uneasy silence. It was Lou who broke into a grin first. Piper felt her relief like a palpable wave. She fell into laughter.

"I'm so glad she's dead," she said. She released her t-shirt, hoping her face was mostly clear now. "You really killed her?"

Lou's smile widened. "I did."

"What about the sister and the minions? Anyone else going to show up and throw people off the building to prove some point?"

"Her sister is alive. But I don't think we have to worry about her."

"That's what you said about Diana."

"She saved my life."

"Diana?"

"No," Lou said. "Her sister. She could've killed me, but she took me to the hospital."

Lou's gaze was suddenly dark and distant. Wherever she was now, Piper couldn't go there with her. *And that's okay*, she thought. *It only matters that I'm here when she comes back.*

She shrugged. "Okay then. You're probably right."

And we're alive, she reminded herself. *We're alive, this is over, and we still have each other.*

Piper wiped at her running eyes. "Hey, how do you feel about cat-sitting?"

44

Italy was often warm in the summer, but on this night, it felt oppressive. Konstantine had taken off his shirt and wore only thin silk pants. Still, he opened the window in his bedroom and invited in the breeze caressing the Arno River. Enticed, the breeze swept through, ruffling his sheets and the book on his bed.

The river itself was beautiful to behold, pulsing with moonlight. The spell was broken by a group of teenagers laughing riotously on the opposite bank.

"Do you still have your medical kit here?" a dark voice asked.

Konstantine turned to see Lou shrugging out of her leather jacket. He hadn't even heard her come in. It had been two days since he'd seen her.

Her hair was down, accentuating the hollow of her throat. She removed her shirt, revealing that she was already braless.

His throat clicked as he swallowed, his eyes tracing from the curve of her breast down to her hip bone. "It's under my bed."

She stooped, hiding the best parts of her. It was enough for him to regain his composure.

The case rattled as it was dragged across the stone floor and into the lamplight. She looked up, met his eyes. "Do you mind?"

He gestured with an open palm, and that was all the invitation she needed to take the kit into the bathroom and shut the door.

The shower ran, then quit. The kit clattered as the lid was thrown open and then she was there again, a towel wrapped around her body.

Konstantine noted the stitches along her leg and knew they weren't Lou's handiwork. He'd seen hers, both on his body and hers.

"Who did those?"

"The hospital."

"You have a story to tell," he said. "Maybe two."

She told him about Diana, Blair, the hospital. Her friends were alive and accounted for. The beast prowling the shores of La Loon was fed.

"It's a good thing I went to the hospital. You don't have the right needles in your kit," she complained, throwing the towel onto his bed. "How do you stock this thing?"

He smiled. "Inadequately. Apparently."

She shot him a look. He crossed to the bed, to what he'd begun to think of as his side, and stretched out on the covers. He watched her arrange the packages in his kit. When her hands faltered, the shadows would shift and she'd disappear, only to reappear moments later with her fists full of sterile white packages, many stamped with red letters and blue trim.

He held up a hand. "Do you mean to tell me that you're appearing and disappearing, *naked*, in some medical supply facility right now?"

She flicked her eyes up to his and smiled. "No. I'm taking it from my kit. I'll restock it later."

"Ah, I see," he said with a touch of sarcasm. "Thank you for making my kit adequate again."

"It was for me," she said. "I don't want to die because you didn't have something I needed."

"Smart move. Anything else?" He was disappointed to see her tug the shirt down over her head and pull on pants.

His eyes traced the last visible stretch of skin between her shirt and hip. "Will you lie with me? I want to tell you what I learned about La Loon."

She crawled into the bed beside him.

LOU HADN'T MISSED THE SHIVER THAT HAD RUN THROUGH him at the mention of La Loon, and she wondered if he'd ever view the place as anything but a nightmare. To Lou it was a haven, strangely familiar, and yet she understood that no one else would ever feel that way.

"The plants on La Loon, including that strange grass we saw, don't photosynthesize. They likely feed on fungi in the ground, parasitically. And the fungi probably feed on carcasses. Perhaps those left behind by your pet or whatever washes up onto the shore."

Lou said nothing. She watched his face as he spoke, tracing his jaw with her eyes.

"The air is 27% oxygen, 71% nitrogen, 1.4% argon and 0.06% carbon dioxide. There are dust particles in the air, but no pollen. There are some other solid particles but nothing we can identify. The soil is volcanic and rich in iron, calcium, magnesium, sodium, potassium, phosphorous, sulfur, and silicon. I wonder if the cliffs we saw were an extinct or dormant volcano."

"Why?" Lou asked.

"The soil shows no sign of eruption. There would be..." He seemed to search for the word. Lou liked his voice, low and soft like a melody. "Sediments. Maybe there are caves underground, carved by lava. I want to try a GPR."

"I don't know what that is."

"Machines that can send pulses into the ground to show us pictures of what's beneath. There could be miles of caves under there."

Warm and relaxed beside him, she began to feel the effects of the Vicodin she'd taken before coming. She hadn't wanted to take it, but her shoulder needed the relief. And so did she.

After two nights of endless assault, Lou could barely move it at all and the swelling had returned.

She hoped she would fall asleep quickly and wake to find her mobility had returned.

Sometimes, after a hard night, the exhaustion of the fight would take her completely. Other nights, the adrenaline pulsing in her veins would fight against sleep. She hoped it wouldn't be that kind of night.

His fingers were in her hair.

"I think the evidence shows your world is not Earth," he said. He said this gently, as if the news might disappoint her.

"You think it's an alien planet?"

"I do. We can never know for sure, but I do."

Her eyes traced the soft, swirling plaster in his ceiling. After a long stretch of silence she said, "I guess that's no stranger than the idea of going forward or back in time."

"No," he agreed. "But are you disappointed?"

He must have heard the hesitation in her voice.

"No," she answered honestly.

"No? Why?"

In truth, Lou's mind had trailed off to other things. "I'm worried about the boy."

"Which boy?"

Lou adjusted herself against the pillow. "The one we saved in the raid."

Konstantine turned on his side so he could look at her face. They lay like that, thighs touching, nearly nose to nose. "Do you think he is still in danger? Do you feel it?"

"No. Not right now."

"But?"

"But..." *Diana said they come back.* Predators remain predators. Their hunger and lust will always drive them to find the kids, the vulnerable and afraid.

Someone out there would love to find Shai, hurt him, and relive their sick fantasies at his expense.

Shai's father was dead, but how many had seen the videos? Who might recognize his face on the street and want Shai for themselves?

"He's so small," she said.

Konstantine pushed the hair back from her face. "You can always check on him."

He was right. She could keep Shai on her radar as well as the others: Piper, Dani, King, and Mel.

Konstantine.

Would it keep extending like this? Her circle?

And why should she prioritize one person above another? One cause above another? Did abolishing the drug trade mean more than saving children from those who'd prey on them?

Was Piper, Dani, King, Mel—or Shai—more inherently valuable than any of the other seven billion people on the planet?

No. But they mattered to *her*.

And that was better than the alternative. The alternative was to be Diana Dennard, or something like her. To care about nothing, no one, but herself.

She had her hunger. She always would. But she also had more.

"You said you understood a woman like Diana?" Lou stared into those green eyes. "Is that because she's like me?"

"No." Konstantine placed a kiss on the tip of her nose. "There's no one on this planet like you."

EPILOGUE

S hai shot up in his bed, his heart pounding in his chest. Whatever dream had been on him the moment before was already fading. What was left was the funny tickle on the back of his neck. Sometimes it kept him awake at night, this tickle. Sometimes when he closed his eyes, he saw his father's face, felt his father's hands on his body.

"Are you there, angel?" He wet his lips. "It's me, Shai."

Shai spoke to the dark, waiting, listening.

As one moment stretched into two, his hopes sank.

She's probably busy. Angels must be very busy.

He'd slid beneath the blankets when he felt a tight pop between his ears. It was like the time he took an elevator to Mommy's work. She worked in an office in a very big building. On the hundredth floor, she'd told him.

His eyes slid to the corner of his bedroom between his closet door and bookcase.

For a moment it was only black. The thick, unyielding shadows were complete.

Then she stepped into the light. The orange haze from

the lamps outside his window cut across her face like tiger stripes.

"Angel!"

His elation threatened to erupt from his chest. He suddenly didn't know what to do with his hands or his body. His legs bounced under the blanket as he reached out for her.

She pressed a finger over her lips.

He covered his mouth and stifled a laugh. He wanted her to come closer. He wanted to touch her again and remind himself that she was real.

She did. She sat on the edge of his bed and placed a steadying hand over his jittery legs.

He tried to make them be still.

"How are you?" she asked.

He liked her voice a whole lot. It was lower than his mother's.

"You came."

"Were you afraid?" she asked. "It felt like you were afraid."

She knows how I feel. She knows everything.

"I was. I get scared in the dark sometimes." He wanted to be honest with her. He wanted to tell her everything. He lay back down. "But you like the dark."

"I do," she said, pulling his covers up and draping them across his chest.

"When I was littler, I used to think there were monsters in the dark," he said. Then he smiled at her. "Is that why there's angels in the dark too?"

Her smile faltered. It hurt his feelings to see it, like maybe he'd said something wrong.

"How do you know I'm not a monster?" she asked.

"No," he said, relieved that it wasn't something he'd said. "Monsters are scary. You don't scare me."

"I don't?" she asked, running a hand through his hair.

His body relaxed against the pillows. "No."

"A little bit of fear is okay," she said. "Sometimes, fear keeps us smart."

"Really?"

She tucked the blanket around his chest, placing a hand on top. "Yes. If we didn't have any fear, we might go too far." She frowned. "Do you understand?"

"Yes," he said. He didn't, but he wanted to make her smile.

And she did. "You're a smart boy already."

A door creaked overhead and soft footsteps started down the hall. Shai knew his mother was coming to check on him. The angel must've known it too, because she stood, her eyes sliding between the door and the dark corner of his room.

"Will you always come when I'm afraid?" Shai whispered. *Please say yes. Please.*

"If I can," she said. "Close your eyes."

He shut his eyes.

When his mother opened the door, Shai was lying perfectly still under his blanket. Through his lashes, he saw that the place where the angel had stood a moment before was empty now. Now it was bright with hallway light pouring in over his mother's shoulder. It haloed her wild hair and thick robe as she lingered in the doorway, watching him sleep.

With a sigh, she pulled the door closed. A second later, the hallway light clicked off and the thin strip of light beneath the door disappeared. He listened to her steps weighing heavy on the stairs before shuffling down the hall overhead, and heard the slight click of her own door closing again.

In the dark, a cool hand pushed back his hair, tracing his forehead and neck. He knew it wasn't his mother's, but he also didn't open his eyes.

Anything to keep her with him for a little longer.

Did you enjoy this book? You can make a BIG difference.

I don't have the same power as big New York publishers who can buy full-spread ads in magazines, and you won't see my covers on the side of a bus anytime soon, but what I *do* have are wonderful readers like you.

And honest reviews from readers garner more attention for my books and help my career more than anything else I could possibly do—and I can't get a review without you! So if you would be so kind, I'd be very grateful if you would post a review for this book.

It only takes a minute or so of your time, and yet you can't imagine how much it helps me. It can be as short as you like, and whether positive or negative, it really does help. I appreciate it so much and so do the readers looking for their next favorite read.

If you would be so kind, please find your preferred retailer at ➜ https://www.korymshrum.com/devilsluck and leave a review for this book today.

With gratitude,
Kory

GET YOUR THREE FREE STORIES TODAY

Thank you so much for reading *Devil's Luck*. I hope you're enjoying Louie's story. If you'd like more, I have a free, exclusive Lou Thorne story for you. Meet Louie early in her hunting days, when she pursues Benito Martinelli, the son of her enemy. This was the man her father arrested—and the reason her parents were killed months later.

You can only read this story by signing up for my free newsletter. If you would like this story, you can get your copy by visiting ➜ www.korymshrum.com/lounewsletteroffer

I will also send you free stories from the other series that I write. If you've signed up for my newsletter already, no need to sign up again. You should have already received this story from me. Check your email and make sure it wasn't marked as spam! Can't find it? Email me at ➜ kory@korymshrum.com and I'll take care of it.

As to the newsletter itself, I send out 2-3 a month and host a monthly giveaway exclusive to my subscribers. The prizes are usually signed books or other freebies that I think you'll enjoy. I also share information about my current projects, and personal anecdotes (like pictures of my dog). If you want these free stories and access to the exclusive give-aways, you can sign up for the newsletter at ➜ www.korymshrum.com/lounewsletteroffer

If this is not your cup of tea (I love tea), you can follow me on Facebook at ➜ www.facebook.com/korymshrum in order to be notified of my new releases.

ACKNOWLEDGMENTS

Every time I write a book, there is always a point (usually around the 60-70,000 word mark of the first revision), that I begin to feel hopeless. *Impossible! This book will never be finished!*

I step away. I take a nap. I walk the dog. Maybe I start to eat a lot of carbs, and drink extra tea. Passing an entire afternoon with a box of truffles, casting despairing looks at my ceiling begins to feel perfectly normal.

It is in these moments, that I need the most help. The front-line supporters arrive right on time: Kimberly Benedicto, Kathrine Pendleton, Angela Roquet, and Monica La Porta. They tell me to take showers, to eat something, to get some sunshine and air. They read the pages and assure me there is something there worth sharing.

With their encouragement, slowly, I get back into the swing of finishing the unfinishable and *more* help arrives! Daily notes from people who love the series and want it to continue. Christian Bentulan provides another gorgeous cover. Toby Selwyn lends his keen editorial eye, and Alexandra Amor swiftly executes all formatting and creeping business tasks that threaten to distract and overwhelm me.

And when I think I can't possibly find any more help and support, there's my street team! They arrive, giddy with excitement, wrench the pages from my (proverbial) hands and eagerly devour the "final book". Within days they dutifully report those stowaway typos, and dispatch the first round of reviews.

Then the curtain falls and I find you. Yes, *you*, the reader. Somehow you found this book and decided to read it. You liked it enough to keep thumbing through the back pages, searching for a little more and discovering instead that you've been a star in this production the whole time.

And here I am, pinning a ribbon to your shirt, shaking your hand vigorously, thanking you for coming, and encouraging you to join us for the cast party.

Because, really, all of this was for you.

ABOUT THE AUTHOR

Kory M. Shrum is author of the bestselling *Shadows in the Water, Welcome to Castle Cove,* and *Dying for a Living* series. She has loved books and words all her life. She reads almost every genre you can think of, but when she writes, she writes science fiction, fantasy, and thrillers, or often something that's all of the above.

She can usually be found under thick blankets with snacks. The kettle is almost always on.

When she's not eating, reading, writing, or indulging in her true calling as a stay-at-home dog mom, she loves to plan her next adventure. (Travel).

She lives in Michigan with her equally bookish wife, Kim, and their rescue pug, Charley.

She'd love to hear from you!
korymshrum.com

ALSO BY KORY M. SHRUM

Dying for a Living series (complete)

Dying for a Living

Dying by the Hour

Dying for Her: A Companion Novel

Dying Light

Worth Dying For

Dying Breath

Dying Day

Shadows in the Water: Lou Thorne Thrillers (ongoing)

Shadows in the Water

Under the Bones

Danse Macabre

Carnival

Devil's Luck

Design Your Destiny Castle Cove series (ongoing)

Welcome to Castle Cove

Night Tide

Learn more about Kory's work at: www.korymshrum.com

CPSIA information can be obtained
at www.ICGtesting.com
Printed in the USA
FSHW021907310520
70451FS

Sometimes revenge is the road to salvation.

Louie Thorne understands this. When her parents were brutally shot dead in their home, Louie found the strength to go on only by armoring herself with the quest for vengeance. She found the criminals that took everything from her—and ended their lives—despite what it cost her.

So when fellow huntress Diana Dennard crosses Louie's path, in pursuit of a dangerous pedophile, Louie refuses to interfere. She understands the need governing Diana's every move—even if the woman's methods toe the line of madness.

As Lou is dragged into Diana's hunt, Diana's mask slips. The game turns dark. Suddenly the bad guys aren't Diana's only target and Lou finds herself between a dangerous and conniving psychopath and the ones she loves.

Will Louie's dark power be enough to protect them? Or will the coldest heart win...

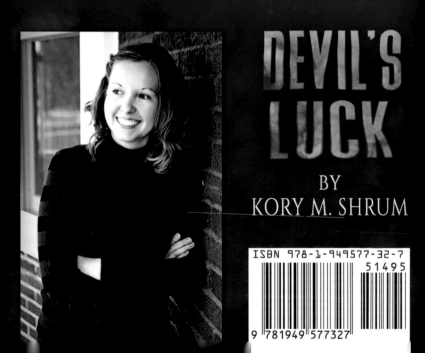

DEVIL'S LUCK

BY
KORY M. SHRUM

ISBN 978-1-949577-32-7
51495

9 781949 577327